Fiddling with the [...] **prayer *kapp*, Amy** [...] **always lived aroun** [...]

"I came here when I was young," Andrew said. "My *vadder* died and *Mamm* met John's *vadder* at a wedding. He was a widower by then. They got married soon after they met."

Amy nodded. "And where did you live before that?"

"We lived in Lancaster right up until we moved here."

Why didn't anyone mention he'd come from the same place as she? "Do you remember anything about it?"

"I was too young, but I'm sure I remember my old *haus* and playing in the snow, running in the fields, that kind of thing. Just vague images."

They smiled at one another, and Amy felt more of a connection to him knowing that he'd come from her hometown.

"Would you do me the honor of allowing me to drive you home after the gathering tomorrow?" Again, he spoke in a quiet voice so the others couldn't hear.

"I'd like that."

USA TODAY bestselling author **Samantha Price** wrote stories from a young age, but it wasn't until later in life that she took up writing full-time. Formerly an artist, she exchanged her paintbrush for the computer and, many bestselling book series later, has never looked back. Samantha is happiest lost in the worlds of her characters. To learn more about Samantha and her books, visit samanthapriceauthor.com.

THE AMISH DEACON'S DAUGHTER

USA TODAY Bestselling Author

Samantha Price

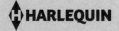

If you purchased this book without a cover you should be aware that this book is stolen property. It was reported as "unsold and destroyed" to the publisher, and neither the author nor the publisher has received any payment for this "stripped book."

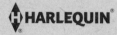

ISBN-13: 978-1-335-49975-2

The Amish Deacon's Daughter

First published in 2018 by Samantha Price.
This edition published in 2020.

Recycling programs
for this product may
not exist in your area.

Copyright © 2018 by Samantha Price

All rights reserved. No part of this book may be used or reproduced in any manner whatsoever without written permission except in the case of brief quotations embodied in critical articles and reviews.

This is a work of fiction. Names, characters, places and incidents are either the product of the author's imagination or are used fictitiously. Any resemblance to actual persons, living or dead, businesses, companies, events or locales is entirely coincidental.

This edition published by arrangement with Harlequin Books S.A.

For questions and comments about the quality of this book,
please contact us at CustomerService@Harlequin.com.

Harlequin Enterprises ULC
22 Adelaide St. West, 40th Floor
Toronto, Ontario M5H 4E3, Canada
www.Harlequin.com

Printed in U.S.A.

THE AMISH DEACON'S DAUGHTER

Chapter One

Amy watched Olive drive her buggy away. She turned and kicked a stone with her black boots as she walked toward her house. It wasn't a good thing for an Amish girl to be approaching twenty with no man on the horizon, something her parents reminded her of almost daily. Being the eldest in a family of six girls increased the pressure on her to find a man.

Her four friends had found men. What was it about her that she was the only one who remained single? For one thing, she was the one whose parents pressured her to be married, and day after day she bore the burden.

Olive and Amy had been with their girlfriends for their usual Saturday get-together at the coffee shop in town. On the way home, all Olive talked about was her upcoming wedding, quite unaware that Amy wanted to talk about anything but. Amy told Olive to let her out way before her house and said she'd walk the rest of the way. She would surely scream if she had to hear more of marriages. For the first time, Amy was the odd one out amongst her friends.

As she moved closer to the house, she heard her sisters before she saw them. When she turned onto the driveway, she saw them playing baseball in the field. It was a new game for them and they played it whenever they could.

"Amy."

Amy looked up from kicking another stone to see Martha running toward her.

When Martha reached her, she said, "I don't know why you never take me to town. I'm nearly the same age as you and I love coffee."

"You're not nearly the same age; you're two years younger. Besides, they're my friends, and they don't bring anyone else. Why should I be any different?"

Martha wrinkled her freckled nose and looked over her shoulder at the other girls who were still playing. She turned back to Amy. "I heard *Mamm* and *Dat* talking about you last night."

Amy stopped still. "Me?"

"Mm-hmm."

"What did they say?"

"It was something about a letter. They got a letter from someone, and then I heard them say you should go." Amy tugged on her sister's arm. "Go where?"

"Ow." Martha rubbed her arm.

"Tell me."

"I don't know."

"Think, Martha, think." Amy slouched to look directly into Martha's green eyes.

Martha's gaze rose to the sky. "It was something about sending you to marry someone."

Amy reeled back and her hands flew to her mouth. *"Nee,* it can't be."

Martha leaned forward. *"Mamm* didn't want you to

go, but *Dat* said there are no men here your age, and if you don't marry someone soon you'll be alone like Marie Byler."

Amy rubbed her chin. Most people were too scared to even speak to Marie Byler. She found something wrong with everything. "They can't send me somewhere, can they? And who is it that they think I should marry? Do they even know him?"

"I don't know, but Amy, you can't tell 'em I told you. I'll be punished for eavesdropping."

Amy looked into her sister's worried face. "I won't say anything. I hope you were having a bad dream."

"Would it be so terrible? They might send you somewhere nice and you'll meet a *wunderbaar* man. There's no reason to think it'll be awful."

"Hush, Martha. It'll be painful. I only know this place; I was born here and I'll die here. I don't want to be anywhere else. Besides, all my friends are here. And you wouldn't want me to go, would you?"

Martha threw her arms around Amy's waist and held her tight. *"Nee,* that would be awful. I want us to stay together forever."

Amy patted Martha on her back. *"Gut.* Now you tell that to *Mamm* and *Dat* if they try to send me away. I'm sure you were dreaming. Did you hear it at night?" Martha nodded and took a step back.

"See? Just a bad dream."

Amy's four young sisters ran to her giggling loudly.

Amy sputtered to Martha before the other girls could hear. "You haven't mentioned this to anyone, have you?"

"Nee."

"Gut, then don't."

Amy stayed outside with the girls for a while before

she went into the house to help with the dinner. While she stood with her *mudder* cutting the vegetables, Amy noticed she was unusually quiet. "Is anything wrong, *Mamm?*"

Her *mudder* shook her head and didn't look at her.

Amy placed the knife on the wooden cutting board. "What is it, *Mamm?*" She could see her *mudder* close her lips together, and then screw up her face.

She looked at Amy with tears in her eyes. "I'll let your *vadder* tell you."

Amy tilted her head. Her heart nearly stopped. Maybe Martha was right. "Tell me what?"

Her *mudder* looked away, but not before Amy saw that a tear had trickled down her cheek. She was not going to get any words out of her mother, that was for certain. Amy left the vegetables and went to look for her father. Just as she stepped out of the house, she saw his buggy stop outside the barn. As she drew closer, she heard her sisters talking excitedly to their father.

Amy strode toward him, determined to get answers. "Girls, *Mamm* wants to see you right now. Leave *Dat* alone. Go help with dinner."

The girls obeyed and went inside the *haus.*

"I've never heard you speak to them with anger before, Amy."

Amy rubbed her temples. *"Mamm* said you had something to tell me. She looked upset."

"Ah."

"Well, what is it?" Amy's body tensed as she waited for an answer.

Her father walked over to his horse and patted him on his neck. "I'll fix you in a minute, boy." His father looked toward the house and then said to Amy, "Let's find somewhere quiet to sit." They walked into the barn and sat on wooden boxes.

Amy's *vadder* took off his hat and rubbed his head. "It's not been easy for us with six girls. I've had to sell half the farm because we don't have a son to help out."

Amy frowned. How was it her fault she wasn't a boy? This wasn't the first time she'd heard her parents' preference for sons.

"That aside, your *mudder* and I are concerned that some of your friends have turned to *Englisch* boys."

"Nee, that was only Claire, and Donovan said he might join us."

"Jah, but 'might' is a long way from making a decision. Olive Hesh is another one."

"Jah, but you know that Blake and Olive are getting married. Blake is getting baptized soon."

"It turned out that way, but what would Olive have done if Blake had changed his mind about joining us? Do you think that she wouldn't have followed him right out of the community and into the outside world?"

Amy shrugged her shoulders keeping quiet, knowing Olive would've most likely followed Blake anywhere; she wasn't going to admit that to her father.

"I've written to a bishop from another Amish settlement. He has a *bruder* who needs a *fraa.*" Her father's face flushed red and even the tips of his ears went red.

"And what does that have to do with me? There would be a lot of *menner* who need *fraas.*"

When her father frowned, she knew her comment bordered on cheeky, so she looked away fearing a reprimand.

His bottom jaw flexed. "You need a husband. You haven't found one by yourself and you'll soon be twenty."

Amy straightened and pulled her shoulders back. "That's not so old. It doesn't matter. I've got my maid job. I'm saving money to support myself."

"I'm a deacon, Amy. It's important my *familye* sets an example for others to follow. *One who is righteous is a guide to his neighbor, but the way of the wicked leads them astray.*"

"I'm a bad example because I'm not married? *Dat,* there are a great many bad things I could be doing, and I don't think being unmarried is one of them."

"I'm not giving you my opinion alone, Amy. The Bible warns us to be careful who our friends are. Look what your friends have done. They've been associating with *Englischers* and looking for husbands among them."

Amy hung her head and covered her face with her hands. This could not be happening to her. She looked back to her father. "What is it you want me to do? Marry someone I don't even know?"

"Bishop John from Wisconsin is expecting you next week. You'll stay with them."

Amy's mouth fell open. "I can't. What about my job?"

"You'll have to leave it. If you find the bishop's *bruder* entirely unsuitable, you don't have to marry him. You must give him a chance first, and get to know him."

Amy rubbed her temples. Martha had been right. "What do you know about him?"

"He's thirty and—"

"Thirty?" Amy shouted. "That's far too old. Why hasn't he found a *fraa;* what's wrong with him?"

"Possibly the same thing that's wrong with you." Amy clutched at her throat, and her voice rose in pitch. *"Jah,* but I'm not thirty." Amy huffed and crossed her arms. "You don't mean it, do you, *Dat?"*

"It's arranged."

She narrowed her eyes. "And what does *Mamm* think about it?"

He slowly nodded. "Your *mudder* and I are always in agreement."

Amy scowled and looked away. What he meant was her mother had been given no choice but to agree to his plan.

Amy had already seen her mother wasn't in agreement.

"Go inside and help your *mudder*. We'll talk later. I have to rub the horse down."

Once back inside, Amy organized a game in the living room for her sisters so she could talk privately with her mother in the kitchen. She was her only chance of escaping this scheme. *"Dat* told me about sending me away."

Her mother nodded and her bottom lip quivered.

"I know it's *Dat's* idea."

"You do need a husband, Amy."

"Jah, but *Gott* can just as easily send one to my door. Why do I have to be packed off to some place I've never even heard of? Where was it again?"

"Wisconsin. I hear it's very nice. It has rivers and fishing and it's north of here and colder… I think."

"I don't like the cold. I hate it. I've been longing for the hot weather to return."

"You don't have to stay long. Your *vadder* and I had planned to talk to you about it after dinner when the girls would be in bed. We'll have no more talk of it now until after dinner."

Amy nodded and turned her attention to slicing the beans. She'd never been away from home or her family.

Chapter Two

When the girls were in bed that night, Amy sat in the living room with her parents.

"Well, what have you got planned for me?" Amy didn't like it, but she saw no choice but to comply with their plans.

"You'll stay with the bishop and his *fraa*. Their names are John and Jane Miller. They have five *kinner,* and you will live with them in exchange for helping Jane in the *haus.*"

Amy tried not to show she was upset. She'd been doing well saving money with her maid's job, and now she was going to be an unpaid maid at a place she didn't want to be at. "How am I going to get there?"

"I'm going out tomorrow to make the arrangements and buy the tickets. You'll catch a train to Wisconsin, and once you're there, you'll get a bus to Augusta, on the Eau Claire line. I've been told it'll be more than six hours on the train and over three hours on the bus."

Mamm added, "You should take some needlework with you."

"That's very far away." Amy looked at her mother. "Do you really want me to go, *Mamm?*"

"Nee, I don't, but your *vadder's* right. It's best for you to go out and find a *mann* and start your own *familye."*

Her father put his hands in the air. "We're not saying you have to marry Andrew Miller, just meet him and see what you think."

"See, Amy? No one's forcing you to do anything," *Mamm* said with a smile.

"I'm sure *Gott* would've placed someone for me closer than Wisconsin. I don't even know where that is. I've never been on a bus or a train before." She breathed out heavily. "What if I get lost? I won't know where to go or what to do." The thought of finding her way among strangers in an unknown place filled her with fear.

Dat said, "You'll find where to go. It'll do no good going back and forth over the matter. The decision's been made."

"Can I ask a question?" Her father nodded.

"What do you know about this Andrew man?" Amy asked.

"Andrew is John's *bruder.* I met John when he came here for Gabe Birchell's wedding two years ago. We often send letters and discuss community matters and the like. I asked him if he knew of any single men looking for *fraas,* and he told me of his *bruder.* He said Andrew is a strong man of *Gott.* He has a sawmill, works hard, and needs a woman in his home."

Amy breathed out heavily. *Why doesn't he get a maid to help him?* That's what she wanted to say to her *vadder.* It sounded easier to stay where she was than be packed off somewhere because the man needed someone to cook and clean for him—being a *fraa* should be much more than that.

What do I know about sawmills, and Wisconsin, and thirty-year-old men? Nothing!

At least her father had said she didn't have to marry him if she didn't like him.

Amy leaned back in the couch aware both parents were waiting for her to say something. Yes, she'd go, have an adventure, and before she knew it she'd be home again. Amy fixed a smile on her face. If they were forcing her, she'd make the most of it.

Poor old Andrew Miller could feel as awkward about this whole thing as she did. Maybe he didn't like the prospect of a wife so much younger. It amused Amy to think that John might be sitting down right now talking Andrew into meeting her. So vivid was the image of that in her mind, she almost felt sorry for Andrew, the middle-aged sawmill owner.

The next Saturday afternoon, Amy was with her friends at the coffee shop.

When she told them her horrific news, Lucy was the first to comment. "You're not going, are you?"

"I have to. You know what *Dat's* like and how he's always saying that his *familye* has to be a *gut* example. He thinks twenty is too old to be single, and he doesn't want me to end up with an *Englischer.* I also reckon he thinks I should be married, so my younger sisters don't take a long time to marry." Amy slumped further in her chair. She might not see her friends for a long time.

"How long will you be gone?" Jessie asked.

"They haven't told me."

Olive rubbed Amy's shoulder. "Do you think it's possible it mightn't be that bad?"

Amy chuckled. "I'm going to a place I've never heard of

and it's probably in the middle of nowhere. I won't know a single person, and they want me to marry an old man."

Jessie fiddled with the strings of her prayer *kapp*. "How old is he?"

"He's thirty."

"That's not too old. Joshua is twenty-eight," Lucy said.

Amy took a look around the coffee shop. It was three-quarters full, and everyone was happily chatting and not taking notice that they were Amish. She would miss her friends and the times at the coffee shop. "I need the largest slice of chocolate cake in the store."

The girls giggled. Amy waved to Dan to take their orders.

Dan strode toward them, smoothed back his hair and smiled down at Lucy. They all knew Dan had a secret crush on Lucy. "Sorry to keep you waiting, girls. Now, what would everyone like today?" He took a notepad and pen from the back pocket of his jeans.

"Amy's father is sending her to Wisconsin, so she needs the biggest slice of chocolate cake she's ever seen," Lucy said.

"Yikes, Wisconsin? Really?" Dan scowled.

Amy nodded and pushed her bottom lip out.

Dan said, "Yours is on the house, Amy, and I'll add an extra couple of scoops of chocolate ice cream."

Amy giggled. "Thanks, Dan."

Once Dan had taken their orders and given Amy a wink, her mood improved. "I'm blessed to have you girls as friends. I'll write to all of you every day."

"Will you work once you get there?" Olive asked.

"I'm working for my board. That's what *Dat* arranged with the bishop. I'll be staying with them and helping Mrs. Miller. They've got five *kinner*."

"You like children, so that's okay," Jessie said.

"Jah, I do. It mightn't be so bad once I get there, and I don't have to stay if I don't like it." Her friends fell silent. "I leave at the end of the week."

"Are you going by Greyhound?" Lucy asked.

"Nee, even the Greyhound doesn't go there. I've got a long train ride and after that, there's a long bus ride."

Olive leaned forward and put her hand on Amy's arm. "Sounds like a true adventure."

"Jah, see it as an adventure. You never know what could happen or who you might meet." Jessie smiled and raised her eyebrows as if she were trying to beam enthusiasm into Amy.

Amy scratched the back of her neck and nodded. She was doing her best to look on the bright side of things.

The hardest part of leaving for Amy was telling the family she worked for she was leaving. They asked her to call them when she returned, but something within told her she'd never go back. She'd tried to explain to her father that a suitable period of notice should be given to one's employer, but her father said a week was enough notice.

The train ride was a disaster. All the while Amy's stomach churned, not knowing how she'd find the bus to start the next leg of her journey. She'd never gone on public transport like this, not alone. When she sat down in the dining car to eat her inclusive-in-the-ticket-price dinner, she had to hurry back to her seat. She'd started to cry and didn't want anyone to see her. Amy was alone, afraid, and wishing she could be anywhere other than where she was right now.

Chapter Three

When she got off the train at the stop she had been told, Amy had managed to find the bus stop for her next leg of the journey, thanks to a helpful employee at the train station.

The bus trip was long and arduous, but Amy had managed to get some sleep. Relief was what she felt when she stepped down from the bus at Augusta. The first thing she did was look for some friendly Amish folk, but no one was there to collect her.

Mentally, she went back over what her father had told her. Yes, she'd been told she'd be met at the bus station. After hours on the train and then more hours on the bus, she would've hoped that whoever was picking her up would've had the decency to be on time. Punctuality and polite behavior had been drummed into her since she was born. Did these Wisconsin Amish have the same standards? Apparently not!

If she wasn't so tired from the trip, she might've made arrangements to go straight home again. Thankful she had the Millers' address, she jumped into one of the two waiting taxis determined not to wait any longer. It was a bad start to her "adventure."

She nestled back into the backseat of the taxi. Was this a sign of things to come? This whole thing had been her father's idea and it was going to be a disaster. Amy reminded herself her parents said she wouldn't have to stay long. She'd stay, meet the poor unfortunate Andrew, who couldn't find a wife, then she'd go home and tell her parents how unsuitable he was. Then, hopefully, her father would not try to play matchmaker again.

Surely her father, as the deacon, should've known things happen in *Gott's* timing. Possibly, *Gott* just wanted her to be older before she met a man; and if her *kinner* turned out anything like those screaming children on the train, she wouldn't mind if she didn't have any at all. With five younger sisters, she was sure that, in time, she'd have plenty of nieces and nephews.

The taxi drove past a row of stores, just like the ones at home. She was homesick already and hadn't even got to the Millers' yet. Before long, fields and farms surrounded her. The taxi pulled off the sealed road and headed down a dirtpacked driveway.

"Looks like this is it," the taxi driver said as he slowed the car.

Amy craned her neck trying to see a house. When they got past a clump of trees, the house came into view. It was a pretty pink two-level house, and it looked small. The lawn and the flowers surrounding it were overgrown, but that didn't detract from its charm.

But wait, would an Amish bishop live in a pink house? Amy leaned forward. "Are you sure this is it?"

"This is the address you gave me."

When the taxi stopped in front of the house, a short

thickset middle-aged woman came out. She was pleasant looking, and dressed in traditional Amish clothing. Amy was pleased to see a friendly face.

"Amy?"

Amy opened the car door and looked up at the woman who had to be Mrs. Miller. *"Jah,* it's me."

The driver helped Amy get her suitcase out, and Amy paid him. Amy was not happy to pay him out of the little money she'd brought with her. She was supposed to have been driven here by one of the Millers—they were the ones who wanted her here, after all.

"I thought you were coming tomorrow," Mrs. Miller said.

"Nee, it was today."

Mrs. Miller took hold of Amy's shoulders and hugged her. Amy stiffened, not used to displays of affection from strangers.

When Mrs. Miller released her, she said, "I'm Jane."

Amy nodded. *"Wie gehts,* Jane?"

"Gut. Now, come along inside and I'll show you your room." Jane leaned forward and picked up Amy's suitcase and walked into the house.

Amy followed, wondering where the five children were. Inside, the house was warm and smelled of freshly baked bread. The house was bare. There were no embroidered Scripture plaques on the walls, and not even cushions lay on the two couches or easy chairs. Amy's pace quickened to catch up with Jane who was already halfway up the stairs at the end of the room.

Once she was at the top of the stairs, Jane turned around. "I've put you in the end bedroom and, from the window, you can see right across the farm."

"Lovely."

Jane placed Amy's suitcase on her bed. "Here's a closet for your clothes, a dresser, and there's a bathroom outside the house. The bathroom's been added on, but John built it like a part of the house."

Amy smiled and nodded as she looked around the room. It was lovely; the ceilings were high, and it was full of light. "Your *haus* is so pretty."

"Denke."

"Am I taking someone's room?"

"It's Gabbie's. She didn't mind staying in the twins' room."

"That's nice of her. *Dat* said you have five *kinner.*"

Jane laughed. "I do. They will be back soon and it won't be so quiet around here, believe me. John's out getting new shoes for the little ones. They're growing so quickly. I'll make you something to eat in the kitchen and we can talk. Unless you'd like to unpack first?"

"Nee, I can do that later."

Over hot tea and cinnamon cookies, Jane talked about her *kinner.* "My oldest is Gabbie; she's eighteen."

Amy pressed her lips together. The daughter of a bishop was eighteen and not married? According to Amy's father, that was close to being a crime. "Is she getting married?" That would only be fair since her own parents had shuffled her off to this distant place.

"Nee not yet, but I'm sure you two will be best of friends."

Amy had friends and had no reason to befriend anyone if she was only going to be there a short while.

Jane continued, "Adam and Job are the twins, they're nine. Joseph is fourteen and Joel is twelve."

Now things were worse. Amy had convinced herself the children would be younger and she'd be able to play with them. She knew nothing about boys that age or how they played, she only knew about girls. Amy took a sip of her hot tea after doing her best to give Jane a smile. Jane was nice and friendly and that made Amy feel better.

Soon, clip-clopping of hooves and laughter came from outside.

"That'll be everyone back," Jane said.

Amy stood up and walked to the window. Three boys leaped out of the buggy before it stopped. Amy winced when she saw them running and tackling each other. When the buggy came to a halt, the oldest boy and the girl got out and then the buggy headed to the barn.

"Come and meet everyone." Jane walked to the door and Amy followed close behind.

Gabbie ran to them. "Are you Amy?" Amy nodded.

"I've been waiting for you to get here." Gabbie's eyes were bright and from the way she moved, Amy saw she had loads of energy.

Jane laughed and turned to Amy. "Gabbie has been excited ever since she heard you were coming here."

"Jah, we'll have loads in common." Gabbie's warm hazel eyes twinkled with enthusiasm.

Amy smiled. "I'm sure we will. My *schweschder,* Martha, is your age."

"Boys, come here and say hello to Amy," Jane called out.

The boys stopped their messing about and walked toward their mother. Jane introduced each boy, who politely responded by greeting Amy nicely. When the introductions were through, the boys went back to playing.

Gabbie rolled her eyes. "Don't mind them; they're just boys."

Jane gave each girl a pat on the shoulder. "Come on you two. You can help me with dinner."

Amy followed Gabbie and Jane into the kitchen.

Jane said, "You have a seat, Amy, you must be tired from your travels."

"I am a little tired; I left in the early hours this morning to get to the train station. I managed to get a little sleep on the bus."

"It's a long way," Jane said, as she placed an assortment of vegetables on the chopping board.

"When does Amy meet *Onkel* Andrew?" Gabbie asked.

"He's coming to dinner tomorrow night."

Gabbie giggled. "I'll show you around the place tomorrow if you'd like, Amy."

Amy looked at Jane, aware that she was supposed to be helping Jane in the house. "I believe I'll be busy working in the *haus.*"

"You can both go after your morning chores. Gabbie will show you what to do."

Gabbie and Amy smiled at each other.

"Are you sure I can't help with the dinner?" Amy asked.

A deep voice sounded from the doorway. "Ah, this must be Amy."

Amy turned to see Mr. Miller walk into the room. She stood up and greeted the short, balding man. He was quite round in the tummy. "Hello, Bishop John."

"Hello. We weren't expecting you until tomorrow."

"Jah, I know." Amy secretly hoped that the man her parents sent her to meet wouldn't look like his *bruder.* She tried not to look at Bishop John too hard; she'd find out soon enough what Andrew was like.

"We're pleased to have you here," Bishop John said.

Amy smiled politely at him. *"Denke* for having me."

"Kaffe, Jane?" Mr. Miller asked, looking up at his wife.

"Jah, I'll bring it out to you." Jane smiled at her husband before he left the kitchen.

Dinner was quiet, with the four younger children at a different table. Jane and John talked about the farm and an upcoming town meeting.

"What's the town meeting about?" Amy asked.

"The sand mines. The miners have moved in and we're trying to stop more coming. There's even a mine across from our *schul,"* John said.

Gabbie leaned forward and said, "It's a terrible thing. The mining causes silica to float around in the air, and it's toxic."

Amy pulled a face and looked back at John. "That's terrible."

John nodded. "And it'll affect the water supply for the whole town soon enough. The miners are offering some people big money for their land. Up to eight times above the regular market value."

"Ach, that's like what's happening in Lancaster County, but it's not miners; it's developers buying up the farmlands for high prices. My friend, Lucy, is very upset about it."

"Seems we settle in one place and then something causes us to move again. We'll surely run out of places to go," Jane said.

Amy frowned. "Are you going to move?" Jane looked at her husband.

John said, "It's been something we've had to consider. We're concerned for our children."

Amy breathed out heavily and considered the coincidence of being sent to a place where the land was threatened much like at home. She hadn't bothered to listen to very much of what Lucy had spoken about, but to see the Miller family affected like this seemed so unfair. Everyone had a right to clean drinking water and fresh, clean air.

Chapter Four

Amy borrowed a spare coat of Gabbie's the next day after Gabbie had offered to show her around. The coat she'd brought with her wasn't warm enough for the colder climate.

"They've sent you here to marry my *onkel,* haven't they?" Gabbie said as they walked.

"I guess that's their plan," Amy said. "What's he like?"

"We could go and spy on him." Gabbie giggled. "His timber mill is only a ten-minute walk from here. Don't worry, we won't let him see us."

"Okay." It was best she was prepared. If he looked anything like his *bruder,* better she find out sooner than later. As they walked along the road, Amy looked at the forest to the left of them. "Are there bears around here?"

"Sometimes, but not too many. No one's been eaten by a bear for years." Gabbie giggled.

"Hmm. Encouraging. So, how are we going to spy on him without him seeing?"

Gabbie skipped away from Amy and called over her shoulder, "There's a hill that looks down over the mill. We're nearly there."

Amy ran to catch her. "They're not trying to marry you off to anyone, Gabbie?"

Gabbie stopped skipping and turned around. *"Nee,* they say I'm too immature and need to grow up." She laughed. "Too silly and too young in the head."

Amy smiled at her. She should have thought of using that as her own excuse and then she might still be home.

Gabbie pointed to raised grounds ahead of them. "It's over that hill."

They climbed through a wire fence, and as they neared the top, Gabbie pulled Amy down. "We don't want anyone to see us."

Lying down and with their tummies pressed against the grass, both girls poked their heads over the top.

Amy saw two chestnut draft horses, and then she saw him. He had hair of gold, he stood tall, and his body was solid but lean. She hoped that was Andrew, but then two other men appeared behind him and they both looked older and not as nice-looking. "Which one is he?" she whispered.

"Guess," Gabbie said.

Amy pushed a hand underneath her to stop the sharp grass sticking her through her clothing. "The one in the light shirt?"

"Jah."

Amy turned to look at Gabbie. Was it another of her jokes and Andrew was one of the plainer men? Her face gave nothing away. "He's not at all like your *vadder,* Gabbie."

"They're step-*bruders. Dat's mamm* died, and my *grossdaddi* married Andrew's *mudder* when Andrew was three. I'm not supposed to tell anyone this, but Andrew's *mudder* ran off with an *Englisch* boy and came back when Andrew was two." Gabbie whispered, "She didn't ever marry the *Englischer*."

"Of course not."

Gabbie looked at her expectantly.

"Oh." Amy took a moment to absorb the information. That meant Andrew's mother had been an unmarried mother when she'd returned to the community to marry Bishop John's father, making Bishop John and Andrew not blood-related at all.

Amy nodded, trying to take it all in and work out who was who. "Does Andrew know?"

"*Jah,* of course. He knows; I'm not supposed to say anything to anyone. They think I gossip." Gabbie laughed. "I suppose I do."

"Do Andrew's *mudder* and John's *vadder* live around here somewhere?"

Gabbie rolled onto her back. "Both are dead."

"*Ach.* That's sad."

"That's life." Gabbie's tone was matter-of-fact.

Amy fixed her gaze back on Andrew. Suddenly, it seemed a good idea to have come all this way to meet him. It was worth the torturous trip. "What's he like?"

Gabbie scoffed. "I guess he's okay."

Amy furrowed her brow. "What do you mean? It sounds like you don't get along with him."

"He's old and he's like every other grown up. Too serious, not any fun."

"You're grown up; you're eighteen."

"I don't feel it, and I don't want to be an adult."

Any other time, Amy would've asked Gabbie why she felt as she did, but as she stared at Andrew, nothing else was important. Amy watched Andrew speak to the workers. Two more men appeared; it seemed he had at least four men working for him. "Where does he live?" Amy whispered.

"Behind the mill, not too far away." Gabbie turned back onto her tummy and looked over the rise again. "What do you think of him?"

"He looks all right. Why hasn't he found a *fraa?*"

"Nothing or nobody is good enough for *Onkel* Andrew, but I guess he'll have to settle for you since they've sent you all the way here."

"It's not like that. I've only come to meet him." Amy pressed her lips together.

"Nee, the wedding is all arranged; it's happening in a week."

"It can't be; my parents won't even be here, and they said I didn't have to marry him if I didn't like him."

"That's how it is. They tricked you."

Amy stood up. *"Nee,* it's not right. I won't do it."

Gabbie took hold of her hand and pulled her back down. "Shush. I was joking." Gabbie peeked back over the crest of the hill then drew back. "He's seen you; quick, let's go." Gabbie stood, pulled Amy to her feet, and ran all the way to the bottom of the hill. They stopped behind a large tree once they were a little distance away.

"He saw us?" Amy held her hand to her fast-beating heart.

"Jah, he was staring up at the hilltop."

"He'll surely think I'm weird for spying on him like this."

Chuckling, Gabbie slapped her on her back. "I was only having a joke with you about the wedding."

Amy rubbed her forehead. "I could strangle you." Amy laughed with relief. She should've realized it was a joke. The rest of the walk home, Amy was silent as she listened to Gabbie chatter about many things.

"I'll show you the apple orchard." Gabbie ran off ahead.

"Wait," Amy called after her. Gabbie wasn't at all like Amy's sister, Martha, even though the two were around the same age.

She turned and ran backward. "I wait for no man. Woman. Whatever." Then Gabbie turned back again and ran faster.

Amy giggled at her; she was fun to be around. Gabbie stopped running once she reached the orchard, allowing Amy to catch up.

"Do you work in the orchard?" Amy asked as they walked along the rows of trees.

"*Jah;* when it's picking time the whole *familye* works. Now, tell me truthfully what you think of Andrew so far?"

"He looks handsome from a distance."

"He's plain. He's not handsome at all. Do looks matter to you?"

"*Nee,* not at all." Amy bit her lip. Looks weren't that important—but she didn't want Andrew to look like his *bruder,* so they must've been of some importance. "What about you? Do you like anyone?"

Gabbie looked up, and then jumped up to pluck an apple from the tree. "There is one boy I like. Only trouble is…"

"What?"

Gabbie stared at Amy. "Only trouble is, he's courting someone." Gabbie took a bite of apple and then promptly threw it away.

Amy looked to where the discarded apple landed.

Wastefulness in Amy's *familye* was frowned upon. *"Ach,* that's a pity."

"What do you think I should do about it?" Gabbie fixed her eyes on Amy.

Amy rubbed her chin. "The apple?"

"No, silly. The boy I like."

Amy shook her head, still wondering why Gabbie had tossed the apple away. "There's nothing you can do."

"I could break them apart."

Amy grabbed Gabbie's arm. "You can't do such a thing."

"Can if I want."

Amy had never met someone with Gabbie's attitude. *"Nee,* just wait, and *Gott* will bring you someone. If you're meant to be with him, it'll happen."

Gabbie jumped up, grabbed another apple and threw it as far as she could. "You can't be happy your parents expect you to marry an old man like my *onkel."*

"I wasn't happy, but maybe it's *Gott's* will that I'm here. I mean, it is—because here I am."

"Then it's His will I break Joseph and Ilsa apart."

Amy was horrified. "You can't do that. You can't interfere in the lives of others in such a way."

"My dear Amy, I believe such things happened in the Bible. People interfered in the lives of others to get their way. There were many schemers."

"Jah, and you should know that they never came to a happy end."

Gabbie threw her head back and laughed. "I'm having a joke with you, Amy."

Amy studied Gabbie's face to see if she was indeed joking, then she laughed with her.

"So you want to marry my *Onkel* Andrew?"

Amy drew in a breath. Now Gabbie was pressuring her about Andrew. "I don't even know him."

"I think you love him, and I think you fell in love with him as soon as you saw him."

Amy looked down as they walked. She would have to be careful what she said to Gabbie; she didn't seem like a person who could be trusted.

Gabbie said, "We had better get you cleaned up and looking nice for when you meet him at dinner tonight."

Amy looked down at her clothes that now had grass stains and dirty marks. *"Jah,* you're hard on my clothes. I need a *gut* cleanup."

When they got back to the house, Amy had a quick shower, while pangs of nerves gnawed at her stomach. The man she'd seen was strong and handsome, and she hoped he wouldn't think she was as silly as Gabbie. If his personality matched his looks, she wanted to make a good first impression. When she'd changed into a new dress, apron and *kapp,* she headed to the kitchen to help Jane just as she'd help her own mother at meal time.

"You're our guest, Amy. For tonight anyway, make yourself comfortable in the living room."

"I do want to help you more around here, Jane. I feel terrible for not being around much today."

"There's always tomorrow." Jane put her hand on Amy's shoulder. "Now, you can set the table if you insist on doing something, and don't forget to lay an extra setting for Andrew."

No, she could not possibly forget Andrew was coming for dinner. Gabbie was helpful to her mother as they prepared dinner and it did not escape Amy's notice that Gabbie behaved better in her parents' presence.

When the sun was disappearing behind the horizon,

there was a knock on the door. Gabbie tugged on Amy's sleeve, and whispered, "That'll be him."

Still in the kitchen with Gabbie and Jane, Amy heard the muffled voices of men in the next room.

Jane said, "We have five minutes to go. Gabbie, you can take Amy out to meet Andrew."

With her hazel eyes twinkling, Gabbie took Amy by her arm and pulled her into the living room without Amy having a chance to straighten her prayer *kapp* or apron.

They stopped in front of Andrew, who sat on a couch opposite John, and Amy was relieved to see he was the man she'd seen from the hilltop. As silly as Gabbie had acted, she hadn't been sure what to expect. Both men stood. Amy looked up into a pair of bright blue eyes that stood out on his tanned face. Her heart pitter-pattered. He was more handsome up close and, when his lips turned upward at the corners, he was even more so. Somewhere in the distance, Amy heard someone speak.

Chapter Five

John said, "This is Amy, Andrew."

Andrew tipped his head. "Hello, Amy. I'm Andrew."

Amy giggled, as John had already said he was Andrew. Could he be nervous too? "Hello." She regretted giggling like a girl, but it was done now. As long as she didn't giggle again, it should be okay.

"Please sit." Andrew motioned to the couch next to him.

Amy shot a look at Gabbie before she sat.

"Mamm said dinner will be in five minutes," Gabbie said.

"Smells *gut."* John rubbed his hands together.

"It certainly does," Andrew added before he looked around. "Where are the boys?"

Gabbie said, "Can't you hear them? They're playing up in their bedrooms."

"You better tell them to get washed up for dinner, Gabbie," Mr. Miller said.

At once, Gabbie obeyed her father. And before long, Amy heard the scurrying of feet from the floor above.

"How are you enjoying your stay, Amy?"

"I'm having a lovely time so far. Gabbie showed me around today."

One of Andrew's eyebrows rose slightly. "Was that you I saw on the crest above the mill?"

Amy stared into his striking blue eyes and noticed a faint smile on his handsome face. "Ah, *jah,* Gabbie was showing me the sights." Amy fiddled with the strings of her prayer *kapp,* hoping someone would change the subject. She was embarrassed to have been caught spying on him and she hoped he hadn't seen them running away.

"Dinner's ready," Jane called from the kitchen, providing the hoped-for distraction.

The sound of heavy footsteps rained down from the stairs as four boys barreled down them.

"No running," John ordered.

The boys obeyed and walked quickly to take their places at their smaller table next to the adults' one. It was a home designed to cater for a great many people.

"Can I help you serve, Jane?" Amy asked.

"Denke kindly."

Amy placed vegetables and meats on the boys' plates, hoping she was giving them enough. She knew growing boys ate more food than girls. When she finished that, she helped Gabbie and Jane place the large bowls of food on the main kitchen table.

Once everyone was seated, they bowed their heads for the silent prayer. Then their eyes opened and everyone passed the food bowls around.

Amy looked across at Andrew when she felt him looking at her. "What are you doing so far from home, Amy?" Andrew asked.

Amy's mouth fell open and she looked at John and when he kept his head down, she looked at Jane, who quickly looked away. She closed her mouth, took a deep breath, and opened her mouth again to give an answer, but no words came out. Didn't he know why she was there?

When she failed to answer, Andrew said, "Here for a time away from home—a vacation?"

In desperation, Amy looked at Gabbie, and she too was of no help. In fact, she smiled as though she enjoyed the awkward scene. Amy looked down at her food. "Something like that."

After no one had spoken for a time, Andrew asked, "Amy, do you have many in your *familye?*"

"I'm the eldest; then there's Martha, Mary, Rose, Lily, and the youngest is Sally. And you?"

"Just my *bruder* here." He nodded his head toward John.

She already knew John was not his biological brother, they were stepbrothers. His mother had been involved in some sort of scandal, but it seemed to have been covered over or forgiven before she married John's father.

The silence was awkward as John and Jane continued to keep their heads down. Gabbie smiled, still enjoying the awkward silence; that was plain to see.

Amy asked, "How long have you had the sawmill?"

"About ten years now. I started working there when I was eighteen. A few years later, the old man who owned it retired and I bought it from him."

Okay, now what else can I ask? Amy looked over at the younger boys, hoping they'd make a noise so they would be scolded. At least that would be a distraction.

Andrew also looked around. "So, Amy, do you work back at home?"

"I had a job with a *wunderbaar Englisch* family. I cooked and cleaned for them. I was their maid."

"Why did you leave?" Andrew asked.

Oh dear, what could she give as a reason for leaving? "Pardon?"

"You said you *had* a job?" Andrew set his fork on the edge of his plate, and laced his fingers together.

"*Ach jah.* My *vadder* thought it not suitable to be spending too much time amongst *Englischers.* My *vadder* is a deacon." It was partly true. She just left out the part about leaving the job to meet a man whom everyone hoped she'd marry—except the man himself, who obviously knew nothing about it.

"*Jah,* it can be hard for the *kinner* of deacons and bishops, can't it, Gabbie?" Gabbie narrowed her eyes at him and Andrew chuckled, and said, "I'm only teasing, Gabbie."

Gabbie remained silent and popped a forkful of chicken pie into her mouth.

When the weirdly quiet dinner was over, Amy and Andrew were shuffled to a separate living room, which the Millers called their sunroom because it had many windows and faced toward the south. In the back of her mind, Amy thought how wonderful it would be on a chilly winter's day.

Andrew leaned across to Amy, and whispered, "What's wrong with them tonight? Have you done something or are they upset with me?"

Amy put her hand to her mouth and giggled. She knew they were embarrassed to be caught out in their scheming. "They aren't always like that?" she said softly. "This is only my second dinner here, and last night I was too tired from the trip to pay much attention."

Andrew leaned back in his chair. "You wouldn't know, would you? *Nee,* they aren't like this and it's odd. Something's going on, I'm sure of it. We're the odd ones out, you and I, and that's why they've sent us in here. They'll be talking about us right now."

Fiddling with the strings of her prayer *kapp,* Amy asked, "Have you always lived around here?"

"I came here when I was young. My *vadder* died and *Mamm* met John's *vadder* at a wedding. He was a widower by then. They got married soon after they met."

Amy nodded. "And where did you live before that?"

"We lived in Lancaster right up until we moved here."

Why didn't anyone mention he'd come from the same place as she? "Do you remember anything about it?"

"I was too young, but I'm sure I remember my old *haus* and playing in the snow, running in the fields, that kind of thing. Just vague images."

They smiled at one another, and Amy felt more of a connection to him knowing that he'd come from her hometown.

"Would you do me the honor of allowing me to drive you home after the gathering tomorrow?" Again, he spoke in a quiet voice so the others couldn't hear.

"I'd like that." After Amy spoke, the rest of the *familye* joined them.

The family played Dutch Blitz and board games for the next couple of hours before the younger children were sent to bed. Then there was a round of coffee and cookies for dessert. When the evening drew to an end, John suggested that Amy and Gabbie go to bed.

Then he had quiet words with Andrew before he left. Was John telling Andrew why she was really there? It was awkward that Andrew hadn't been the one to instigate her coming there. Did he even want a wife? Was coming all this way a total waste of time?

As she changed into her nightdress, Amy prayed there would be a *gut* outcome from her visit. She decided it didn't matter if she might be wasting her time regarding Andrew; she was meeting different people and seeing a different part of the world. Her *vadder* always said you could learn from every experience. Amy rubbed her bare arms and reprimanded herself for not bringing a warmer nightdress. She jumped into her bed and moved her legs quickly in an effort to warm the bed.

As she closed her eyes, her lips turned upward into a smile. She was going on a buggy ride with a man. She had never been on a buggy ride or any kind of date with a man before. Amy took a deep breath and imagined Andrew's handsome face. His coloring was unusual with dark gold-blond hair, tanned skin, and those blue, blue eyes. When he had smiled, he'd revealed even white teeth.

"Wake up, Amy. You have to get ready."

Amy opened one eye to see Gabbie, fully dressed and ready. Amy threw the bedcovers off and sat up. "Morning already? Am I late?" Amy looked at the window and saw that the sky was already light.

"Nee, but you will be if you don't get up now. I'll brush your hair."

"Okay, *denke."* Amy slid out of bed and changed into her grape-colored dress. After she pulled on her over-apron, she unbraided her hair. She loosely braided her hair every night so it would not get into knots and tangles during the night.

"Sit here." Gabbie used her foot to push a chair toward Amy.

Amy sat, and Gabbie ran the brush through her hair. "This is nice. My little *schweschder* used to brush my hair for me. She's about your age; I think I told you, her name's Martha."

"I suppose you miss them all."

"Jah."

Gabbie said, "Sometimes *Mamm* lets me do her hair." After she firmly braided Amy's hair, she said, "We fix our own breakfast on Sundays."

"We do at home as well," Amy said while pinning up her hair.

"We have to be quick because when *Daed* says it's time to go we have to leave right then."

Amy placed her prayer *kapp* on and then followed Gabbie down the narrow, wooden staircase, and into the kitchen. The boys sat quietly while they ate their breakfast. Gabbie handed her a plate and both girls sat.

"Mamm makes this every Saturday so we can have it for breakfast on a Sunday. It's baked eggs with vegetables, and it's got small pieces of bacon in it. Sometimes we don't have bacon and it's chicken or sausage instead."

Before long, John appeared in the kitchen. "Five minutes, then we're going."

The boys rushed to the sink to clean their own plates while the two girls stayed sitting.

"Are you looking forward to seeing Andrew today?" Gabbie asked with a twinkle in her eye.

"I've not thought much about it."

Gabbie chuckled and spooned the last portion into her mouth.

"Are you ready, girls?" Jane bustled into the kitchen and spooned some egg casserole into her mouth. She put the leftovers into the refrigerator. "Got to go now," she said as soon as she had swallowed.

Gabbie stood and took Amy's plate and her plate to rinse them off.

"Denke, Gabbie."

Gabbie grabbed Amy's arm. "Let's go."

Although the buggy was a large one, it was still crowded with so many of them in it. Amy was squashed against one side of the buggy, which she much preferred to being squashed in between two of the boys.

Ten minutes later, they arrived at the Schrocks' house where the meeting was being held. The wagon with the wooden benches was already there, and six men were carrying the benches into the house.

As they walked toward the house, Gabbie whispered to Amy, "Sometimes people come early to talk to *Dat.* He hears everyone's problems." Gabbie grabbed Amy's arm. "Quick, let's hurry inside; it's cold."

Warmth engulfed them when they stepped into the house. A fire roared in the fireplace at the far end of the room. Gabbie took Amy to meet Mr. and Mrs. Schrock and then they sat at the back of the room. Gabbie stood and took off her coat and, when she sat back down, she spread it across her knees. Amy was still chilly, so she kept her coat on.

As people walked through the door, Gabbie told Amy about nearly every one of them. A tall boy walked in and Gabbie fell silent.

"Well? Who's he then?" Amy asked.

Gabbie's gaze flicked to the ceiling and back to Amy. "That's the boy I told you about."

"He looks nice."

"*Jah,* he is, and he's the only one I like." Amy giggled into her hand.

"What's funny?"

"Just like at home. I've got four friends and there were no *menner* in the community for us—not any our age."

Gabbie blew out a deep breath. "So that's why they sent you here?"

Amy nodded. "That and my *vadder* didn't want me to spend time around *Englischers*. One of my friends just married an *Englischer*."

The boy looked over at Gabbie then quickly looked away.

"He just looked over here," Amy whispered. "Did you see that?"

Gabbie shrugged. "He's still courting someone else."

Amy held her peace. She didn't want to give Gabbie any encouragement in the wrong direction.

Andrew walked in the door and waved to the two of them and they waved back.

When Andrew got talking to someone, Gabbie said, "He was looking around for you."

"You think so?"

Gabbie nodded.

The number of people in attendance was much smaller than the meetings back home. Everything was run much the same, though, with the hymns sung in German, the prayers, and then Gabbie's father delivered a sermon. There were only about twenty people who stayed through the afternoon for the nightly singing. Gabbie had gone home with her parents, but since Andrew was taking Amy home, she had to wait until he was ready.

Andrew stood beside her at the drinks table when the last of the singing was over.

"How did you enjoy our gathering?"

"I enjoyed it very much."

"Are you ready to go?"

She was on her first date. *"Jah."*

He walked her to his buggy and once they were away from the Shrocks' *haus,* Amy's heart pounded. It was awkward with him not knowing why she'd come. How was it that he didn't know? She should've asked John or Jane why he hadn't been told, but she didn't want to be disrespectful. From how her father had spoken, Andrew had requested help in finding a wife.

Chapter Six

"I like this time of year," Andrew said above the horse's gentle clip-clop sounds on the road.

"You do? I don't like the cold."

"I think there's something nice about it being cold outside when you're warm and snug inside."

"It's not horrible to be cold."

He chuckled. "*Jah* it is. What are your plans while you're here?"

She had to think fast; she couldn't tell him she'd been planted there for him. "I hope to help Jane in the *haus* and maybe help make a nice garden. Although it's not the season to plant."

"You like gardens?"

"I love flowers. I like growing vegetables too. There's something satisfying about seeing things grow."

He laughed as he drove. "I'm taking you up here a little way. There's a place where we can see the town lights." Andrew pulled the buggy off to the side of the road. "It's a short distance up here."

Amy got out of the buggy and looked up into the dark

night sky. The moon was luminous and seemed larger than it did at home.

"The moon is beautiful, isn't it?" he said when he joined her.

"It's huge."

Andrew turned his face toward the sky once more. "It doesn't normally look as big. Must be a full moon tonight, or nearing a full moon."

He walked on, and Amy walked beside him trying to keep up with his long strides. A few more steps and the lights of the nearby town lit up the darkness.

"See?" he said.

"Ach, that's very pretty."

"I thought you'd like it. I could show you around the town. John and Jane mightn't have the time, and I don't think they let Gabbie go too far."

"Jah, I'd like to have a look around."

"I'm busy tomorrow and the next day. How about Wednesday afternoon?"

"I'll look forward to it."

"There are many things to see."

Amy trembled and pulled her coat tighter around her waist.

"Cold?"

Amy nodded.

"Best we get back into the buggy and get you warm."

Disappointed their time together would be so short, Amy walked back to the buggy with Andrew.

As they traveled back to John's house, Andrew told Amy about the history of the town. Once they arrived, Andrew stopped the buggy and said, "I had a nice time with you, Amy. There's something calming about being around you."

Amy smiled. "I had a good time too."

He lowered his voice. "I'm looking forward to seeing you on Wednesday."

"I should check that it's okay with Jane." Amy remembered she was to help Jane in exchange for board.

"I'll call in on Tuesday night after dinner to make sure it's all right."

Amy smiled. "Okay."

As she stepped down from the buggy, Andrew said, "I'll walk you to the door."

He joined her outside the buggy and they walked up to the house. The front door swung open and John stood in front of them. "Don't mind me. I heard a noise and didn't know it was you two. Come in."

"I won't stay. I'm just delivering Amy home."

John nodded as Amy walked through the doorway. *"Denke,* Andrew."

"Bye, Amy."

"Goodnight, Andrew."

Seeing no one in the living room, Amy walked upstairs to her bedroom all the while listening to the muffled conversation of John and Andrew.

Once she'd closed the door, she leaned against it until she heard Andrew's buggy leaving. She was half expecting Gabbie to burst through the door any minute to find out how she'd gotten along with Andrew. Changing into her nightgown, she knew she had to put Andrew out of her mind. It would be hard, and she wouldn't see him for two whole days.

When she was lying beneath the covers in the slowly warming bed, her thoughts drifted again to Andrew. He was older than the husbands and boyfriends of her friends, but none of that mattered anymore. Tingles of satisfaction spiraled through her body knowing she was to see him on Wednesday. Tonight had been the best night of her life.

The next morning, Amy was determined to help Jane as much as she could. She sprang out of bed at first light and went into the kitchen. Jane was already cooking breakfast and John sat at the kitchen table. "I'm sorry, I wanted to wake earlier."

"We rise early here," John said.

Jane pointed to the table. "Sit and I'll get you some breakfast."

"Nee, let me do something," Amy said.

"You can help me later today. Sit and I'll fix you some eggs. You can help me make breakfast for the boys when they wake."

"Okay." Amy sat opposite John.

"How do you like it here so far?" John took a mouthful of coffee.

"I like it very much." What she meant was she liked Andrew very much—and what she'd seen of the town so far was all right.

"I'm glad you like it. And Andrew?"

"John, don't put Amy under so much pressure. You told her *vadder* you wouldn't."

Amy's eyebrows rose at Jane's comment. She didn't think her *vadder* would've considered such a thing important. Now that they had raised the subject of Andrew it was a good time to voice her concern. "It surprised me that Andrew doesn't know why I'm here."

John looked away from her then stared into his mug of coffee. After a moment, he looked up at her. "Andrew's a complex person. He wouldn't like this. That's why we didn't say anything when he came here for dinner."

Amy twisted her lips. "I understand that but who decided I should come here? I was told there was a *mann* looking for a *fraa*. I thought he was the one who wanted me here." Couldn't anyone see how awkward she felt?

"He's alone, and he needs a *fraa.*" Jane placed a mug of coffee in front of Amy.

"Denke, Jane." Amy placed her hands around the mug and looked across at Bishop John hoping for answers.

"It's a difficult situation, but that's the way things are." John looked again into his coffee.

"I feel like I'm keeping a secret from him and that makes me tense. I guess… I am keeping a secret from him."

Jane cleared her throat. "He would not have done this for himself, Amy. He's been too long by himself to know what's good for him."

Amy was now in a difficult position and she hoped both Jane and Bishop John knew how awkward she felt about this. It wasn't fair that she was now forced into a position of keeping their secret. Would Andrew be upset when he found out this had all been arranged behind his back?

When Bishop John left, Jane went back to cooking the eggs and Amy drank her coffee.

When the younger boys had gone to school and Bishop John had left for work, taking Joseph with him, both Amy and Gabbie gave the house a thorough cleaning.

When their work was done, Amy went to her room and wrote to her friends. Firstly, she wrote to Claire, who was newly married to Donovan, the *Englischer.*

Claire's marriage to Donovan was partly what had spurred Amy's father to send her away. Amy figured she could just as easily meet an *Englischer* where she was right now, but her father seemed convinced otherwise.

Amy pulled a chair near the window, so she could write and look out over the land at the same time. After her letter to Claire, she didn't want to write much anymore, so she addressed an envelope to Olive but wrote one letter to her and Jessie and Lucy, so the three of them could all read it together at the coffee shop. In her letters, she told her friends about the family she was staying with and how different it was there, but she did not tell them about Andrew. That kind of thing couldn't be explained so easily in a letter. Lastly, she finished with a letter to her parents.

Gabbie burst into her room as she was sealing the envelopes. "Do you want to do some quilting?"

"Jah, I'd like that. I haven't done any for a while."

"Mamm's helping me make a quilt. You can help me, too." Gabbie giggled.

Amy stood and placed her envelopes on the top of the dresser where she would see them and remember to post them. She followed Gabbie downstairs and into the sunroom. Cut pieces of fabric lay on the small table near two couches. When Amy sat down next to Jane, she looked out the two large windows, which looked over the Millers' land and across to the forest.

"Have you done much quilting, Amy?" Jane asked.

"Mamm and I used to do a lot, but we haven't done any lately."

Jane loosely tacked the fabric pieces together.

"I do cross-stitch mostly and embroidery," Amy said.

"I brought some with me so I could do it on the train, but I didn't get to it."

"Why ever not?" Jane asked.

Amy smiled. "I didn't feel like it. All I did was look out the window trying not to be sick."

Gabbie giggled. "You were train-sick?"

"I think so." *More like homesick.*

Chapter Seven

❧

For two whole days, Amy had looked forward to seeing Andrew again and he'd said he'd stop by Tuesday evening. It was after dinner when Gabbie and Amy were busy cleaning the kitchen that Amy heard Andrew's voice coming from the living room.

"Andrew's here," she said to Gabbie.

"Go then; I'll finish this."

"Denke." Amy wiped her hands on a cloth, straightened her prayer *kapp* and licked her lips before she walked into the living room.

"Ah, here she is. Hello, Amy. I told you it would be all right," Andrew said, smiling.

"I wanted to be certain," Amy said.

"You're not a prisoner here, Amy, you can come and go as you please. You're a guest," John said.

Jane stood up. "I'll make some hot tea. Amy made an apple pie today." Jane winked at Amy as she walked past. All Amy had done was wash and peel the apples.

"Sit with us, Amy," John said.

As Amy sat on the couch, she was relieved to see Gabbie come out of the kitchen and walk toward them.

"The boys are quiet again," Andrew said.

Gabbie sat down with them. "They're playing in Joseph's room before bedtime, and that'll be very soon."

John chuckled. "That's why they're quiet. They know if they're too noisy they'll be sent to bed earlier."

"Would you like to have your own *kinner, Onkel* Andrew?" Gabbie asked.

Amy frowned at her, but Gabbie had her eyes fixed on Andrew.

Jane returning with a tray of tea was the perfect interruption. "Gabbie, go fetch the milk, please."

Amy wriggled in her seat. "Can I do anything, Jane?"

"Nee, that's all that's lacking."

Gabbie scowled and took her time leaving the room, but was back in no time with the milk, placing it on the coffee table.

Once everyone had a cup of tea in hand, Amy was pleased Gabbie's question to Andrew had been forgotten about.

When Andrew finished his tea, he slapped his hands on his knees. "I won't hold you up. I only came to ask about stealing Amy away tomorrow." Andrew stood. "Would you show me out, Amy?"

Amy noticed everyone's smiling faces as she rose to her feet. *"Jah,* of course."

"Take your time, Amy. Gabbie and I will clean up here."

"Denke." She walked with him to the door. When he opened it, a cold draft swept through the house.

He quickly closed it and they remained in the house, but still, they were far enough away from prying ears. "Don't come out with me; it's too cold. I wanted to see you alone to tell you I enjoyed our time on Sunday night."

"I did too."

He seemed relieved when she said so. "I've not been able to think of much else. I'm looking forward to tomorrow."

Amy smiled and nodded. "Me too." *Arrghh, think of something to say rather than keep on agreeing with him,* Amy chided herself.

They stared into each other's eyes for a second before he opened the door fully and left her gazing after him. Her body flooded with a strange sense of calm as she closed the door, knowing she'd met the man she was going to marry.

"Gut nacht," Amy called to everyone before she hurried up the stairs. Rather than talk with the others, she wanted to savor the moment by herself.

Everyone bidding her a good night echoed around her head as she climbed the stairs. Amy changed into her nightdress and flew under the covers, snuggling into her pillow. She replayed every word he'd said from the moment he'd entered the house. After all these years without a beau, who would've known love could be so easy?

The next morning, Amy worked hard doing the chores, so she wouldn't feel guilty about spending the whole afternoon with Andrew. It was right on one o'clock when Amy heard Andrew's buggy outside the house. She hurried upstairs and gathered up her letters.

She swung her coat over her shoulders as she heard Jane call, "Amy, Andrew's here."

"I'm coming." Amy walked downstairs trying to

steady her rapid breathing and when she got to the bottom there stood Andrew with his hands on his hips. "Hello." She nervously held up her letters. "Can we stop somewhere to mail these?"

"Jah, we'll go to the post office."

Once they were a little way from the house, he said, "I forgot to tell you not to eat much today."

She giggled. "I haven't had much."

"That's *gut.* I'd like to take you to a little restaurant I know. Actually, it's not so small." He chuckled. "I go there often. After that, I'll show you around, and we can mail those along the way."

"Sounds good."

As the buggy traveled down the roads, which were not dissimilar to the ones at home, Andrew talked about the climate of Augusta and what it was like in every season. Amy tried to look interested when all the while she was admiring his large hands and strong legs.

"Give me the letters," he said, as he stopped the buggy unexpectedly.

Amy handed the letters to him, he got out and she watched him drop the letters in a box, just two stores up. When he jumped back into the buggy, he rubbed his hands together before he picked up the reins. "It's chilly out there. Not far to go now."

A little way up the road, Andrew parked the buggy behind the restaurant and covered his horse with a blanket. "Quick, let's get inside. We'll try to get a seat near the fire."

The tables close to the fire were taken, so they sat opposite each other in a booth in one corner. Andrew handed Amy one of the menus already on the table. "They have an all-day breakfast here. They also have delicious muffins and we must take a dozen away with us."

Amy giggled at his excitement over the muffins. "Okay."

"Don't laugh. These aren't just any muffins. You'll see when you taste one."

"Can't wait." Amy scanned down the menu. The "big breakfast" was two pancakes, two eggs, hash browns, bacon and sausages. "Someone would have to be hungry to order the big breakfast."

"I usually have the steak."

"I think I'll have a salad sandwich. Tuna."

Andrew's mouth turned down. "Is that all?"

Amy looked up from the menu. "What would you suggest?"

"Corn-beef hash, ham and cheese omelet. Anything other than a boring salad sandwich."

"Okay, then I'll have potato pancakes with applesauce." Amy closed her menu.

"Fine."

The waitress took their order, and then they were left staring at each other across the table.

Nervousness caused Amy to break eye contact, and then she looked around the restaurant to find something to talk about. The walls were brightly colored and two walls were covered in brightly painted murals. When she looked back at him, he was still smiling. "Do you eat out much?"

"Nee. When I do, though, I come here."

The waitress placed their coffees on the table.

Amy warmed her hands around the cup. "This place reminds me a little of the coffee shop I meet my friends at every Saturday."

Andrew leaned his head to one side. "Is that right?"

"*Jah.* Why do you look surprised?"

"It's just that your *vadder* is a deacon and I thought he wouldn't allow you to go to such places. Unless, of course, you went there accompanied."

Amy screwed up her nose. "My friends are there."

"I see." Andrew stared into his coffee. "I mean an older *bruder* or your *vadder.*"

Amy sipped her coffee and then swallowed quickly. "I don't have an older *bruder.* If *Dat* had to go with me, I wouldn't go. It would make my friends uncomfortable." When Andrew didn't comment, she asked, "Has John told you anything about me or my *familye?*"

Andrew laughed. "Only things that have come up in conversation. If I want to know about you, I'm quite capable of asking you myself." He moved in his chair and his lips turned upward at the corners. "I would like to know more about you." He took a sip of coffee while keeping his eyes fixed upon her.

She placed an elbow on the table and placed her chin on her knuckles. "What would you like to know?"

"I'm intrigued about your adventurousness. You've come all this way for no reason in particular. I admire that."

She had to change his line of thinking before she had to tell him that he was the reason she was there. "It took a long time to get here. Tell me about you."

"There's not much to know. The mill keeps me busy. I've got a small home." He leaned forward with a smirk hinting around his lips. "A home that needs a woman's touch." Embarrassment caused her to look away.

He continued, "And I find peace in walking in the

woods or driving my buggy down quiet roads. You can probably tell that I've grown used to my own company."

Amy studied his face. Was he telling her he wasn't marriage material and was happy on his own? No, he had made that comment about his house needing a woman's touch.

He then shook his head. "Don't get me wrong. I don't want things to stay like this."

"How would you like your life to be?" Amy asked.

The waitress placed their food on the table.

"Ah, this looks *wunderbaar.*" Andrew picked up his knife and fork. "To answer your question, I'd like to have a *familye*. And have someone to share things with and have someone to talk to."

Amy nodded. She had her *schweschder* and her friends to confide in and ask advice of. It must be awful to have no one. "What about friends; can't you talk to them?"

"I've got friends and then there's John, but they're all busy with their own families."

"Why have you never been married?" Amy poured the applesauce over her pancakes.

He stared at what she was doing, as though he'd never seen anyone have that combination. Then he looked up at her. "I could ask you the same question."

"I'm a little younger than you."

He chuckled. "That's true enough." Andrew breathed out heavily. "I can't really say I've ever met a woman I've felt strongly enough about to share my life with. There have been some who were nice enough, but each time I felt that something was missing."

Amy looked back at her food and cut a portion of

pancake. "That makes perfect sense." She looked up at him and they smiled at each other.

"And what's important to you, Amy? What do you want?"

"I'd like a *familye* too."

"Ah, we have something in common." He cut a piece of steak and when he had swallowed it, he said, "Maybe *Gott* sent you here for a *gut* reason."

His smile sent shivers through Amy. She blinked rapidly and looked down into her coffee.

"I do have to tell you that these last two days that I've waited to see you again have been hard for me." Andrew rhythmically moved his fork through the air as he spoke, as though to emphasize the words.

Amy frowned. "In what way?"

"I wanted to see you Monday. It was all I could do to stop myself visiting you, but I don't want you to get tired of seeing me."

Amy gave a little giggle.

"I'm sorry, Amy. You don't mind me saying these things, do you? I don't want you to feel uncomfortable if you're not feeling the same things I am."

Chapter Eight

Amy's heart pounded within her chest; she could barely draw a breath. She slipped her hands under the table and pushed a fingernail into the palm of one hand. She steadied her breathing, trying to take her mind off how handsome the man across from her was. Maybe her father had been right to send her here; perhaps he'd been following God's plan and hearing His voice.

Andrew stared at her, waiting for an answer. He'd said he couldn't wait to see her and wanted to know how she felt. Slowly, she inhaled and then exhaled. "I feel the same."

His face relaxed into a smile. "That makes me a very happy man."

Amy put her hand to her mouth and giggled.

He nodded toward her food. "Keep eating. We've lots to see when we finish here."

When they had eaten their meal, Andrew ordered a dozen assorted muffins to take with them. When they walked out the door, Andrew handed her the paper bag of muffins.

"Try one."

Amy took the bag in one hand and her other hand flew to her tummy. *"Ach,* I couldn't possibly find the room."

He smiled. "Maybe later." Once they were seated in the buggy, he said, "I could take you to the farmers markets or to look at the stores, but they don't seem very special. I'm taking you to my favorite place."

"Where's that?"

"Hiking."

Amy looked up at the gray sky. "In this cold?"

"We can't let a little frost stop us."

"It's too cold for the horse, isn't it? He'll be standing while we walk."

"I've got a decent blanket for him, but you're most likely right. I'll drive you down past the road where the walking trail begins. We'll walk there when the weather is warmer. How's that?"

"Okay. Tell me what it's like." Amy didn't do any walking for pleasure at home. The only walking she did was for the purpose of going somewhere, but she could get used to it and accompany him on his walks.

He glanced over at her. "You'll love it. There are butterflies, all kinds of birds...and the trail winds up and down, over old wooden bridges and around steep rocks. The views are spectacular."

Amy smiled at the thought of a grown man taking pleasure in watching butterflies. "I like to watch birds. At home, I leave a bird feeder in a tree to distract them away from my vegetables. I often sit and watch them."

"Isn't it insects that eat the vegetables?"

"Birds do too and I keep my vegetables almost insect free. I plant flowers, marigolds and other plants that the insects don't like, in between the vegetables. I also make a garlic spray to keep them away."

Andrew stopped the buggy in the middle of the deserted road. "See." He pointed to a dirt trail that led downhill. "That's my favorite place to walk, down there. This is where the trail begins."

"I'd like to walk it sometime."

"You will. The weather will improve in a few weeks. Since you're too scared of the cold, I could show you around the mill and show you my workshop."

"I'd love to see where you work. What do you do in the workshop?"

"I try my hand at making furniture."

Amy sat up straight. *"Jah,* I'd like to see that."

"Let's go then." Andrew clicked his horse forward.

Fifteen minutes later, they were at the sawmill and Andrew showed Amy through to a workshop at the back of the mill. She walked into the huge barn of a room and looked at rows of furniture. "Is this all yours?"

"Jah." He chuckled.

"I was expecting to see one or two pieces of half-made furniture."

"I've had a fair amount of time on my hands. I've never sold any. This is my way to pass the time." He beckoned to her and pointed out one of the dressers. "This is a traditional style dresser with the four small drawers at the top and the four large drawers below."

"The wood is beautiful." Amy ran her fingertips over the grain.

Andrew placed his hat on the top of the dresser. "It is beautiful. It's high-grade red maple. It's softer than other maples and it's a little more difficult to work with."

"It's so nice."

"It's my favorite wood. I like the color and how the grain's so close."

He opened one of the drawers and she stepped closer to look. "The insides of the drawers are made from pine. Using pine on the inside has two advantages. Pine is less costly, and it's lighter. If it were all made from maple, it'd be hard to lift."

"How long would it take to make one of these?"

"It takes me many weeks; I don't know how long it would take anyone else." Andrew pointed to the sides of the drawer.

"You see here?"

She leaned over and looked.

"I use the old half-blind dovetails, which is the traditional method."

"Ah." Amy straightened up and nodded.

"I'm sorry; I'm sure you can't be interested."

"Nee, I am. I'm interested. Please, keep telling me about them all. I'm impressed that you've made all these and made them so well."

Andrew looked surprised.

Amy continued, "It must have taken a long time to learn how to do it."

"It did, and many failed attempts." He smiled as he rubbed his jaw.

The next hour flew by with him showing her his furniture.

When he was down to the last piece, she said, "How did you get interested in making furniture?"

"My *vadder* was a cabinetmaker." He sat on one of his small chests and she sat beside him.

Amy's eyes traveled around the warehouse. Which *vadder* was he speaking about?

"I don't know if you're aware, but John and I had different *vadders*. *Nee,* I believe I told you that."

"Jah, you mentioned it to me."

"My mother was unmarried when she had me." He looked at the floor.

Amy raised her eyebrows as if she were unaware of such a thing. "You were innocent of anything that happened...like that."

"I know, but I'm sad for the hard times my *mudder* went through before she married my *vadder*. It wasn't easy for her to return to the community and repent in front of the congregation, so she'd be allowed back in."

"Nee, that would be difficult for anyone."

"She was shunned for a time. That was hard, she said, and after that things got better. John's *vadder* and my *mudder* were happy together." Andrew smiled and dug her in the ribs lightly. "I know that Gabbie would've mentioned something to you. Whatever's in her head comes straight out her mouth."

"Just a little. And your *mudder* told you your *vadder* was a cabinetmaker—or was it your step-*vadder* who was the cabinetmaker?"

"My real one, biologically speaking."

"Is it in your genes then?"

"It could be. It's calming and a bit like your gardening. You like to see something grow from a small seed, and with this, it's seeing something grow out of the rough timber. Something that's practical and looks nice."

"I understand." Amy was glad he opened up to her about his *vadder* and his past. "What was it like growing up with a step-*vadder?"*

"I couldn't ask for a better *familye*. I was loved and

cared for and both my parents were kind and understanding. You asked me something earlier today."

"Jah, what?"

"You asked me why I've never married." He took a deep breath and laughed. "Why am I telling you all these things?" Shaking his head, he said, "I'm hesitant when it comes to committing myself to someone and I think it stems from what happened to my *mudder.*"

Amy sat on her hands. "You mean how you came to be—your biological father and everything?" Andrew nodded.

"Did your *mudder* tell you much about what happened?"

Andrew ran a hand through his hair. "A little information here and there. She never sat me down and had a long talk with me and told me what her situation was or how I came to be. The only thing I know was that he was a cabinetmaker and she only told me that after I got interested in wood." Andrew stood up and beckoned for her to follow. Soon they were in the lunchroom. "It's small, but we don't need much. Just a place to sit and eat when it's too cold out." Amy sat on one of the four chairs.

"Tea or *kaffe?"* he asked.

"Tea, please. Do you want me to get it?"

"Nee. You relax; you're my guest."

Amy smiled at him before he turned around to make the tea. She peeked out the door and into the mill. "I thought it would be noisier than this."

"It's deafening at times." He looked at the clock on the wall. "We've about twenty minutes before the noise starts."

After he placed two cups of tea on the table, he sat

opposite. They looked at each other and smiled again. They'd barely finished their tea when the noise started.

"Told you," he yelled.

She covered her ears.

"C'mon, let's go."

They hurried out of the work area and when she was about to get into the buggy, she paused; she didn't want the day to end. She looked over at him. *"Denke* for today. I enjoyed it."

"Me too. We have to do this again soon."

"I'd like that."

He reached for her hand and held it firmly. Her body warmed in response to his touch; she looked down to see her hand concealed in his.

"Your hand's cold."

Happiness filled her and she had to stop herself from giggling like a young girl. "My hands are always cold."

They looked into each other's eyes some more and smiled again.

As they traveled back to Bishop John's, Andrew said, "I'm happy you decided to come for a visit. It was meant to be."

"I was thinking the very same thing."

After a while of peacefully listening to the horse clip-clop down the road, Andrew eventually spoke. "And, you haven't told me why you've never married."

"Oh, there's no one around for me. At least, that's what I thought."

He glanced over at her. "You thought that before you arrived here?"

She beamed a smile at him. He knew exactly what

she meant and she was letting him know she liked him. "That's right."

"Maybe we both won't be single for much longer." Their eyes met. "Maybe."

She was disappointed when they got back to John and Jane's house. She wanted their time together to continue into the night. "Are you coming inside?" Amy was aware that someone from the house might be spying from the window if they weren't quick to get out of the buggy.

"I will, but I won't stay for dinner. I've taken up enough of your time."

"Please stay," Amy said.

"Nee, I won't. I'm forewarning you because Jane and John will do their best to persuade me to stay."

When they stepped through the front door, the aroma of a baked dinner wafted under their noses.

"Andrew, stay for dinner?" Jane asked. "It's nearly ready and it's your favorite, roasted rosemary lamb."

"Nee denke. I must go and see to some things at the mill. It smells delicious."

"Come and warm yourself with some hot tea with me then," John called out from the couch.

"Okay, just a quick cup then."

"Sit with us too, Amy," John said.

Amy sat down with the two men, and Gabbie, who had been playing with the boys in the sunroom, came into the living room. She looked at Andrew then Amy. "Are you two getting married?" she asked as she flopped onto the couch.

"Gabbie!" John's head swiveled to his daughter.

Gabbie leaned back. "Well, that's why she's here."

Andrew looked at John and when John looked away,

he frowned. Andrew asked Gabbie, "What are you talking about?"

Gabbie rolled her eyes. "Is it that hard for you to see? Amy's been sent here to be married off and not to just anyone, married to *you.*"

Andrew's jaw dropped and he looked at Amy. Knowing he'd feel betrayed, she didn't know what to do or say. "Amy?"

All Amy could do was shrug her shoulders. She should've told him the truth as soon as she found out he didn't know.

Andrew turned to John. "Is this true?"

Chapter Nine

John sucked his lips in. "We were going to tell you…"

"You were? That's a *gut* thing to know." He looked back at Amy. "And what part have you had in all this deception?"

"It's not as it sounds," is all she could think to say.

Andrew bolted to his feet. "On second thought, I've no time for tea. I'll be on my way. Tell Jane goodbye for me, will you?" he asked no one in particular before he walked out of the house.

John glared at Gabbie, and all she could do was pull a face. "Well? He had to know, didn't he?"

"Not like that he didn't," John said.

Amy stayed still licking her lips. What a mess things were. This was the first man she'd ever liked and now it was over as quick as it had started.

"Where's Andrew?" Jane walked toward them with a tray of hot tea.

"He's gone," Gabbie said. "He said to say goodbye to you."

John sprang up from the couch; his hands curled in

anger. "Go to your room, Gabbie. Stay there all night and don't come down."

"Not even for dinner?"

"Nee!"

Gabbie stared at him, stood and then walked up the stairs to her room with no signs of remorse.

John threw his hands up in the air before he sat back down. "I'm sorry, Amy."

Amy took a deep breath. Now, maybe she could go home at least. "That's all right. Things always work out how they're meant."

John explained to Jane what had just taken place. Jane said comforting words to Amy and handed her a cup of hot tea as though that would make everything better.

John muttered, "She's a very headstrong girl."

"Why would Gabbie say such a thing?" Jane asked.

"She might think that he should know," Amy said. "When I arrived, I thought Andrew himself wanted a *fraa*. I was shocked he didn't know why I'd come. He would feel he's being pushed into something, and he'd feel people were conspiring behind his back. I know exactly how he'd feel. I'd be feeling the same." The sad thing for Amy was, he thought she'd been a part of it all.

John and Jane were silent as they sipped their tea.

When dinner was over, John allowed Amy to take Gabbie's dinner to her room.

Amy stood outside Gabbie's closed door. "I've got your dinner here, Gabbie."

"Come in."

Amy placed the tray of food on the bed beside her.

"Denke, Amy. Did Andrew come back?"

"Nee, he didn't." Amy sat on the edge of Gabbie's

bed. "Why did you say that to him? You didn't mention anything of the kind when he came to dinner the other night."

Gabbie placed the plate on her lap. "I don't know."

Amy's eyes wandered to her hands that were on her lap. "I'll leave you alone then." Amy leaped up and headed out the door.

"No wait, Amy."

Amy stepped back into the room. *"Jah?"*

"I'm sorry I said those things."

Amy frowned. "Why did you?"

"I don't know. I really don't know."

Gabbie looked so distressed that Amy sat down on her bed again. "Don't upset yourself. What's done is done."

"You're not mad?" Amy shook her head. *"Nee."*

A tear fell down Gabbie's cheek.

"What's wrong?"

"I hate this place. I want to leave."

"You're old enough to do that if you want. Your *vadder* would know many people you could visit."

Gabbie's lips turned down at the corners. "I don't want to visit stuffy people that *Dat* knows. I'm too scared to leave. I don't know what I'd do. I could go on *rumspringa,* but I don't know anyone."

"Jah, that would be hard. What about visiting a different community?"

Gabbie sniffed. "Like where?"

"You might be able to come back with me when I go back."

Straightening her back, she said, "Really?"

"If it's okay with our parents I don't see why not. And don't forget my *schweschder,* Martha, is the same age as you."

"That would leave *Mamm* alone here with the boys."

"It would just be a visit and then you could come back."

Gabbie smiled. *"Denke,* Amy."

"Now, eat your dinner." As Amy walked out the door, she hoped she hadn't said something silly. Did she really want Martha being influenced by Gabbie's brash and forthright ways? A change of scene might do Gabbie some good, though.

After breakfast the next morning and after the boys were at *schul,* Jane whispered to Amy, "You're going to bake an apple pie."

"I am?"

Jane continued, "Then you're going to take that apple pie to Andrew."

Amy's hand flew to her mouth. "I couldn't. He's best left alone until he calms down."

"You can and you will. In my experience *menner* like pie, in particular, apple pie."

Amy tipped her head to the side. "I don't think pie will make up for him being deceived."

Jane stepped closer to Amy. "You'd be surprised what pie and a pretty face will do to a *mann."* Amy giggled.

"Now come on. I'll help you."

"Nee, I really think it's not a *gut* idea. I'd feel awkward, and he blames me for not telling him why I'm here. I should've told him at the start as soon as I found out. He's right. I deceived him."

"Well, you didn't tell him, and you can't change that. What you can change is what you do right now." Jane took hold of Amy by the elbow and guided her into the kitchen. "Trust an older lady to teach you about men."

"You think he'll see the pie and forget the deception surrounding my being here?"

"Jah." Jane nodded. "Or at least decide you're not responsible for it."

Amy and Jane left Gabbie happily quilting in the sunroom while they made a large apple pie. Amy hoped she wouldn't be further embarrassed when she brought the pie to Andrew.

"How am I going to get there?" Amy asked as the pie cooked in the oven.

"You can take a buggy. We have a second one and a second horse, Silver."

"Okay, *denke.*"

When the pie came out of the oven, Jane wrapped it in a cloth. "Take it over now while it's warm. It smells delicious."

"I'll hitch the buggy," Amy said.

"Get Gabbie to help you."

The two girls went out into the barn.

"Did *Mamm* tell you Silver's flighty?"

Was this another of Gabbie's jokes? Amy looked at the horse standing with his head hung low. "He doesn't look as though he is."

"Sometimes he's all right, but he's easily scared by things. That's why he's not our main buggy horse. *Dat* bought him at an auction and they were going to sell him for dog meat. He used to be a harness racer."

Once they had Silver hitched to the buggy, Jane met them outside with the pie. Amy was tempted to ask Jane if the horse was safe, but surely she would've mentioned if he wasn't.

The horse clip-clopped toward Andrew's house and Amy hoped that she wasn't making a big mistake by seeing him again so soon. If she didn't have to report back to Jane, she would've made a detour and gone somewhere else for the day. And, if Andrew was upset with scheming, how much more upset would he be when she brought the pie to him?

She went straight to his house, and when she stopped outside, he came out to meet her. Andrew came right up to the buggy door and stood beside it.

Honesty was the only way. "Andrew, I've been involved in another deception."

"What is it this time?" he asked trying to look stern despite his lips curving upward.

She glanced at the pie beside her, pleased he was acting friendly. "It involves apple pie."

He looked at the ground, scratched his cheek and looked up at her again. "And is the apple pie deception entirely your own idea?"

Amy shook her head.

"Apple pie does sound like the kind of deception that might be acceptable."

She stared into his blue eyes and his face softened.

"Come inside." He opened the buggy door.

She reached across to the pie and handed it to him. "This is the peace offering that I'm to give you."

He took it from her and nodded. "Gladly accepted from whoever forced you to bake it."

She climbed down from the buggy and they walked inside.

He set the pie down on his kitchen table. "I guess we should have some pie before it cools."

"Sounds like a good idea." Amy sat at the table and as he set about gathering plates and forks, Amy said, "I want to apologize for not telling you why I'm here.

My parents didn't want me to marry an *Englischer* like some of my friends had. Well, one of my friends. The other friend's boyfriend converted. Anyway, without me knowing, they wrote to John and before I knew it the plan was hatched and I was sent here. It's none of my doing except to go along with my parents' wishes." Amy breathed out heavily. At least he knew now. "When I got here, I thought I was coming to meet a man who was asking to meet potential *fraas*. I didn't know you were being…"

"Set up?"

"Jah."

Andrew looked at her, then stood over the pie and cut it into pieces.

Amy continued, "I had no idea you didn't know about it until dinner when you asked why I was here."

"Ah. I thought you looked somewhat startled when I asked you that." Andrew sat down. "It must've been a shock for you when you realized I didn't know."

"It was, and then I was too shocked and didn't know what to say. I couldn't say I'd been sent here hoping to marry you, or that everyone else was hoping we'd marry. I mean, they were sitting right there and weren't saying anything."

Throwing his head back, Andrew laughed heartily. "Now I can see what an awkward position you were in. No wonder John and Jane seemed so odd that night."

"I'm glad you understand." Amy relaxed into the chair.

"I don't understand why they did it, but I can see the funny side." Andrew pushed his fork into the pie. "I must apologize for my reaction." He popped the pie into his mouth.

Amy shook her head. "It was understandable."

He swallowed another mouthful of pie, and said, "This is very *gut* pie. It could cover a pretty big deception."

"Jane and I made it. Although, she might say that I made it all by myself." Amy giggled, happy that they were back on track with their relationship. At least, she hoped they were.

Chapter Ten

Three weeks along, Amy and Andrew were seeing each other every other day. In their most recent private moment together they'd both expressed their strong feelings.

"Letter for you, Amy," Jane called out one afternoon.

Amy hurried downstairs anxious to read news from home. She recognized the handwriting of her father. That was unusual because it was mostly her mother or one of her sisters who wrote. She sat on the couch and tore the envelope open only to learn her mother was sick and asking for her. Amy put her head in her hands. *Mamm* couldn't have been that sick, or they would've called John's phone in the barn. This had come at the very worst time.

Reading further, she knew she had to return. Amy folded the paper and popped it back into the envelope, and then dragged her feet into the kitchen to tell Jane she had to go home.

Jane was sitting at the kitchen table also reading a letter and she looked up at Amy when she walked into the room.

"It's from your *vadder* and he wants you home." Amy nodded and sat opposite.

Jane sighed. "He said your *mudder* is not seriously ill, but she has been pining for you."

"Mamm gets very emotional."

"They've bought your tickets and you leave on Friday."

Amy gasped. "That's only three more days."

Jane nodded. "We'll be sad to see you go. You've fit in with the *familye* so well."

"Jane, do you think that one day Gabbie might be able to visit? My *schweschder*, Martha, is her age, and I'm sure they'd get along. They're very similar except for Martha being a little quieter."

"That might do Gabbie some good. We'll think on that when your *mudder* gets well."

"We might have to bake another pie for when I tell Andrew the news."

"I don't think he'll be happy you're going, but you'll be back, won't you? As soon as your *mudder* is better?"

"Denke, I hope so. You wouldn't mind if I come back?"

Jane reached over and patted Amy's hand. "I would love you to come back whenever you want. Why don't you go over and tell Andrew now?"

"He'll be working."

"He won't mind."

Amy bit on the inside of her lip. "You think so?"

Jane nodded. *"Jah,* go on. Take the buggy."

Amy had wasted no time hitching the buggy. When she stopped near the mill, Andrew caught sight of her and jogged over to greet her.

"Is everything all right, Amy?"

Amy shook her head, opened the buggy door and stepped out. "I have to return home to Lancaster County."

"Why? You've only just arrived."

"*Dat* wrote and said *Mamm's* sick and needs me."

"I'm sorry to hear that. What's wrong with her?"

"She isn't seriously ill, but what am I to do? I have to go." A tear trickled down Amy's face.

"Come into my office."

Amy followed Andrew into a small portable building beside the mill. He faced her after he closed the door behind them. She turned toward him, and he stepped in close and carefully wiped the tears away from her cheeks.

"I don't want to go, Andrew. First, they force me to come here when I don't want to, and now they want me back when I want to stay. I feel as though I have no say over my own life and I'm over eighteen. I'm an adult."

"I don't want you to go either, but they are your parents." He enclosed his arms around her, and she sank her head into his chest. "Come back to me, Amy." Andrew continued to hold her tight.

She turned her head to look up into his eyes and as though it was the most natural thing in the world, he lowered his head until his soft lips touched hers. With eyes closed, she savored the velvety sensation of his lips. When she realized she was kissing, she stepped back and her hand flew to her mouth.

"I'm sorry, Amy." He looked at the ground.

Her heart beat wildly. "It's okay." She had wanted to save that first kiss for the man she'd marry, and he hadn't even asked her.

"I'm going to miss you. You'll be back, won't you?"

Amy nodded as she wiped another tear from her eye. "And I'll write."

"I've never met anyone like you, and I don't want to lose you. But Amy, I have one serious concern with us."

"What is it?"

"Our ages. I might be too old for you."

"Nee you're not. I think your age is perfect. We're perfect together, and everyone else thinks so too, that's why I was sent here."

He smiled. "I'm ten whole years older than you."

"How do you know how old I am?"

"John happened to mention your age, and it's clear you're much younger than I am."

"Does it matter so much?"

Andrew looked down and rubbed his forehead. "My only concern is for you. It's something you have to consider."

When Amy pushed her bottom lip into a pout, Andrew stepped closer. "You have a chance to go away and forget me. You can meet someone your own age or nearer to your age. Take this time as a chance to think about what you want. Time away could be good for the both of us."

Amy was not pleased to hear his words. *"Nee,* Andrew, none of that matters and I could never forget you. I'll come back as soon as my *mudder* is better."

Andrew put his hand on her shoulder and his fingers trailed down her arm. He picked up her hand. "We haven't known each other long enough to make any promises."

Amy could barely speak, but inside she felt like screaming. She wanted him to promise her something.

Why didn't he propose right now? Her mother would understand why she couldn't come home if she said she was marrying Andrew. Then she might be allowed to stay.

"When do you leave?" he asked.

She sniffed and tried to be brave. "I have to leave on Friday."

"Can I take you to the bus stop?"

Fighting back tears, Amy nodded.

"Let's get out of here." Without waiting for her to speak, Andrew guided her out of the office past the mill and into the buggy she'd driven there. He sat in the driver's seat with Amy beside him.

"Don't you have to work?" she asked.

He clicked the horse forward, turned to her and said, "I'm the boss, remember?"

"Where are we going?"

"Somewhere, anywhere; I don't know." He looked over at her and laughed.

She forced a smile back at him, pleased for any time alone she got to spend with him.

"I'm just driving," he said. "I'll show you the river."

Amy pulled her coat tighter around herself wondering if he might kiss her again. Next time, she wouldn't pull away.

He glanced over at her. "Cold?"

"Nee."

Minutes later, he pulled the buggy to a halt. They walked hand in hand down a hill until they reached a river.

"It's pretty here."

"I'm going to miss you so much, Amy. You've lit up my life like a warm glowing candle in a darkened room.

Never doubt how I feel about you. What I feel is real. I've never felt this before."

The mellow tones of his voice made her body tingle. "I didn't know I could feel this way about a man until I met you."

"If only you were older, Amy."

Amy narrowed her eyes. "Andrew, what does age have to do with anything?"

He placed his arm around her shoulder, and whispered, "Possibly nothing, but I worry you might feel forced into things by your *familye,* and that might've clouded your judgment over me."

"That's not so at all."

"Time apart will help you find your true feelings."

Amy shook her head. "I don't want time apart." Didn't he feel the same? If he did then surely he'd never allow her to leave. He'd call her family and explain that they would marry and she'd have to stay.

"With age comes a more even temperament. You learn that sometimes it's best to wait and not rush into things." He ushered her closer to the river's edge.

Amy watched the water lap at the small plants that grew on the edge of the riverbank. From his words, Amy knew he wasn't going to propose.

"I'm busy, with a large order that's just arrived, for the next couple of days, Amy, but I'll see you Friday."

Thunder clapped in the gray sky overhead, and the rain pattered down upon them.

"We should head back," Amy said. She was too upset to enjoy their time together, and an hour later they were back at the mill.

Andrew got out of the buggy and looked a little sad when he said goodbye, but he'd said his part and she didn't want to feel any more rejection. With tears in her eyes, she headed back to John and Jane's house. What possible reason would he have for not seeing her in those last two days? He'd said he was the boss, couldn't he delegate the work? And, surely he could come to dinner on one of those nights before she left, couldn't he? It seemed he was letting go already.

The next days were a blur for Amy, and on Thursday she had Jane send Andrew a message that Gabbie would take her to the bus on Friday. She did not think she could say goodbye to Andrew without crying and causing a scene. It would be easier if Gabbie took her.

As Gabbie stood beside the bus, Amy said, "I'll miss you, Gabbie, but I'll come back as soon as I can."

"I'll miss you too. You've been like a big *schweschder* to me."

Amy smiled. "I'll write as soon as I get there."

"I'm going to go home right now and start writing you a letter."

The girls hugged before Amy boarded the bus. As the bus pulled away from the stop, Amy looked back to see that Andrew had just arrived in his buggy. She saw him jump out and run up behind Gabbie, pointing to the bus. Amy could've stuck her head out the bus window, could've waved as it drove away. Instead, she sank down in her seat so he couldn't see her.

Her stomach churned for the hours on the bus. Once she got onto the train, she pressed her head back into the headrest. Andrew had said that they shouldn't promise each other anything. He could be keeping his options open in case he met someone else; that's the only reason that made sense. Amy tried to put him out of her mind.

She could not afford to see a future with him in case he met someone else. As much as she tried not to, every moment with Andrew replayed in her mind. He'd had the chance to ask her to marry him, but he hadn't taken it. He as good as said that he was in love with her, and they'd even kissed. The only reason she could find was that his love for her wasn't as strong as her love for him.

When Amy wasn't crying she was sleeping, so the journey home was quicker than the one to Augusta. She was pleased to see Martha and her father when she got off the train in Lancaster County.

Martha ran to her and threw her arms around her neck.

"Don't ever go away again," Martha said.

Something inside her relaxed when she saw her family again. She laughed and her father walked up to her and put his arm around her. "We've missed you, Amy."

"You didn't have to come all the way here. I would've got a taxi by myself. You shouldn't have wasted the money on taxis both ways."

"We were looking forward to seeing you and couldn't wait another minute, that's why," Martha said.

"How's *Mamm?*"

"She's out of bed now. She was quite sick there for a while," her father said.

"Jah, she's okay. She's been crying because she wants you home," Martha said.

Her father frowned, obviously not pleased with the dismissive way Martha was speaking about her mother.

They'd barely gotten out of the taxi at home when her mother came running out to see Amy. She threw her arms around her daughter. "I never should have let you go so far away." Her mother finished her embrace and stood with her hands on Amy's shoulders. "You've lost weight."

"Nee, I don't think I have."

"I think you have, Amy," Martha said.

Amy frowned at Martha. Her mother didn't need to worry about her weight.

"Well, you have," her sister said.

Her father took Amy's suitcase inside, and the women followed him into the *haus*.

"Are you better now, *Mamm?"*

"I got out of bed just this morning."

"She's been in bed for a good three weeks," Martha said.

"I'm better now you're home. I'm sorry we ever sent you to Augusta. You didn't want to go, and we should've listened."

"You look a little pale, *Mamm*. Why don't you go up to bed and I'll bring you up a cup of hot tea? Martha and I can cook the dinner."

"Martha's been doing it all herself since I've been unwell. Okay, I'll lie down. Then you must tell me all about your trip."

While Martha fixed her mother a cup of tea, Amy sat and watched.

"What happened?" Martha asked. "What was the man like?"

Amy put her hand on her head. Where would she start? Should she tell them she hadn't wanted to return because she was in love? It wasn't fair. She'd left Andrew, and her mother didn't appear ill enough for her to be called back. "He was the nicest man I ever met. I want to marry him."

Martha nearly dropped the teapot. "What?" She rushed at Amy and sat next to her. "Tell me more."

"He's kind, thoughtful, and sometimes he's serious and sometimes he's funny." Amy couldn't help smiling.

Martha frowned. "Is he handsome?"

Amy's eyes twinkled. "Very. He's tall and tanned with the most incredible blue eyes."

Gasping, Martha covered her mouth. "Does he want to marry you too?"

There it was. The thing that irked Amy. He wasn't as keen. "We never spoke of marriage, not much. I wasn't there long enough, that was the problem." Amy swallowed hard.

He'd had every opportunity to ask her.

"You'll have to go back, Amy, if you love him."

Amy giggled. *"Jah,* I'll go back as soon as I can. I miss him already. Now, hurry up and make that tea and we'll take it up to *Mamm."*

The girls took tea up to their *mudder* who was in bed, propped upright with pillows.

As soon as Martha sat on her mother's bed, she said, "Amy's in love."

Her mother's eyes grew wide. "Are you?"

Amy grimaced. She'd forgotten to tell Martha to keep it to herself. "I like the man you and *Dat* sent me to meet. I really like him."

Their mother pressed her lips together. "He's not a suitable match because he lives too far away."

Amy's mouth fell open. "But…you and *Dat* sent me there."

"It was your *vadder's* idea, and he made me think it was a *gut* one, but he sees now that it wasn't."

Amy pressed her lips together and looked over at Martha.

"You will allow her to go back though, right? She misses him dreadfully already," Martha said.

Mamm passed her cup back to Martha. "We can talk about it later. I'm feeling poorly and need to sleep. *Gut nacht.*"

Amy closed her mother's door, and she and Martha made their way downstairs to get the dinner ready.

"Don't worry, Amy, they'll let you go back."

"Jah, I know. *Mamm's* a little upset. I don't think that *Gott* would've let me meet him if I couldn't marry him. *Gott* will make a way. I know it."

"That's right. He will."

The younger sisters came in from playing and helped with the evening meal.

Dat didn't mention Augusta over dinner. It was best to leave the subject alone for a time, Amy thought. Their mother did not come down for dinner and stayed in her room the rest of the night.

After dinner, Amy wrapped herself in her thick coat and sat on the porch by herself. It was the first time alone since she'd gotten off the train. Her mind and body gave way to numbness.

Her father came out and sat next to her. "Cold out here, isn't it?"

"Jah it is. I'm just thinking here quietly, away from the noise of the girls."

He chuckled. "Martha tells me you're sad because you want to return to Augusta, and she said you've fallen in love."

Amy looked straight ahead. "That's true enough."

"It's not practical that you be away from the *fami-lye* now."

"Why, *Dat?* You and *Mamm* were the ones who wanted me to find a *mann,* the ones who sent me away against my wishes, and when I do go and find a *mann,* you send for me to come back. Are you saying that I can't go back—ever?"

"Not for the time being. Your *mudder* will tell you why tomorrow, and then you'll understand."

Looking out into the darkness of the night, Amy knew nothing either of her parents would say could keep her from Andrew.

"Gott can find you a man here."

"Jah, but I don't want just any man, *Dat."*

"All things are possible to those who believe."

Amy furrowed her brow. When things got too difficult for her *vadder* to explain he always resorted to quoting Scripture. "I don't know what *Mamm* can say that'll make me want to stay."

"I understand you think that now, but wait and see what your *mudder* has to say." He stood and walked back into the *haus*.

Closing her eyes in the quiet of the night with the cool breeze stinging her face, she remembered the feel of Andrew's lips against hers. Would she ever taste his sweet lips again? She placed her fingertips on her lips and imagined that he was right there with her.

Chapter Eleven

It was after breakfast when Amy and Martha were sitting in the kitchen that their *mudder* delivered the news. "I'm having a *boppli*."

Amy raised her eyebrows. "Another one? Aren't you too old?"

"*Nee,* I'm not and *Gott* has blessed us with another child."

"That's great, *Mamm*," Amy said without making the effort to sound genuinely pleased.

"Yeah, great," Martha said with less enthusiasm than even Amy had expected.

Mrs. Yoder frowned. "I thought you girls would be delighted."

"Is this why I have to stay here? Is this why I was told I had to come home; to help you look after another *boppli?*"

"Aren't you pleased?" Mrs. Yoder smiled.

"I'm shocked." Amy rubbed an eyebrow. This couldn't be happening. "I want to be pleased, but it doesn't seem right." Amy looked over at Martha.

Martha licked her lips. "How could this happen? It's not right. Aren't you too old or something?"

"Nee, your *vadder* and I have wanted another *boppli* for some time now. This child is a blessing from *Gott,* and you're both acting spoiled. I thought you both would've been pleased."

"But, *Mamm,* Amy is nearly twenty—it seems she should have her own *bopplis* soon and…well, it seems weird," Martha said.

"James Byler is twenty-two years older than his *bruder,* Thomas, and none of you has ever thought of that as weird." Their mother spoke of their neighbors.

"You're old enough to be a *grossmammi,*" Martha said, ignoring her mother's words. "I'm eighteen, and if I get married now I could have a *boppli* in a year, so my *boppli's onkel* or *aente* would only be a year or two older. I don't like it; it's not right." Martha planted her feet firmly on the floor and placed her hands on her hips.

"You and *Dat* told me I had to find a *mann* to start my own *familye,* and when I try to do that, you stop me." Amy rose to her feet, walked downstairs and right out of the *haus*. She knew she should've been happy to have another *schweschder,* or a *bruder,* but she wasn't; not when the *boppli* was keeping her away from Andrew.

It was a week later that Martha came running through the door with a letter from Andrew. "Amy, quick, where are you? I have a letter and it's from him, I'm certain of it."

Amy grabbed the envelope from her sister. She recognized the writing as his from when she'd seen things he'd written at the mill.

She hurried to the privacy of her bedroom where she could read every word carefully.

His handwriting was smooth and flowing. To savor every moment, she brought the paper to her nose and inhaled, then she held it close to her heart. She knew he wouldn't speak of promises or love—he'd made that clear before she left.

He wrote of how he'd enjoyed her company. It didn't matter the words he wrote, all Amy cared about was that he had written and that meant he hadn't forgotten, nor had he met another.

She would write straight back to him. Sucking the end of the pen, she wondered what to write. She could not tell him of her mother's news, of the *boppli*. Although many women in the community had *bopplis* when they were older, Amy never thought it would happen in her *familye*. Finally, Amy wrote telling him about how she would come back very soon. Yes, if she wrote it, then it might just happen.

It wasn't until the next day that her mother broke the news that Amy was expected to stay in Lancaster County and not return to Augusta. Ever.

Weeks turned into months, and the letters between Amy and Andrew became fewer. There was little for Amy to write to him about; every day was the same. She'd had to leave her job as a maid before she left for Augusta, and her *mudder* had been bed-ridden since she'd come back. Amy had become the one who ran the whole household.

Once the boppli is born, things will return to normal, Amy hoped. The lack of letters worried her, and she wondered whether Andrew's feelings for her had dimmed. It preyed on her mind that he'd thought it too soon to make promises to her. It also disturbed her that he thought her too young.

Today was the first Saturday in months that she was able to get out of the house and see her friends in town back at their favorite coffee shop.

"I can't believe I'm back here. I haven't been here in ages."

Amy had missed going out with her friends. It seemed so long ago that she had been carefree and not encumbered with her *mudder's* burden of running the house and looking after the *kinner*.

"Are you still writing to Andrew?" Jessie asked.

"His letters haven't been as frequent. Now, I wait a long time before I write back. I don't want it to seem like I'm anxious. I don't want to scare him away." Amy straightened her prayer *kapp*. "He should be the one who is keen."

"He's in Augusta and you're here, I don't think you could do anything to scare him any farther away," Olive said dryly.

"Well, in the last two months I've only had two letters and they've both been short." Amy looked into her coffee. "I think he's lost interest. Who wouldn't? It's been so long and I haven't told him why I can't go back. I promised him I'd return as soon as my *mudder* got better."

Jessie fixed her large green eyes upon Amy and grabbed her arm. "You must tell him, Amy, or he'll think you have no interest in him."

"I agree; you have to," Olive said.

"What reason have you given for not going back?" Lucy asked.

Amy took a deep breath. "None really." The girls looked at each other.

"I don't want to tell him my *mudder's* about to have a *boppli* at her age. I'm embarrassed."

"It's a normal thing," Lucy said.

Amy shrugged her shoulders. It might be normal for others, but it did not seem right. "He thinks he's too old for me."

"Nee, he'd only be saying that for your sake. He wouldn't mind you being younger," Lucy said.

"That's right," Olive said.

They could be right, Amy thought, as she took a mouthful of coffee.

"You girls will have to be attendants at my wedding," Olive said. "We're getting married in nine weeks."

"The *boppli* will be born by then," Amy muttered to herself.

"Jah, we will, Olive, we'd love to," Lucy said.

While the girls chattered about Olive's wedding to Blake, Amy tried to appear interested and happy. All she could think about was Andrew. It didn't seem fair to meet a man and then be whisked away from him.

When the talk of the wedding had died down, Jessie turned to Amy. "You know, Amy, my *bruder* has been asking questions about you."

"Mark?"

Jessie nodded. *"Jah;* I thought if you're not thinking too much about Andrew, I reckon Mark might be interested." Jessie giggled.

"Did Mark ask you to find out about Amy?" Olive asked.

All eyes fixed upon Jessie.

Jessie giggled and said, "He might have."

Amy's eyebrows rose. She'd never considered Jessie's *bruder* because he was so much older, but he wasn't as old as Andrew.

"Just letting you know that Mark might talk to you at the gathering tomorrow," Jessie said.

The girls oohed and aahed, and then giggled.

"Thanks for letting me know, Jessie," Amy said. Maybe Mark would help her get over Andrew since she'd most likely never see him again.

Chapter Twelve

Amy drove the buggy home thinking about Mark. He was a nice man, and now, his age wasn't an issue. Could *Gott* have sent her all the way to Augusta to meet Andrew with the sole purpose of opening her eyes to Mark? Mark had been there all the time, and she'd overlooked him.

The next day at the gathering, Amy knew that Mark was interested in her by the way he continually glanced in her direction. Of course, she didn't look his way but kept a watch on him out of the corner of her eye. It wasn't until the meal after the service that he approached her.

"Hello, Amy."

"Hi, Mark." Amy had no idea what to say to him because she didn't really know him.

He scratched the back of his neck and looked around. "It's a lovely day."

"Jah, it's nice once the cold weather goes."

He swallowed hard and rubbed his jaw. "Amy, I was wondering if you might like me to drive you home tonight?"

She had to give him a chance. *"Jah,* okay." She nodded and smiled knowing he was nervous. "Have you tried these little sausages? They're lovely." Amy turned back to the table, stabbed a sausage with a toothpick and handed him one.

He took it from her and popped it into his mouth. As he chewed, he nodded then when he'd swallowed, he said, "Very nice."

"I made them." She smiled up at him.

"Ah." He laughed. "Good thing I liked it, then, isn't it?"

As Amy was about to say something else, Martha rushed toward them. "We have to go home now, *Mamm's* feeling poorly."

"Mark's taking me home later."

Martha looked at Mark, gave half a smile and left them.

"You can go with your *familye* if your *mudder's* sick, Amy."

"Believe me, *Mamm* is always sick; it's nothing out of the ordinary." Amy shook her head.

When Mark frowned, she realized how uncaring she sounded. "I mean, in her condition, it's normal to feel ill some of the time."

"Ah." Mark nodded.

By now, it was plain for anyone to see that her mother was expecting. Even though pregnancies weren't spoken about openly between men and women, it was a fact of life. Days away from having the *boppli*, *Mamm* had gone back to spending nearly every day in bed except when she forced herself out for meetings.

"I'll come and find you a bit later then?" Mark asked.

Amy looked up at him and nodded. When he was gone, she looked for one of her friends to speak with. She found Olive, and all Olive could talk about was her up-coming wedding, which was a nice distraction for Amy.

Once the meeting was over, Mark approached Amy. "Are you ready to go?"

"*Jah.*"

They climbed into his buggy and he clicked his horse forward. It seemed strange to be with another man. This was only the second man she'd ever gone on a buggy ride with and she was twenty already, now that her birthday had just passed.

"How did you like your trip away?"

"I enjoyed it. I didn't think I would, but the *familye* was lovely. They have a *dochder,* Gabbie, the same age as Martha. She's going to visit us soon, hopefully." Amy glanced across at Mark. He had the same coloring as Jessie, thick, wavy light-brown hair and green eyes. He was a solid, well-built man.

He looked over at her and she smiled and looked away.

"Your broken leg has completely recovered I see," Amy said.

"*Jah,* that was a long time ago. My leg is better than new. Except when the weather is about to change—then I have my own weatherman."

Everything about the buggy ride reminded Amy of Andrew. She closed her eyes and remembered how it felt to sit next to him.

"Are you okay, Amy?"

Amy cleared her throat. "Yes, a little tired I guess. I've been waking through the night to make sure *Mamm's* all right." She hoped that might redeem her from her previous comment regarding her mother.

"It must be hard for you to take your *mudder's* place in the household now she's not feeling well."

"She was a little better for the past couple of weeks; she's gone downhill again over the past few days."

"Looks like it's about to rain."

Amy put her hand out of the buggy. *"Jah,* it's already raining." Even the rain reminded her of Andrew. It'd rained when they were at the river the last time they had been together.

"We might call it a night and I'll take you straight home since it's raining."

"If you want to."

"Do you want to?"

"We can go a little farther." Amy guessed Mark sensed her lack of interest in him and she felt a little embarrassed. She wanted to like him. "How's the farm doing?"

"Great, at the moment. Last year we prospered and we're hoping for the same this year." After a silent moment, Mark said, "What do you like to do in your spare time?"

Amy chuckled. "I haven't had a lot of that lately, but I do like to sew—embroidery and needlework rather than clothes. Although, I just finished making new dresses for three of my sisters. When I sew samplers, I can make them different every time. Whereas dresses are all the same."

"I have to wonder, Amy, why you have never married."

Amy giggled. "What about you? You are a little old to be unmarried, don't you think?"

"That's true enough. Perhaps you and I have to be more practical in our choices."

Amy looked at him. He stared straight ahead at the road. What did he mean? Did Jessie tell him she was in love with Andrew and Mark knew it was never going to happen? "I've never made a choice, so I don't know how I could make a more practical one."

"What I mean is, that you and I are unmarried. We're both from the same community and both our families know each other very well. You and my *schweschder,* Jessie, have grown up together. I was hoping you'd consider me as a possible choice for you."

"*Ach.*"

He looked over at Amy and she twisted her mouth.

He gave a half-hearted chuckle. "I'm not speaking my mind very well. I guess I'm not good at this kind of thing. I need a *fraa* and you're single and I thought that you and I might make a pair."

"*Jah,* I see what you mean. Well…this is all sudden."

"*Nee,* Amy. I don't mean to put you under pressure. I'm not asking you to marry me right now. I was hoping your mind might be open to the possibility of that happening." He glanced at her and put his hand to his head. "I've made a complete hash of things. I'm taking you home."

"You haven't made a complete hash of things. I'm glad you spoke your mind. I will consider what you've said."

He turned the buggy and headed toward her *haus.* Once he was outside Amy's house, he drew the buggy to a halt. "I would be pleased if you gave it some thought, Amy."

Mark smiled at her and his eyes were kind. Amy smiled back. "I will, Mark."

Amy walked into the house and went straight up to see her *mudder*.

Martha was there, sitting on the bed. She looked up when Amy walked in. "The midwife is coming soon."

"Is the *boppli* coming?" Amy asked.

"Jah, Mamm said that the *boppli* should be here by morning."

Chapter Thirteen

Amy sat on the other side of the bed and stroked her mother's head. "I'm sorry I took so long to come home."

Her mother reached her hand up and patted Amy's hand as if to say it was okay. Amy knew she should've gone home with the *familye* and not gone on that buggy ride.

When June Byler, the midwife, arrived with her assistant, the two girls were shooed out of the room. While the younger girls slept, Martha, Amy and their father waited in the living room. The three of them dozed in the early hours of the morning and were woken by the broken cries of a newborn.

They ran up the stairs with *Dat* leading the way. The girls stayed back as he opened the door and after a few minutes, the girls were allowed in to find they had a *bruder*. The Yoders finally had their first son after six girls.

Their smiling mother kissed the red, wrinkly baby on his head. "I don't know what to do with a boy. I'm used to girls."

"You'll soon learn," their father said with tears of joy still lingering on his cheeks.

"He's so tiny," Martha said.

Amy looked at the tiny person who was the cause of her separation from Andrew. She wanted to resent him, but he was simply too cute.

The midwife and the assistant cleaned the room around everyone before they left.

With some hours of darkness still left, Amy fell into bed pleased she still had time for some sleep. She could snatch a few hours before she had to wake for the younger girls, to see that they did their chores before getting them off to *schul*. Amy was too tired to think of what Mark had said and too tired to think of Andrew.

The next time Amy saw Mark was when she went to Jessie's house for the last fitting of her attendant's dress for Olive's wedding. Jessie was the best seamstress in the group of friends, so she was the one who had offered to sew the attendant's dresses. Olive sewed her own dress and the suits of the male attendants.

It was a Saturday afternoon and, because the wedding was on the next Thursday, the girls had skipped their normal get-together at the coffee shop to meet at Jessie's house. Amy hoped she'd see Mark, but wasn't sure if he'd be there.

Mark had been the first person she'd seen when she stopped her buggy outside Jessie's house.

"I hear your *mudder* had a boy?"

Once Amy got out of the buggy, Mark took the reins to tie the horse up.

"Jah, they've called him Micah."

He looked up from looping the reins around a post.

"That's nice."

"I've been thinking about what you said to me last week, Mark."

"You have?"

"I… I don't see things the way you do."

He crossed his arms. "What do you mean, Amy?"

"I want to marry for love."

"We're all *Gott's* children and have love for one another."

"Not that kind of love. I'm speaking of romantic love."

He sighed and rubbed his neck. "I know how you girls think, and you might be looking or waiting for something that doesn't exist."

It did exist. Amy knew it because she was in love with Andrew, but she couldn't tell Mark that. Mark would ask why Andrew and she weren't married if their love was that strong. "I believe that it does exist."

Mark nodded. "The offer's there, Amy. Jessie's waiting in the house for you."

Although Amy had as good as rejected him, Mark stayed polite and friendly. It was at least nice to know that she had some sort of offer if she started to get cranky like old Marie Byler.

Jessie had already made the dress. Amy pulled the blue dress on over her head. "It's nice, but it's a little long, isn't it?"

"Jah, I'll need to take it up a little. I think that's all that needs doing to it."

Amy searched for something positive to say. "It's a pretty shade of blue." *Just like Andrew's eyes,* she thought.

"Stand straight and I'll pin the hem."

While Jessie leaned down and pinned the hem, she said, "I saw you and Mark speaking."

"He took me home from the gathering on Sunday. You knew that, didn't you?"

"Jah, I saw you in his buggy. Do you like him?"

"I wish I did. That would make things so much simpler. I do like him, but not in a romantic way."

"Okay, you can take it off now. Careful of the pins."

Amy took off the dress and then pulled her own dress over her head. "I'm excited about Olive's wedding. She's the first one out of the five of us to get married. Well, the first Amish one, if you don't count Claire's wedding."

"Elijah didn't want to get married until we had a *haus.* I told him I wanted to get married sooner than that. Now we're the next ones to get married after Olive."

"I'm the last one. What if I never get married?" Amy placed her prayer *kapp* back on.

"You will; we all thought that we might never and then someone appeared for each of us."

Amy nodded, still unconvinced.

When Amy was at Olive's wedding, her mood hadn't improved. She sighed. Here she was at another wedding and it wasn't hers. She'd watched Blake and Olive get married, while Blake's mother, an *Englischer,* had cried into a white lace handkerchief throughout the entire lengthy service. Blake's small son, Leo, sat well-behaved next to his grandmother doing his best to comfort her by patting her arm.

When will it be my turn?

She felt as though her youth was slipping away. The girls hardly ever met at the coffee shop now that the others were occupied with their men. Claire was still trying to talk Donovan into joining the community, but all Claire's friends knew he never would. He'd refused to come to Olive and Blake's wedding, so Claire had come on her own.

Amy desperately wanted a family of her own. She was busy with a household, her mother's household, when she should've had one of her own. It all seemed so unfair. And, still, she hadn't heard from Andrew in weeks.

Chapter Fourteen

Months have passed.

"Gabbie's coming to stay with us," Mr. Yoder announced over the evening meal.

Martha clapped her hands. She'd been writing to Gabbie since Amy had come home and told her about Gabbie, but they'd never met. "Is she staying a long time?"

"Her *vadder's* allowing her to stay here to help us out while your *mudder's* feeling poorly." Mr. Yoder smiled lovingly across the table at his wife.

"I can manage," Amy said.

"You can do with doing less than you are." Mrs. Yoder smiled at Amy, and then said to Martha, "I've not been the same since Micah was born. I might have to start taking the tonic Nellie Byler keeps telling me about." Micah, the Yoder's only son, was now nearly a year old.

"Jah, do that, *Mamm."* Martha's green eyes fixed on her father. "When is she coming? I just got a letter from her and she hadn't mentioned anything about it."

"Her *vadder* thinks it best that she comes here for a time." Martha studied her father's face. She knew he was keeping something from her. There was a definite reason Gabbie was being sent away from Augusta, just as there had been a purpose when Amy had been sent away from home over a year ago. Martha chewed on a piece of fried chicken while she tried to figure it out. It didn't make sense. Amy had been sent there to find a husband, but there was no man here for Gabbie. "So that's it then? She's coming here to help *Mamm?*"

Her father looked down at his food and nodded. Martha knew that he always looked away from her when she asked a question that he didn't want to answer. She glanced across at Amy and knew she was wondering the same thing. She and Amy were perfectly capable of looking after the whole family when *Mamm* had one of her sick days. Although, it would be good to have an extra pair of hands especially when Micah got fussy and cried during dinner.

Mary's face beamed. "That will be nice, won't it, Martha? Your best friend in the whole world is coming to stay with us."

Martha smiled at her little sister and nodded. "I'm looking forward to it."

"You only met her through writing letters, so how can she be your best friend?" Rose, another sister, asked.

"She is my best friend. We write to each other nearly every day."

"Now girls, no more talk about it over dinner." Mr. Yoder's stern gaze moved to each girl in turn.

Martha narrowed her eyes at Rose when her father wasn't looking. She hadn't even had a chance to learn when Gabbie was arriving and now she'd have to wait to find out.

Mr. Yoder looked at his wife. "Did you hear Mr. Glick broke his leg?"

"Nee, I didn't know. Who's helping him on the farm? He's got no sons; he's only got Anna," Mrs. Yoder said.

"He's got his *fraa* as well," Martha said.

Mr. Yoder stuck out his chin. "He needs a man to help him. His *fraa* and *dochder* will be no *gut* to him with the farm work. He's got people who helped him today, and he's got his nephew coming from Ohio tomorrow."

Mrs. Yoder raised her eyebrows and gave a quick glance in Martha and Amy's direction. "And how old is his nephew?"

Mr. Yoder's face lit up. "Twenty-five, I'd say."

"Ah." Mrs. Yoder nodded.

Martha noticed a slight smile twigged at the corners of her mother's mouth. *"Mamm,* Amy and I can find our own husbands." Martha breathed out heavily.

"What makes you think I was thinking of you? Rose is nearly eighteen; she might beat you both and get married first."

Mary giggled and Martha looked across at Rose, who gave her a look as if to say, "so there." Amy didn't laugh at all and Martha knew she was still pining for Andrew from Augusta. One day, Amy might make it back there to see him if *Mamm* ever allowed her to leave again.

Mr. Yoder put down his fork and raised his hands. "That's enough of that topic at the table."

Mrs. Yoder turned to her husband. "As soon as Mr. Glick's nephew gets here, I'll have him to dinner. We've got girls and none of them are married yet. Surely, you wouldn't deny Amy this chance?"

Amy frowned and took a gulp of water.

Mr. Yoder made a gruff sound from the back of his

throat while Martha knew to keep quiet; there was no use arguing with her parents, it had never worked for Amy.

"What's his name?" Mrs. Yoder's face contorted as she tried to contain a grin.

"His name's Michael Glick," their father said.

Martha pushed the food around on her plate wondering what Michael Glick would think of being their chosen topic for the over-dinner conversation.

It was only after her mother and siblings went to bed that Martha had a chance to speak to her father in private. *"Dat,* when's Gabbie arriving?" She sat down on the couch next to him.

Mr. Yoder looked up from his Bible. "She'll be arriving this Saturday, and since Micah is now sharing Amy's room, Gabbie will share your room. I'll move another bed into your room tomorrow."

Martha was pleased they'd be sharing. They'd have so much fun and could talk into the night. "Is there a reason she's coming? Has she been sent by her folks like how you sent Amy to Augusta?"

Closing his Bible, Mr. Yoder said, "Gabbie's *vadder* thought it best she go somewhere different for a time. He didn't tell me his reasons, and I didn't ask."

Martha knew from the tone in his voice he thought her too nosey. Why wouldn't she be inquisitive regarding her best friend in the world?

"Saturday's only two days away, which is enough time for me to arrange my bedroom comfortably to fit the two of us." Moving to the comfortable chair by the window, she wondered why her father wasn't anxious to marry her off. Amy had been nearly twenty when she'd been sent away, and Martha had just turned nineteen. Maybe they were content that at least they'd tried to marry Amy off, or maybe *Mamm* secretly wanted them all to live at home forever.

Martha rubbed her neck in frustration. She had not even been on a buggy ride with a boy.

As her father quietly read his Bible, Martha's thoughts drifted to Gabbie. The only reason that she could think of for Gabbie being sent there was to keep her away from Joseph. In her letters, Gabbie had confided she was in love with Joseph, but he was marrying Ilsa. Was Gabbie's father trying to keep her away from trouble? Martha was sure that was the reason, and her father probably knew it too by the way he avoided eye contact.

"Are you doing a Bible reading with me?" Her father's voice cut through her thoughts.

"Err, yeah." Martha rose to her feet and opened the nearby drawer of a bureau where her Bible lay. She opened the large, black leather book and looked at the page on which it had fallen open. Her Bible always opened to her favorite Psalm.

Martha enjoyed the quiet times she had with her father since Amy spent most of her time sulking in her room. Her mother always went to bed after the after-dinner cleanup, leaving the girls with their father, and Martha was always the last of the girls to head to bed.

An hour later, Martha yawned and was ready for sleep. She closed her Bible. *"Denke* for letting Gabbie stay here, *Dat."*

Looking up, he gave a smile and a quick nod. "You're off to bed?"

"Jah."

"Gut nacht, Martha."

"Gut nacht, Dat."

As Martha climbed the stairs to her bedroom, she

thought about what Amy had told her about the Millers'
house. It was larger than their house but sparse and open.
The weather was much colder and the community much
smaller than theirs at Lancaster County. Amy longed
to go back and be with Andrew, but Martha knew she
could never move so far away, no matter how much in
love she was with a man.

On Saturday night, Martha and her father traveled
in the taxi to meet Gabbie at the train station. As soon
as Gabbie saw Martha, she ran toward her and wrapped
her arms around her.

"Hello, Mr. Yoder." Gabbie tipped her head after she
finished hugging Martha.

"Nice to meet you, Gabbie." He looked down at her
suitcase. "Is this all you brought with you?"

"That's it."

Mr. Miller picked up her suitcase. "The taxis are this
way."

Martha and Gabbie smiled at each other. "You look
just the way I imagined you," Gabbie said.

"You too." Both girls giggled. *"Dat's* moved a bed
into my room for you," Martha said.

"Wunderbaar. Denke, Mr. Yoder."

Martha noticed an amused smile on her father's face.
It was hard not to smile when Gabbie was around; she
was full of enthusiasm.

"Are you weary, Gabbie?" Mr. Yoder asked.

Gabbie's hazel eyes sparkled. *"Nee,* I slept nearly all
the way. I've got plenty of energy."

Gabbie hoped her stay in Lancaster wasn't going to
be too boring…boring like the Yoder girls. She did like

Martha, from her letters, even though she might be too goody-goody.

That's what Amy was like.

Throughout dinner the first night, Gabbie stayed bright and happy on the outside, but on the inside, she was seething at having been sent away from Joseph. Her father had to know she was in love with Joseph and instead of helping her get him, he had sent her miles away—a day's journey. She would never be so awful to her children if she ever had any. And, thanks to her father, she probably wouldn't because Joseph was the only man for her.

She did her best to look on the bright side. *While I'm here, I could meet a man who'll take my mind off Joseph. Another man would be the best thing I can hope for, and it would serve Mamm and Dat right if I marry a man from Lancaster County and never return.*

After dinner with Gabbie, it was all Amy could do to wait until she got to her room before she cried. Gabbie reminded her of her stay in Augusta and that reminded her of Andrew. Secretly, she'd hoped Gabbie would deliver a message to her from Andrew, or a letter, but there was no word from him. He didn't even ask Gabbie to say hello to her. It seemed he'd forgotten her completely.

She would've heard if he'd gotten married. Why had their correspondence ceased? She couldn't start writing now that she'd stopped, and anyway, he should be the one to chase her.

Chapter Fifteen

"I'm so glad you're here, Gabbie." Martha sat cross-legged on one of the two beds in her room. She slowly unbraided her hair as she spoke.

Gabbie lay on the other, on her tummy and with her feet in the air. "Me too."

"I've been asking you to come for ages. What made your *vadder* suddenly decide to let you?"

"It's because of Joseph. *Dat* found out I like him, and that's why I'm here. He wanted me out of the way."

Martha drew a brush through her long hair. "I thought it might be something like that."

Gabbie rolled onto her back and huffed. "I don't know what to do, Martha. I'm so in love with him that it hurts."

"I've never been in love."

"If Joseph marries Ilsa, he'll be lost to me forever. I'll be forced to marry someone boring, someone I don't love at all."

Martha licked her lips trying to think of a comforting thing to say. "Things will happen how they're meant to. You could meet someone else, someone you'll love even more than Joseph."

Gabbie sat bolt upright. "What if *Gott* is punishing me?"

Martha gave a giggle and then glanced at Gabbie's face to see she was serious. *"Nee,* I don't think *Gott* would punish you. What for? Have you done something terrible?"

"I don't think so. Not something terrible, just the usual stuff." Gabbie tore her prayer *kapp* off.

Martha frowned and wondered what she meant by "the usual stuff." She placed her brush down on the bed and sectioned her hair ready to braid. *"Gott* forgives, He doesn't punish."

"Do you want me to plait your hair?"

"Okay." Martha turned around and placed her feet on the floor, sitting at the side of the bed while Gabbie came to kneel behind her.

"I love fixing hair. I wish I could've had just one *schweschder."*

"You've got me." Martha giggled.

"Hold still." Gabbie yanked on Martha's hair.

"Ow."

"If you move I won't be able to do it properly."

"I only want it braided so it doesn't tangle during the night. It doesn't have to be perfect," Martha said.

"Dat says if you're going to do something, do it the best you can."

Martha could tell from Gabbie's dominating and bossy manner she was the eldest child. Even though they were the same age, Gabbie was bossy toward her.

"Tell me about this boy who's coming to dinner next week."

Martha drew her eyebrows together. "You've heard about him?"

"Your *mudder* told me there's a new boy in town, and he's coming to dinner next week."

Martha rolled her eyes. "He's come here from Ohio because his *onkel* broke his arm—no, I think it was his leg or something. Anyway, he's helping him on the farm."

"You've met him?"

"Nee, not yet. We'll most likely see him at the meeting tomorrow if you're not too tired to go."

Gabbie scoffed. "That's never an option where I come from. We always go even if we're sick. Anyway, I slept most of the way today. I might not sleep at all tonight."

When the lights went out, Martha kept talking, but after a short while the responses stopped and all Martha could hear was Gabbie's deep breathing. She'd fallen asleep before Martha.

Sunday-meeting mornings were always hectic, as Martha's parents tried to get everyone out of the house for the early morning meetings. Other mornings were more organized because Amy was up early and in charge. The girls were all old enough to get themselves ready on a Sunday while Amy rested.

"Let's go, Gabbie. You've got to wake up now if we're to get there on time."

Gabbie opened one eye and then the other. It seemed the long trip from her home was catching up with her.

Martha continued to stare into Gabbie's face. "Everyone's downstairs already."

Gabbie sat up in bed and stretched her arms over her head. "Brush my hair for me?"

Without wasting time, Martha took Gabbie's brush

and drew it through Gabbie's long hair. After a few strokes, she said, "There," and handed Gabbie the brush.

"I'm so tired. Do I have to go?"

Martha scoffed. "You said that you always have to go at home, even when you're sick. And *jah,* you do have to go. There'll be a lot of people who want to meet you." Besides that, she'd already told her father that Gabbie had said she'd go.

Gabbie huffed and changed into her dress. "At least braid my hair? I'm way too tired."

Martha had finished dressing, so she didn't mind helping Gabbie. "We won't have time to eat at this rate. That is if there's anything left by the time we get downstairs." Gabbie remained silent.

Once Martha had braided and pinned Gabbie's hair, she popped her prayer *kapp* on top of her head. "There, finished."

"Let's go," Gabbie said and pulled on Martha's arm. They walked arm in arm down the stairs.

Martha's younger sisters were making a ruckus in the kitchen.

"I never knew girls could make so much noise," Gabbie said.

"They'd never get away with it if *Dat* were in the *haus*. He must be out hitching the buggy."

Amy walked in and hushed her sisters, and they immediately fell quiet.

"Where's *Mamm?*" Martha asked Amy.

"She's not come down yet."

Martha pulled a face. "I'll go up and see if she's okay."

"Why wouldn't she be? Has she been sick?" Gabbie asked.

Martha nodded but didn't want to say too much in front of the girls. "You eat, I'll run up and see her."

As she rounded the corner of her mother's doorway, she saw her mother lying in bed with Micah playing on the floor beside her. *"Mamm,* are you sick?"

"I just feel a little tired. Can you take Micah for me today? He's had breakfast already. I'll feel better if I have a *gut* rest."

"Of course, *Mamm.* Do you want anything before I go?"

"Your *vadder's* already made me a cup of tea."

"Come on, Micah." Martha put her arms out and he jumped into them. She carried the heavy toddler down the stairs.

"She's not well?" Gabbie asked when she saw Micah in Martha's arms.

Martha shook her head. "She's staying here, and we're taking Micah."

"I could stay and look after her," Gabbie suggested.

Amy shook her head. *"Nee.* She'll be okay. She'll just sleep while we're gone."

"Here, you eat, Martha, and I'll take him." Gabbie clapped her hands and then reached toward Micah. He giggled and leaned toward her.

But Martha had no time to eat anything, as her father already had the buggy at the front of the house. "Time to go." Mr. Yoder strode through the *haus* clapping his hands as he did every meeting-Sunday morning to hurry the girls into the buggy. The younger girls ran ahead with Amy following, leaving Gabbie, Micah and Martha the last ones.

Rose ran back into the house. *"Dat,* what's wrong with *Mamm?"*

"She's sick again. I'll have Martha take her to see about that tonic later in the week."

"Okay, *Dat,*" Martha said.

The gathering was held at the Zooks' house, a thirty-minute buggy ride away. The younger girls hurried out of the buggy excited to see the Zook girls who were around the same ages.

"Do you want me to carry Micah, Gabbie? He gets quite heavy," Martha said.

"Nee, he's okay for a while."

When they were seated, Gabbie whispered to Martha, "Are there always this many people, or are there visitors from another community?"

"Nee, it's always this size."

"It's three times as many people as we have."

"I know, Amy's told me all about it." Martha's eyes were drawn to a man who walked through the door. He was one of the tallest men at the gathering; his dark wavy hair fell just above his shoulders and from the distance she was to him, his eyes were dark. "That must be the new *mann* there now." Both girls looked at the young man. "I've never seen him before." Martha studied him.

"He's handsome," Gabbie whispered behind a cupped hand.

Martha gave a quick nod with her eyes still fixed on him. He walked with purpose and confidence, walking forward to shake her father's hand and then the hand of the bishop.

"I'm glad I came when I did," Gabbie said.

Frowning, Martha couldn't help but be annoyed. Gabbie was already in love with someone else or said she was. How quickly she had forgotten Joseph.

"Don't you think he's handsome, Martha? Look how

fine and tall he is. I'd say his voice will be deep and smooth."

"I guess he's all right."

Micah squirmed out of Gabbie's lap and climbed into Martha's arms.

"So, you don't like him?" Gabbie asked.

Martha knew Gabbie was asking hoping Martha didn't like him, that way Gabbie would have a green light. "I don't know him. I haven't met him yet."

"Gut. Then you won't mind if I get to know him, will you?"

The first halfway decent stranger to visit in ages, and now Gabbie was going to get in first? "What about Joseph?"

"He's marrying someone else." The annoyance in Gabbie's voice was clear.

Martha let out the breath she'd been holding on to. "He's coming over for dinner this week, so I guess we'll both get to meet him then."

A smile spread across Gabbie's face. "I must ask your *mudder* what day he's coming and I'll cook the entire meal."

"I do that," Martha said while making signs with a finger over her lips telling Micah to stop squealing.

"You and Amy can have a rest, and I will cook." Gabbie put her hands together and rubbed them briskly.

Before Michael sat down, his eyes swept across the women's side of the room.

Gabbie dug Martha in the ribs. "Did you see him look at me?"

Martha pressed her lips together. "He looked this way, that's all."

"You don't think he stopped and gave me an extra

look? I mean, didn't his eyes linger when he saw me?" Unable to speak, Martha shook her head.

Gabbie whispered, "He was looking over at the women, so that means he's looking for a *fraa.*"

"That's understandable at his age. I wonder why he hasn't married."

"You think there's something wrong with him, Martha?"

Martha put her finger up to her lips again, this time to shush Gabbie. If her father found out she'd been whispering, she would never hear the end of it, not for weeks. Now that Martha was older she, just like Amy, had the pressure of being a good example to her younger sisters and the rest of the community. Being a deacon's daughter wasn't easy sometimes.

Rather than the bishop speaking, Martha's father delivered the sermon. Martha loved to hear her father preach God's word. Thankfully, Micah had gone to sleep in her arms.

When the service was over, one of the older ladies minded Micah and the other little ones so Martha and Gabbie could help the ladies with the meal afterward.

"Your *mudder's* not having another *boppli,* is she?" Gabbie asked Martha when they carried bowls of food to the trestle tables.

Martha's jaw dropped. "What? Have you heard something?"

Gabbie laughed. "Would that be so terrible?"

"She's old, so *jah.* I think it would be. She's been feeling so poorly, and she only had Micah a little over a year ago."

"Girls, I'd like you both to meet Michael Glick," the bishop said as he caught Martha's eye.

The girls had been so busy talking they hadn't noticed the bishop approach with the "new man in town."

Gabbie gave a giggle. "Hello, Michael."

The bishop said, "This is Gabbie and this is Martha."

Michael tipped his head. "Pleased to meet you both."

"Martha's the deacon's second-oldest *dochder,* and Gabbie's *vadder* is Bishop John in Augusta."

"I liked your father's sermon, Martha."

Martha smiled. *"Denke.* I did too."

"Does your family live close by?" All Martha could do was nod.

"I'm from Augusta," Gabbie said as she stepped forward.

"You're a long way from home," Michael said.

"I've just arrived, and I'm to stay awhile. I'm staying with Martha and her *familye.* That gives us something in common. We're both new to the community."

The bishop put his hand on Michael's shoulder. "I'll introduce you to some others."

The girls watched Michael walk away.

"Why didn't you speak to him, Martha?"

"I did."

"He'll surely think you find him uninteresting. Is that it, is that why you didn't speak?"

"I think he's fine, but I didn't have a chance to say much." Truth was, she couldn't find words other than to say hello and answer his questions. "He was talking to you and then he had to go with the bishop."

"We had a real connection. Could you feel it too; did you see the look in his eyes when he spoke to me?" Gabbie clasped her hands to her chest in a dramatic fashion.

Annoyed, Martha pulled on her arm. "C'mon. We've work to do."

Chapter Sixteen

When Michael was coming for dinner, Gabbie had pushed everyone out of the way and cooked everything herself. Amy had been glad for the break and went to her room, while Martha did what Gabbie ordered her.

"I can't wait until he arrives." Gabbie gazed out the kitchen window, which overlooked the driveway and gave a clear view up the road.

Martha set the main table and a second table for the younger girls. Whenever they had guests, the younger children sat at the smaller table.

The hymn Gabbie hummed while she put the finishing touches on the meal grated against Martha's nerves. "Do you have to hum, Gabbie?"

Gabbie spun around. *"Nee,* I don't. I'm just happy, that's all. I prayed for a husband and then *Gott* sent me here to meet Michael."

Martha's mouth fell open. *Mamm* and *Dat* were clearly trying to match Michael with her, not Gabbie. Gabbie had been sent to avoid trouble in Augusta, not to steal the boy she might like. "I prayed too, and so did Amy."

"He's too young for Amy. She's more suited to Andrew. I think they're secretly in love, but she can't move there and he can't move here. So, it's never going to work for them. Anyway, aren't you happy for me, Martha?"

Martha pulled a face. "You don't even know him, and what about Joseph?"

"Why do you keep asking about Joseph? You know he's getting married. He made his choice."

Martha took a step closer to Gabbie. "It's just that you switched off of him pretty quickly, and now you say you like Michael when you don't even know him."

Gabbie smiled. "I know him, in my heart."

Rubbing her forehead, Martha turned back to finish setting the tables. What chance would she have to get any attention with Gabbie around?

"He'll be here soon, girls."

Both girls looked across to Mr. Yoder in the doorway.

"Everything all right in here?"

"Jah," both girls chorused at once.

He eyed them carefully. "Your *mudder* is coming down in a minute after she puts Micah to bed."

"Jah, Dat," Martha said. "We've nearly got everything ready, haven't we, Gabbie?" Gabbie nodded.

At the sound of hoofbeats, both girls raced to the window.

"He's here," Gabbie said.

Martha looked over to where her father had been standing to see he'd already gone to welcome their guest at the front door.

Gabbie immediately straightened herself by pushing stray hairs under her prayer *kapp* and adjusting her apron. Martha took a deep breath. She knew she stood no chance against the bright and bubbly Gabbie. At that moment, she wished Gabbie had stayed in Augusta.

When they heard two male voices in the other room, Gabbie and Martha went to the living room to greet Michael.

"Hello, Gabbie." He nodded at Gabbie who was right in front of him. He looked at Martha. "And…?"

Martha's heart sank. He didn't even remember her name, but he'd remembered Gabbie's.

"Her name is Martha," Gabbie said before Martha had a chance to form a sentence in her head.

Great, now he thinks I can't put two words together, Martha thought while returning Michael's polite nod.

"Now, everyone sit in the living room, and I'll call you when dinner is ready," Gabbie said.

Martha took her chance and sat on the couch next to Michael.

Gabbie rushed to Martha and pulled her off the couch. "Not you, Martha, I need your help in the kitchen. You're assisting me, remember?"

Martha and Gabbie retreated to the kitchen just as Mrs. Yoder and Amy came down the stairs. Martha heard muffled conversation coming from the living room as she and Gabbie dished out the hot food.

Gabbie whispered, "Did you notice he remembered my name?"

Prickles ran along Martha's neck. *"Jah,* I did."

"It's a *gut* thing you don't like him because I like him a lot."

Martha pursed her lips. She never said she didn't like him. In fact, she wanted to get to know him, but how would that be possible now?

Once the silent prayer of thanks for the meal was over,

Gabbie was the first to speak. "What do you think of the town here, Michael?"

"I've hardly seen much of it. I've been working pretty hard since I got here. I'll have a chance to have a look 'round soon, I'd say."

"I'll show you around," Gabbie said.

"I'm sure you don't know the town well enough, Gabbie, since you've only arrived yourself," Mrs. Yoder stated. "Both of you girls can show Michael around when he's got the time."

Martha glanced up at her mother who raised her eyebrows.

Michael spooned chicken casserole onto his plate. "I'd appreciate that very much. I could come by here Friday midafternoon, and drive you girls around. You can direct me where to go."

Martha was pleased she'd see him again in just two days' time.

Mr. Yoder laughed and slapped Michael on the shoulder. "These girls can drive a buggy as well as any man if that concerns you."

"Nee, I just prefer to do the driving." He looked at Martha and then at Gabbie. "Especially when I'm driving young ladies."

Gabbie put her hand over her face and giggled. Mrs. Yoder popped a piece of chicken into her mouth, frowning in Gabbie's direction.

"Is the farm you're staying at far from here?" Amy asked him.

"It's the farm next door. Just a ten- or fifteen-minute walk to the *haus."*

"Oh, I didn't realize where you'd be staying."

"That's because you don't listen, Amy," Gabbie butted in. You haven't changed since you visited us two years ago."

Martha felt sorry for Amy. She didn't need to be reminded of how long it had been since she stayed with Gabbie's family. It hadn't been two years, not two fully, only about eighteen months.

Michael popped a portion of buttered bread into his mouth. "This food is very *gut.*"

"Denke, I cooked most of it, but Martha helped," Gabbie said.

When Martha looked up, she saw her mother staring at her and making faces. She knew her mother wanted her to speak. She hadn't said two words to Michael since he'd arrived. "Are you a farmer in Ohio too, Michael? Or are you doing that to help your *onkel* out?"

"My parents have a farm, and I've worked on it all my life. I don't help much on the farm anymore; I've been working construction the last couple of years."

Martha nodded, and before she could say more, Gabbie took over the conversation by asking, "And what kind of farm do your parents have?"

"We've got mostly barley fields, but also corn and oats."

Gabbie was quick to add, "We've got an apple orchard back home. Last year's drought really affected it though, and we didn't get as much as we would've liked."

Michael nodded. *"Jah,* same with our crops in Ohio. The drought allowed the weeds to grow through the crop. We ended up just baling it for our own use. We've got fifteen acres of corn, too, and forty dairy cows. The crops here look good so far."

Gabbie had not taken her eyes from him. "Sounds like you'd be very busy at home."

"I like it that way," Michael said before he took another mouthful of food.

Martha knew she had to add something to the conversation, either that or look like she never spoke more than two words. "Do you milk all the cows yourself, Michael?"

Gabbie laughed. "That's too much for one person, Martha. He couldn't possibly do that and the other work."

"Um, I know that, but... I just wondered..." Now Martha felt worse; maybe she should've kept quiet.

"Nee, that's a *gut* question, Martha. My *mudder* and older *schweschder* do the milking nowadays. We used to milk by hand years ago, but now we've got a diesel engine that runs the milking equipment. It saves us time and the women can handle it."

"You've got more than one *schweschder?"* Mrs. Yoder asked.

"I've got one older and two younger, and one older *bruder."*

"And why are you working in construction since there's plenty of work on the farm?" Gabbie asked.

"With the drought, I thought I should look for something else. I've always liked to build things, and a friend of mine got me a job with his *vadder.* He only employs Amish workers. They've given me time off to come here for however long I'm needed. They're good like that."

When the first part of the meal was over, Gabbie, Martha and Amy cleared the plates, ready for the dessert.

"I made whoopie pies," Gabbie told Michael.

"I love all sweet things." Michael smiled up at her.

Once dinner was over, the younger girls were sent to bed while the adults had coffee in the living room. Mrs.

Yoder told the girls she'd clean the kitchen and do the washing up, but Martha insisted on helping.

When Martha finished helping *Mamm,* she went into the living room to join the others. Gabbie had sat herself opposite Michael and, not wanting to sit next to him, Martha sat on the end of the couch next to Gabbie. Amy excused herself saying she was going to check on Micah. Martha knew she wouldn't be back. She was really going to her room to think about her lost love. That's all she seemed to do these days. Mrs. Yoder joined them, sitting in her usual chair opposite her husband.

"Gabbie's just been telling me about where she comes from," Michael said.

"It's a fine place and so different from here." Mrs. Yoder smiled. "I've never been there before, but of course, Amy told us all about it."

Michael stood. "I should go now. I've got an early start in the morning."

"As have we all." Mr. Yoder rose to his feet.

"Denke for having me for dinner, and Gabbie, *denke* for a *wunderbaar* meal."

Gabbie stood up and smiled at him. Not wanting to be the only one who remained seated besides her mother, Martha stood up as well.

"We'll see you Friday afternoon then, Michael," Gabbie said excitedly.

"Jah, I'm looking forward to it."

Martha remained silent and watched as they all walked him to the door. Disappointment gnawed at her stomach.

Why wasn't she talkative like Gabbie?

Chapter Seventeen

The next day was Thursday, and Thursday in the Yoder household was laundry day.

Mrs. Yoder pulled Martha aside while Gabbie took one load of washing to the machine. "Martha, you could have said more to that boy last night."

"Mamm, I can't think quickly, and I'm not so sure of myself like Gabbie is."

"You'd better get sure of yourself pretty fast, or Gabbie will snatch him out from under your nose. Is that what you want?"

Her mother's words gave her a pain in her stomach. Surely, love was not like this? Was this how it was between men and women? Martha never thought she'd be in a competition for love. If she were meant to be with Michael, she would be, and if not, it wouldn't matter if Michael and Gabbie got married. Did her mother want her to fight and jostle for a man to notice her?

"Come on, Martha, help me. I want to get all this finished," Gabbie called out.

"I'm coming."

The girls washed the clothes and fed them through the wringer before pinning them on the line.

"It's a lovely sunny day for drying, isn't it?" Gabbie said with her face turned to the sky.

Martha looked up at the sun. "It is."

Hours later, Gabbie said, "Well, I'm done with the morning chores. I think I'll go for a nice stroll."

"*Gut,* I'll come too," Martha said.

Gabbie stepped back. *"Ach, nee."* Martha frowned. "Do you mind if I go alone?"

Maybe she's upset with me. "You can go alone if you want to. Don't get lost. You don't know these parts."

"I'll go in a straight line and come back the same way. I'll walk along the roadway."

Martha scratched her chin and figured she'd write to her pen-pal cousin while Gabbie walked. "Okay."

Gabbie smiled, turned and began her walk.

Martha climbed the stairs to her bedroom, took out paper and pen and sat by the window thinking what to write. With the pen resting on her lips, she looked outside and noticed that Gabbie was not walking by the roadway as she had said. In fact, she was heading straight to the Glicks' farm. She would have to follow her to see where she was going. If she were going to try to see Michael, why wouldn't she have told her straight out?

Changing quickly into shoes more suited for walking, Martha grew more annoyed with Gabbie and then ran down the stairs hoping her mother wouldn't hear. The younger girls were already in school and her baby brother was the only child at home—apart from Amy, who was out visiting one of her friends.

Martha walked in the direction she'd seen Gabbie heading, but now she'd lost sight of her. She was sure if she headed for the farm next door, she'd soon catch sight of her. A couple of minutes later, she saw Michael mending a fence and he was speaking with Gabbie. Squinting as hard as she could, Martha saw Michael had a smile on his face.

Her heart sank as she wondered if they'd arranged last night to meet in secret. *No,* she decided, *they wouldn't have had a quiet moment together without anyone overhearing. This has been all Gabbie's idea. She was hoping to bump into him. Two can play this game,* she thought as she walked toward the two of them.

"Hello," Martha yelled out as she approached.

Michael looked over at Martha and waved. Martha smiled and waved back. Gabbie spun around and then turned back to Michael and said something.

Martha said to Gabbie, "I didn't know you were walking in this direction." Before Gabbie could reply, Martha looked at Michael, "Did that tree knock the fence over?"

"Jah, the heavy wind during the night broke a couple of old posts and knocked it down."

With her hands on her hips, Gabbie said, "You did too know I was walking this way."

"You said you were walking by the roadway. Anyway, what does it matter?"

"It's nice to see both of you girls again so soon."

"Nice to see you too, Michael. Well, we'd better leave Michael to get on with his fencing, Gabbie."

"Nee, I'll think I'll stay and talk to him for a while."

Michael looked up from his fencing. "You go with Martha, and I'll see you tomorrow. I'm nearly finished up here and I've got a lot of work with the cows as soon as I'm done here."

The usual confidence had left Gabbie's voice when

she replied, *"Jah,* okay, Martha and I have quite a lot to do as well."

"I'll see you girls tomorrow then."

Gabbie flashed a smile at Michael before she turned and took hold of Martha's arm. "Let's go, Martha."

Martha was nearly toppled off balance. "Bye, Michael."

As the girls walked away, Gabbie hissed, "Couldn't you see that we were having a moment?"

"Nee, I couldn't."

"He wanted me to stay but didn't want you to. Why did you have to come?" Gabbie's usual smile was replaced by a frown.

"Why shouldn't I come and speak to my friends? He's not yours, you know."

"Not yet." Gabbie's face scrunched further. "I wish you'd never come here. He didn't want you here."

"Gabbie, that's a horrid thing to say." Martha studied Gabbie's angry face, and then Gabbie walked away. Martha hurried to catch up with her.

"You followed me, and you are trying to ruin things between me and Michael."

Martha kept silent even though she wanted to point out that there was as yet no "me and Michael."

When they got back home, Martha's *mudder* met them. "I need you to drive me to Nellie Byler tomorrow to see about a tonic. *Nee,* I'll go Monday if you can take me or maybe the Monday after that."

"Of course, *Mamm,* you let me know when you want me to take you," Martha answered, quite used to her mother not being able to make a firm decision.

"You should go to a doctor if you're not well, Mrs. Yoder."

Mrs. Yoder looked taken aback by Gabbie's tone. "I don't wish to go to a doctor. I would rather try a tonic. It's done well for me before."

"It worked, did it?"

"It seemed to."

Gabbie shrugged. "Just trying to help."

"I can take you there tomorrow first thing, *Mamm.*"

"We'll see." Mrs. Yoder eyed them carefully. "You two look as though you've been up to something."

"We've just been for a walk," Gabbie said.

"Jah…and we ran into Michael," Martha said.

Mrs. Yoder frowned and looked at each girl in turn. "Must have been a long walk."

Gabbie said, "He was repairing a fence on the property border."

"I've got more chores, but there's something your *vadder* wants you to do first, Martha."

Chapter Eighteen

"What is it, *Mamm?* What does *Dat* want?" Could she be in trouble for something? Had her father seen them speaking to Michael when he was repairing the fence?

"Your *vadder* wants you to go into town to get coffee and honey."

"Okay." Martha looked at Gabbie. "Do you want to come with me?"

"*Jah,* of course I do."

Gabbie stomped out to the barn behind Martha to help her hitch the buggy for their trip to town. Why did Martha have to barge in and ruin her time with Michael? How was she going to get a boyfriend with Martha around her all the time? Martha had pretended not to like Michael when she did. Why couldn't she be truthful and admit she liked him? Martha's family was strange. Her mother was not running the household properly; she left everything to Amy. Amy was trapped here helping the family when it was obvious she wanted to go back to Andrew.

"Martha, why does your *vadder* have to say what food to get? Isn't that your *mudder's* job? Or even Amy's?"

"Sometimes *Mamm's* a little vague. *Dat* helps out too."

Gabbie's mother would never be like that. "Is there something wrong with her?"

Martha shook her head. *"Nee,* she's just tired and has a lot on her mind with the new *boppli."*

"He's hardly new."

Martha shrugged and remained silent.

"Seems like there's something amiss. I mean, she couldn't be just plain lazy, could she?" Gabbie studied Martha's shocked face waiting for her to explain.

After a while spent controlling her irritation at Gabbie's insult to *Mamm,* Martha said, "She's not lazy. She wasn't always this way; ever since this pregnancy started, it seems, she's often tired and sometimes she can't even get out of bed."

"And what about Amy?"

"What about her?"

"She's hardly said anything to me and we were such good friends when she lived at my *haus."*

"You and I are better friends. We're pen pals. She probably doesn't want to be around us. She's never spent time with me and my friends and she likes her own company."

"Hmph. Likes her own room, more like it."

Martha didn't want to say anything to Gabbie about Amy's broken heart. Gabbie had arrived with no news of Andrew, and that had upset Amy even further.

On the way into town, the area where they had been

speaking to Michael came into view. Gabbie craned her neck, and Martha glanced over. Michael had gone.

Martha felt bad over the harsh words she'd had with Gabbie and for interrupting her talk with Michael. "After we collect those things for my *daed* we can go to a café if you'd like."

"Jah, I'd like that *denke."*

Careful to keep the conversation on something neutral, Martha said, "Do you miss your family?"

"Not really. I haven't been away long enough. I like being away. Amy invited me a long time ago and it took that long for my folks to let me come here."

After they got the things her father wanted, Martha took Gabbie to her older sister's favorite coffee shop.

Dan, the manager, approached them once they'd taken a seat. "You're Amy's little sister, aren't you?" he asked Martha.

"Yes, that's right. I've been in here a couple of times."

"Double shot latte on skim?" Dan asked.

Martha's jaw dropped. "How could you possibly remember that?"

"It's my job." He turned to Gabbie. "And what will you have?"

"You tell me since you look like you're a 'people and their coffee expert.' What do I look like I'd have?" Gabbie had leaned forward and was clearly flirting with Dan.

Dan laughed. Whether it was out of shock, or he thought Gabbie was funny, Martha couldn't tell.

"Espresso?" Dan asked.

Gabbie giggled. "Way wrong. A chocolate milkshake, please. I don't even drink coffee."

Dan nodded and walked away chuckling.

"He's nice, for an *Englischer.*" Gabbie stared after him.

Martha giggled. *"Jah,* he is." When Martha looked up, she saw a familiar woman walk through the door. Martha grabbed Gabbie's arm. "Look, Gabbie. It's Anna, Michael's cousin."

Gabbie turned around to look while Martha rose a little in her seat and waved to her. Anna smiled and walked over to them.

"Sit with us, Anna. Are you alone or are you meeting someone here?" Martha said.

"Denke. Nee, I'm here alone. I've just been to get some fabric from the store to make some dresses for my wedding."

"Did you meet Gabbie at the gathering?" Martha asked.

"Jah, we met. Hello again, Gabbie."

Gabbie nodded and smiled. "You're getting married soon?"

"Jah, I'm getting married in six months. Everyone tells me I've plenty of time, but I want to make sure everything's right."

"And is Michael staying with you?" Gabbie asked.

Anna nodded. *"Jah,* he is."

Gabbie looked at Martha.

"Do you want to see my material?" Anna said, already undoing her package.

"Ach, jah," Martha said.

Anna pulled the dark blue material from the corner of the package.

"It's beautiful." Gabbie ran her fingertips along it.

"It has a slight sheen, and, oh, it's so soft. Who are you marrying?"

"I'm marrying Marvin Zook. We grew up together."

"That's nice," Gabbie said, still looking at the fabric.

"Do you have a special someone back home, Gabbie?" Anna asked.

Gabbie's lips pouted slightly. *"Nee,* I don't."

"Are you looking for one?" Anna asked.

"Jah, I'd like to be married. Of course, I would."

Anna put her hand to her mouth and giggled. "I mean, is that why you're here staying with Martha's family; because you're looking for a husband?"

"My family wanted a break from me." Gabbie giggled.

"How did your *vadder* break his leg?" Martha asked Anna, purely to change the subject.

"He doesn't know; that's the funny thing. He slipped in the rain and it hurt a bit, but it wasn't until days later that he found it hard to walk."

Dan brought their drinks to them and took Anna's drink order. "Are you girls having anything to eat today?"

"I'll have a lemon meringue pie," Martha said.

"Me too, Dan, with ice cream," Gabbie added.

"Make that three, and I'll have ice cream with mine too." Anna giggled.

Dan said, "Which flavor ice cream? We also have a lemon sherbet that goes very well with our lemon pie. Might you prefer that to ice cream?"

Gabbie and Anna agreed to try it, and Martha decided to add it to her order as well.

When Dan left their table, Gabbie leaned across to Anna. "Would you like some help with the sewing? I'm a very *gut* seamstress."

Anna's eyes sparkled. "Really? I'd like that, *denke*. That'll save me time. I've so many things to do and my *mudder* doesn't have a lot of time since she's looking after *Dat.*"

Martha knew Gabbie offered to help just so she could be in the house where Michael was staying. If she got close to Anna, that would give her more access to Michael. "We had your cousin, Michael, over to dinner last night," Martha said, quite forgetting she wanted to keep their conversation off him.

"Jah, I wondered where he was. I've been so busy helping *Mamm* with *Dat,* and planning for the wedding that I didn't think to ask where he was. He works very hard; I barely see him."

A waitress brought their lemon meringue pies to the table.

"Does he have a girl at home?" Gabbie asked as each took her first bite of pie and sherbet.

"Nee, I don't think he does. Wow. This tastes really good." Anna looked up at Gabbie and then across to Martha as they both nodded agreement. "Do one of you girls like him?"

"I do," Gabbie said before Martha had a chance to nod, much less speak.

Martha would never admit to liking a man, fearing he might not like her back. That would be too embarrassing.

"I'll help you," Anna said.

Martha was upset she'd missed her chance.

"I'm going on a buggy ride with him tomorrow afternoon," Gabbie said.

Anna laughed. *"Ach,* you don't need my help then."

Gabbie's lips turned down. "I do; Martha's coming too."

Martha scrunched up her nose and said to Anna, "It's not that kind of buggy ride. I'm showing him around, and Gabbie around, at the same time, since they're both new. I would've taken my buggy, but Michael wanted to take his own. Well, I suppose it's one of your *vadder's* buggies he'll be using."

Anna frowned and looked away from Martha to Gabbie and then back to Martha. "Do you like him too, Martha?"

"Nee. I mean, he seems nice, but…"

Gabbie interrupted. "Now, Anna, tell me how you're planning to make your dress."

Anna forgot her question to Martha, and in full detail described how her wedding dress and the dresses of her attendants would look. She went on to tell them that she'd already sewn Marvin's wedding suit.

Martha's mind was elsewhere; there were not many ways one could sew a wedding dress when one was Amish. Before Martha knew what was happening, Anna arranged a time that Gabbie should go to her place to sew. She daren't offer to go as well or Gabbie would be upset with her. For just a moment, she let herself enjoy that idea.

The girls arrived home to find Michael had visited to cancel their Friday afternoon together.

Just as Martha's parents were out of earshot, Gabbie said, "He wants to be alone with me and that's why he canceled. He wants our first buggy ride together to be special." Martha was lost for words.

Gabbie continued, "You could see how he was speaking nicely to me before you came along, Martha."

Martha recalled that she had seen a smile on Michael's face. Maybe Gabbie was right. Martha wanted a man to love her for herself, and if Michael liked Gabbie there was nothing she could do about it.

Gabbie stuck out her chin. "Nothing to say?"

Martha shook her head and headed up the stairs to her bedroom to finish writing a letter to her other pen pal who was also her cousin.

Chapter Nineteen

Later that same night, after dinner, Gabbie and Martha sat with Martha's father in the living room.

"You two might want to offer to help at the sewing room on Saturday. They need more workers," he said.

"I told Anna I'd help her sew her dresses on Saturday," Gabbie said.

Mr. Yoder rubbed the side of his forehead. "You can't be in two places."

"I'll go, *Dat,*" Martha said.

"Okay, and take Rose and Mary with you. They can sew as *gut* as anyone and they're old enough to be doing more volunteering."

"*Jah,* I will."

"What's the sewing room?" Gabbie asked.

"It's a place where the ladies go to make quilts and sew things for charity. We also collect unwanted clothing and package it. There are people who still need help from the big tornado we had some time back," Martha explained.

Mr. Yoder said, "Things are made and auctioned and the money goes to help those who need it."

"Sounds like a good cause," Gabbie spoke vaguely as though her mind was elsewhere.

When Saturday came, Martha took Gabbie to Anna's house before she and her two sisters headed to the building they called the "sewing room."

Just as she was tying up her horse, Amy's friend, Olive, walked out of the sewing room and called out to her.

Martha looked up. *"Jah?"*

"Can you collect some clothes from Mrs. Hershberger's *haus?"* Mrs. Hershberger was one of the ladies in the community who collected unwanted clothing.

"Jah, of course, I can."

"Do you want me to go with you?" asked Rose, looking back at Martha.

"Nee, denke, I'd like time by myself. You go inside." Martha set off to Mrs. Hershberger's *haus,* glad to have some time away from chattering women. Gabbie staying in her home wasn't as much fun as she thought it might've been. The two had gotten along well in their letters, but now a rift was developing.

After Martha had collected the clothes from Mrs. Hershberger, she turned the buggy onto the road and then saw Michael's buggy coming toward her. Martha gave a quick wave when he came closer.

He signaled her to stop, and then he pulled his horse to a halt beside her. "Hello, Martha. What are you doing out here?"

"I'm collecting some clothes for the sewing house. They collect clothes and sew things for charity."

"Jah, I've heard of it. You're by yourself, I see."

Martha nodded. "I've taken Rose and Mary to the

sewing house, and Gabbie's helping Anna with the sewing for her wedding."

"I'm sorry I had to cancel our ride the other day. Perhaps you and I could reschedule for next Saturday?"

"That would be perfect."

"We didn't have much time to speak over dinner the other night. I hear there's volleyball on Monday night, will you be going?"

"Ach, I forgot it was on. *Jah,* I'll most likely go."

"Do you like volleyball?"

"I do, but I'm not good at it," Martha said.

Michael laughed. "I'd ask you if we could do something together now, but I've too many errands to run and I've got to make it back to the *haus* at three."

Martha nodded. "And I've got to get back to the sewing room. Some of the ladies are waiting to package the clothes I've got in the back."

"I'll see you on Monday at the volleyball?"

"Jah."

Michael clicked his horse onward in the direction of the Hershberger's *haus,* and Martha headed back to the sewing room. Martha wondered why Michael hadn't suggested doing something the next day. The next day was Sunday, and since it was the second Sunday no gathering was held. It would've been a perfect day for going for a drive or even having a picnic.

After Martha and her sisters had finished a long day at the sewing room, they went home by way of the Glicks' house to fetch Gabbie.

When Martha's buggy stopped outside the front door, Anna came out.

"Hello, Martha. Are you looking for Gabbie?"

"*Jah,* I told her I'd fetch her when we finished sewing today."

"She left some time ago. Michael drove her home."

Martha frowned. "I told her I'd call for her."

"I'm sure there must have been a misunderstanding," Anna said.

"You're right." Martha smiled at Anna, while inside she was seething. It was one thing if Michael preferred Gabbie and it was another thing entirely that Gabbie had plotted to have time with him.

"I guess she forgot you were coming for her," Anna added.

"*Jah,* that must be it. Did you get a lot of sewing done?" Martha asked.

"We did. Do you want to come in and have a look?"

Martha looked at her sisters and neither looked as though she would object. "Sure, we'd love to." Martha tied up her horse and she and her two sisters went into the *haus.*

"It's nice to see you girls," Anna's mother said.

"Hello, Mrs. Glick. We've come to have a quick look at the dresses," Martha said.

Mrs. Glick asked, "Can you stay long enough for iced tea and cookies?"

Martha's sisters stared at her with wide eyes. They'd had little to eat all day.

"We'd love to, *denke,* Mrs. Glick," Rose said before Martha could respond.

Anna led the way to show them her dresses. "I've got the dresses in here; you girls sit down on the couch and I'll show you."

The three girls sat on the couch and Martha looked around the room. It had been a while since she'd been to their house. Anna opened a large drawer and unfolded a loose brown paper package. She pulled out a dress, held it at the shoulders and let it unfold.

"It's lovely," Rose said.

"It certainly is," Martha agreed.

"When it's finished, it'll be lovely, but it's just tacked together at the moment." Anna handed Martha the dress, turned and got something else out of the drawers. "Today I made the prayer *kapp.*" Anna held a sheer white organza prayer *kapp* in her hands.

"That's pretty. You're a *gut* seamstress," Martha said.

"Denke."

"Into the kitchen girls," Mrs. Glick called out.

While Anna packed the dress and *kapp* away, the Yoder girls walked into the kitchen.

"How's Mr. Glick?" Martha took a sip of iced tea.

"He finds it hard not to do anything, but the doctor said he mustn't do anything or he could make things worse," Mrs. Glick said.

"It's great that Michael could come and help you," Martha said.

"He's been a blessing. I've never seen anyone work as hard as he does."

As Martha was leaving the *haus,* Mrs. Glick pulled her aside. "Martha, I should have you and Gabbie over for dinner one night."

"That would be lovely. Let me know when," Martha said.

Chapter Twenty

Martha giggled, as she watched Gabbie get out of the buggy and run through the green grass. "Wait for me," Martha called after her. When it was just the two of them, they had fun. They were the first to arrive at the field where the volleyball tournament was to be held.

Gabbie spun in a circle with her arms outstretched and then fell onto the ground.

Martha sat next to her. "I'm glad to get out of the house." She ran her hands over the freshly mown grass, while a smattering of rain fell on them in tiny droplets.

"Will the game continue if it rains, or will it be canceled?" Gabbie asked.

Martha looked up at the gray sky. "I don't think it'll rain too much. We don't often get rain in the evening this time of year."

That night, both girls were disappointed because Michael didn't go to the volleyball. Anna had told them he had been invited somewhere for dinner and felt he couldn't get out of it. She then invited the two girls for dinner the next night. Halfway through the night, Gabbie begged Martha to go home.

Martha came downstairs as soon as she heard someone in the kitchen. It was her mother. "I didn't expect to see you awake so early."

Mrs. Yoder yawned and then rubbed her eyes. "I've come to fix a cup of herb tea. I couldn't sleep last night. I'm going back to bed after I drink this, before the younger girls wake."

"I didn't get you that tonic. I'm sorry; I completely forgot."

"That's okay. Amy ended up getting it for me. I can't say it's working."

"You'll have to give it a little time. They don't work immediately."

"I know."

Martha moved to the kettle and poured herself a cup of tea and sat down next to her mother.

Mamm took a sip of tea and then placed the cup back into the saucer. "I was at the market yesterday and overheard Mrs. Glick say that Michael has his eye on a girl. That'll be you, Martha."

Martha pushed out her lips. "It could be Gabbie, or maybe someone else entirely."

Mrs. Yoder scoffed. "He wouldn't be interested in a girl like Gabbie. She's far too forward. I don't know why her parents didn't teach her that she needs to be quiet sometimes to allow others to speak."

"She's different in front of her parents, Amy says. Gabbie's very nice sometimes, but it's awful now that we both like the same boy."

"Don't you be worried. If he's not for you, *Gott* will

bring someone else. I'd reckon he is the one for you, I can feel it. Don't you let Gabbie get in the way."

Martha didn't know how she'd go about stopping that, and she was confused by her mother's conflicting comments.

Mamm added, "You might find out which one of you he likes when you're both at the Glicks' for dinner tonight."

Martha pulled a face. "I don't see how. He can't invite me anywhere in front of Gabbie. Every time he speaks to me, Gabbie jumps in between us. He must know she likes him."

"Sometimes men don't like a woman who's too forward. They don't respect anything they don't get from doing some hard work. They think, if it's too easy they don't want it."

Martha frowned and whispered, *"Mamm,* that sounds like game-playing."

Both women went quiet when they heard footsteps. Gabbie walked into the room rubbing her eyes. "Morning, all. Can I do anything to help, Mrs. Yoder?"

"Morning, Gabbie. I'm back to bed as soon as I drink this. I know it's morning, but I have to catch naps where I can. You can help Martha with the breakfast when the girls wake."

Gabbie yawned and then nodded. "Did Martha tell you we've been invited to the Glicks' for dinner?"

"Jah, Martha told me last night," Mrs. Yoder said. "Let's make pies to take, okay Martha?"

"What a good idea," Martha agreed.

"After breakfast is over, you can." Mrs. Yoder rose to her feet and then tipped the rest of her tea down the sink. "I'll see you girls later."

* * *

That evening, Michael called for Martha and Gabbie to take them back to the Glicks' house for dinner.

"You weren't at the volleyball game," Gabbie said as soon as she climbed into the front seat of the buggy, leaving the back seat for Martha.

"Jah, I'm sorry. I got there after you left. I found out about a dinner invitation I'd forgotten about. After that, I went to the fields and they were packing up. Did you both go?"

Gabbie said, *"Jah,* both of us went. Martha got bored, and we had to go very early."

Martha's jaw dropped. Gabbie had been the one who wanted to go early. "That wasn't what happened at all." Gabbie turned around and glared at Martha.

"I know Martha doesn't have much interest in volleyball, she told me that," Michael said.

Martha's heart raced; she knew she should've defended herself better against Gabbie's words, but didn't want to appear as though she was angry in front of Michael. "I said that I wasn't good at it, but I don't mind watching it."

When they arrived at the Glicks' home, Anna came out to greet them. "I'm so glad you two could come to dinner. Come through to the kitchen. *Mamm's* got the dinner nearly ready."

Martha walked up the front steps and turned to see where Gabbie was. She was waiting by the buggy.

Anna looked for Gabbie as well. "Don't wait for him," Anna called to Gabbie.

Gabbie walked toward them looking down at the ground.

"I'll see to the horse, and then I'll be along in a minute," Michael said.

The girls walked through to the kitchen after saying hello to Mr. Glick, who was sitting on the couch with a red and black checkered blanket over his legs, reading a paper.

"Can I help you with anything, Mrs. Glick?" Martha asked.

"Nee, it's all done. We're waiting on Michael." Mrs. Glick arranged food on a tray and handed it to her daughter to take out to her father.

"He still can't move around very well?" Gabbie asked.

"He's getting better, but he won't be able to do the farm work for a while yet. Michael's offered to stay here with us as long as we need him," Mrs. Glick said.

Martha noticed a smile on Gabbie's face on hearing the news.

Talk of Anna's wedding, the sewing of the dresses and the suits, dominated the dinner conversation. After the meal was over, they stayed and talked in the living room.

When it was time to go, Michael said, "The girls said they'd show me around this Saturday. Is that okay with you, *Onkel* Peter?"

Peter Glick laughed. "You're not captive here, Michael. Of course, go."

On the way back to Martha's house, Gabbie made sure she was the one to sit next to Michael in the buggy. When the buggy stopped outside the Yoders' house, Gabbie said, "Are you coming in to say hello, Michael?"

"Jah, I will."

Martha got out of the buggy first and headed to the

front door. She heard a scream and turned around to see Gabbie on the ground holding her ankle.

Martha rushed to her. "Gabbie, what's wrong?"

Gabbie sat on the ground holding her leg. "My leg, I've hurt it badly."

"Can you stand?" Martha asked.

Michael stood behind Gabbie. "What's happened?"

"I've hurt my leg." Gabbie sobbed with the pain.

"I'll help you inside," Michael offered.

"Denke."

He did his best to help her to her feet and on the other side, Martha was helping.

Gabbie squealed again. *"Nee,* I can't walk on it. Can you carry me, Michael?"

Michael lifted her with one arm around her back and another under her legs. Martha frowned, seeing the way Gabbie placed her arms around his neck and put her head against his chest. She was enjoying it, and that led Martha to wonder whether she was injured at all.

Martha pushed the door open. "Put her on the couch please, Michael."

Michael walked up the porch steps, through the door and placed Gabbie on the couch.

Martha turned to her father who was running down the stairs. "Gabbie's hurt her leg."

Mr. Yoder rushed to Gabbie's side and, by that time, she'd taken off her lace-up shoe and was clutching her stockinged foot.

"It's not swollen," he said after he'd examined it.

Gabbie held it and moaned. "It hurts so much."

"Can you wait until morning, Gabbie, or shall we take you to the hospital tonight?" Mr. Yoder asked.

"I can wait, I think."

"She'll need ice on it," Michael said.

Mr. Yoder said, "We've got some ice. Martha, go fetch it."

Martha hurried to the kitchen and opened the gas-powered freezer and took out a large piece of ice. Placing it on the wooden block near the stove, she smashed it into pieces. Martha took several small pieces and wrapped them in a clean dishtowel and hurried back to Gabbie. She didn't like doubting Gabbie and wanted to believe her.

"Oh, that hurt," Gabbie said when Martha placed the cold pack on her foot.

Mr. Yoder glared at his daughter. "Be careful, Martha."

"Sorry, Gabbie, I put it on as gently as I could."

"That's okay, you can't help it if you're heavy-handed," Gabbie said between sobs. "You've got large hands, like a man's."

Martha frowned. Gabbie and her father were making her look uncaring and clumsy. Martha looked down at her hands. Were they that big?

"Can I get anyone tea?" Mrs. Yoder asked.

Martha turned to see her mother at the bottom of the staircase. "Gabbie's hurt her leg."

Martha's mother rushed to Gabbie and made a fuss over her.

"I'll be okay." Gabbie sniffed, as she held the ice pack to her foot.

"What about a hot cup of tea, Gabbie?" Mrs. Yoder asked.

Gabbie nodded. "That would be nice, and maybe a couple of chocolate cookies."

Mrs. Yoder looked at Michael. "How about you, Michael?"

"I'll have to go now. I've got an early morning planned tomorrow." Michael took a step to the door.

"As have we all, Michael." Mr. Yoder walked him out.

It seemed to Martha that even her father was conspiring against her. With Gabbie on the couch, she could've been the one to see Michael out, and it would've been just the two of them.

Mr. Yoder came back a couple of minutes later. "Any better with the ice on it, Gabbie?"

"I think it's a little better."

"Can you make it up the stairs, or would you prefer to sleep on the couch for the night?" he asked.

"I think my leg is too bad to make it up the stairs, Mr. Yoder."

"I'll have Martha bring you a quilt and pillows. Where is that girl? Martha?"

"I'm right here, *Dat.*" Martha pressed her lips together. Was she invisible to all men? She'd been there the whole time, sitting on the chair when he'd walked back into the room.

Mr. Yoder turned around. "What are you waiting for then? Fetch some things to make Gabbie comfortable."

"Right away, *Dat.*" There was no use arguing. She couldn't accuse Gabbie of pretending the injury so she could lean against Michael's chest and be held in his arms.

Gabbie was pleased her act had worked. Michael was so strong; she had found that out when he'd swept her up and held her close. His chest was hard and muscled, and she had pressed her cheek against it. One day soon they'd be together. Nothing could stand in her way of winning his heart. God had arranged for her to be sent to Lancaster County at the very time he'd come from Ohio. It was too much of a coincidence to be anything other than God's will and His planning. Gabbie knew love could be helped along, and that was just what she planned to do.

After making her visitor comfortable, Martha needed some big-sister sympathy. She knocked quietly on Amy's door, so she wouldn't wake Micah who'd be asleep.

"Come in."

As soon as Martha opened the door, Amy asked her what all the fuss downstairs was about. Amy was in bed with her bedside lamp on, reading, and she closed her book just as Martha sank onto the bed to sit next to her. Martha told her everything, and then asked, "Do you think she's faking it?"

"Only time will tell."

Frustration welled within Martha. "What can I do? Everything seems hopeless. He can't see me because Gabbie's always jumping in front, talking over the top of me or making me look a fool. Tonight, she even said I have men's hands." She held up her hands. "Do I?"

Amy giggled. *"Nee,* they're perfectly beautiful women's hands."

"I don't see why you think it's funny."

"I don't. Not really."

"What should I do?"

Amy shook her head. "You're asking me? I'm no expert. Or maybe I should give you advice and then you do the exact opposite of what I say."

Martha felt more sorry for Amy than she did for herself. "Oh, Amy…why don't you write to him again? Or call him at the mill where he works?"

"I don't know." Amy sighed. "It's all just awkward now. Too much time has gone by."

"How do you know he isn't thinking the same thing?"

"Now you're sounding like Olive."

"Oh, she said a similar thing?"

Amy nodded. "Practically the same."

Martha stayed longer to talk with her sister and found she was the one comforting Amy instead of the other way around.

Chapter Twenty-One

The next morning, there was a miracle in the Yoder household. Gabbie's leg had healed. She made her way into the kitchen and sat down with Martha, and Martha's parents, who were eating breakfast. "I'm better now, Mr. Yoder."

"All the same, I'll take you to the doctor," he said.

Gabbie shook her head. *"Nee,* I'm sure there's no need. Look, I can put all my weight on it. It healed overnight."

"Is there a swelling or mark on your ankle?" Mrs. Yoder asked.

"Nee, it's as if there was never anything wrong."

"Must have been the night's sleep on the couch that cured you," Martha said.

"The body heals itself." Gabbie grinned. "That's how *Gott* designed it."

"That's very true. I'm glad you're better." Mrs. Yoder turned to her husband. "If her leg's better there's no reason to see a doctor."

"Okay. You'd know best."

* * *

Later that day the girls were fixing lunch when they saw Michael's buggy heading toward the house.

"He's coming to see if I'm better," Gabbie squealed.

Mrs. Yoder glanced out the window at the buggy, and then said, "Girls, I need you both to fetch me some coriander and dill from the garden."

"Can we talk to Michael first?" Gabbie asked.

"Nee, do as I ask, and you can see him soon. If you get stuck talking to him, I'll never get my herbs."

The girls walked into the herb garden, both unhappy about not being able to see Michael right away. They were silent until they reached the garden.

"What do you think was wrong with your leg?" Martha asked as she plucked dill and placed it in her wicker basket.

"Most likely, I twisted my ankle. It was very painful."

They walked back to the house, and when they were through the back door, they saw Mrs. Yoder sitting with Michael at the kitchen table, and Amy was there feeding Micah his cereal.

"There you are," Mrs. Yoder said, as she turned to look at them. "Michael and I have had quite a talk."

"It must have been a quick one because we were only gone for five minutes," Gabbie said.

Mrs. Yoder ignored her cheeky comment, rose to her feet, and took the wicker basket from Martha. "Ah, my garnishes. *Denke,* girls. Do you have time to stay for a cup of *kaffe,* Michael?"

"Jah, I do."

Both girls sat opposite him.

"My leg's better," Gabbie told him.

"That's good, I was going to ask about your leg.

You've made a marvelous recovery. I thought you might've broken it or at least sprained it."

"I'm very tough." Gabbie laughed.

"I didn't know your leg would be better, Gabbie. I've come here to ask you, Martha, if you'd come to the charity auction with me on Friday."

"Jah, I'd like that," Martha said.

"Good. I know you're interested in charitable works. My *onkel's* volunteering me to take lots of things to the auction and I thought you might help?"

Gabbie pushed out her bottom lip and glared at Martha. Martha knew Gabbie hoped she'd refuse his offer. "I'd really like that, Michael. *Denke* for thinking of me. I'd love to help."

Michael's face beamed, and Martha realized she might yet have a chance with him. Maybe he liked her and not Gabbie.

Mrs. Yoder carried the coffee cups to the table and placed them down just as Micah began crying. "He's been fussy. I think it's his back teeth."

"Two year molars?" Amy asked.

Mamm nodded and then leaned forward and picked him up out of his highchair. "And I'd say he needs a diaper change."

"I'll do it," Amy said.

"You can come and distract him for me."

Martha wasn't happy her mother and sister left the room leaving her to deal with Gabbie. "I'll get us some cookies," Martha said.

While Martha went to the pantry to get the cookies, she heard Michael ask, "How long will you be staying here, Gabbie?"

"I'm not sure. I might have to leave soon."

"That's too bad."

Martha came back and placed the cookies in the middle of the table and sat back down next to Gabbie.

After Michael bit into a cookie, he moved uncomfortably in the chair.

"Weren't you going to do some gardening, Martha?" Gabbie asked.

"*Jah,* but I'm visiting with our guest now. I'll do the gardening later." Martha fixed a smile on her face.

Gabbie raised her eyebrows. "You sure? It'll be time to help prepare dinner soon."

Michael took a huge gulp of coffee. "Well, I'll be heading off soon and then you'll be able to garden."

"Already? You haven't even finished your cookie." Gabbie's eyes fixed on the half-eaten cookie on his plate.

He picked it up and stood. "Thank your *mudder* for me, Martha. Tell her I'm sorry I had to leave so quickly." He popped the rest of the cookie into his mouth.

Martha nodded and both girls followed him to the door. They stood and watched as his buggy moved away from the house.

"I don't know why he asked you, Martha. It's me he likes."

"I'm sorry, Gabbie, but he thought your leg would still have been hurting you."

"That's okay. It's good that he's getting to know my friends. I'm sure that's what he's doing."

"You think so?"

Gabbie nodded. "It's the only thing that makes sense."

"You don't think that he can like me as a potential *fraa?*"

Gabbie put her hand over her mouth to stifle giggles. "I'm sorry, Martha, I don't mean to laugh. You're just so funny sometimes. Don't worry. You'll find someone. Michael is so kind and considerate, don't you think?"

"Jah, he seems very kind. He likes to help the poor and the needy. I like that."

"And the way he's spending time with you is so sweet." Gabbie sighed.

Doubts crept into Martha's heart. *Is Gabbie the woman he prefers and he's taking the long way around?* Gabbie was by far the brighter and more outgoing of the two as far as personalities were concerned. Martha knew she lacked the energy and spark that Gabbie had.

Gabbie went up to the bedroom to get away from Martha for a while. It wasn't fair that Michael asked Martha, but he wouldn't have known her leg would be "miraculously" better. Anyway, she had gotten to feel the hardness of his chest and put her arm around his neck, and that's something Martha would never do. Gabbie giggled as she flung herself on her bed. She wondered for a moment if Michael could like Martha but quickly dismissed the idea. Martha wasn't much fun, so what could Michael see in her?

Chapter Twenty-Two

At one o'clock on Friday afternoon, Michael arrived to take Martha to the charity auction. As they set out, Martha noticed the buggy was indeed full, but another person could've easily fit.

"How long have you known Gabbie?" Michael asked.

"I only met her recently, but we'd been writing to each other for months. Amy met her when she was on vacation there some time ago."

"She's a different girl. Different from anyone I've met before."

"She is." Martha agreed trying to hide a frown. She didn't want their time to be spent speaking about someone else, especially Gabbie.

"She helped Anna quite a bit with the sewing the other day," Michael said.

"*Jah,* Anna showed me when I went there to fetch Gabbie." Martha remembered how Gabbie had tricked Michael into driving her home. She couldn't say as much to Michael. He would know Gabbie liked him; she was making it obvious enough for everyone else to see. "Maybe Gabbie could've come with us today. There seems room enough in the back."

Michael laughed and glanced over at her. "I wanted to have some time with you, away from Gabbie."

Martha looked away from him and stared at the road ahead.

"I hope that's all right?" Michael asked.

Martha smiled and nodded, wishing she could say something witty or clever.

"When Gabbie's around, it doesn't give you a chance to speak, and I'm sure there's a great deal you'd want to say," Michael said.

She glanced back at him, their eyes locked for a second before she looked away.

"I'm not much of a talker. I mean, not when I first meet people," Martha said.

"Then you need more practice."

Once they arrived at the charity auction, Michael wasted no time unloading the buggy while Martha was dragged into one of the tents by a couple of the women. They needed another volunteer to serve the teas and the coffees, and Martha was it.

Martha heard the noises from the auction for the next two hours and she hoped that they were raising a good sum of money. She looked up from behind the counter and saw Anna walking toward the refreshment tent.

Martha stepped over so Anna could see her, and waved.

"Hello, Martha, I didn't expect to see you today."

"I wasn't coming this year with Gabbie visiting, but Michael said he'd bring me."

"Gut. Where's Gabbie?"

"She's at home," Martha said.

Anna frowned. "She didn't want to come?"

Martha shook her head. "Don't think so."

"That's odd."

Martha wondered why she thought it odd, but remained silent. She didn't want to get into another conversation about Gabbie.

"She was such a *wunderbaar* help to me. I might ask if she'd like to help me put the finishing touches on everything. *Jah,* I will. I'll have her come to the house when I have my attendants for their final fittings if she's still in town."

Martha smiled and tried to be happy. "I'm sure she'd love that. She had a good time the other day at your *haus.*"

"I should go and catch the auction before it finishes. Are you staying for the dinner afterward?"

"I think so," Martha said.

Anna smiled and walked on. Martha had spent the entire time in the refreshments tent. She was pleased to see Michael coming to get her after the auction, and they got to know a little more about each other at the meal afterward.

On the way home, Michael asked, "Would you go on a buggy ride with me, Martha? Just you and me, one night soon?"

"Jah, but I don't know when." Martha's insides tingled with excitement, but then nerves got the better of her. "My *mudder's* been sick. I'm taking her to get a tonic on Monday. She tried one, but it's not as good as the ones she used to get from a different place." As soon as Martha spoke, she knew it was no excuse at all. Her mother being sick hadn't stopped her from going any-

where else. She was nervous about being with him, and that was all.

"Where are you taking her for the tonic?" Michael asked.

"There's an old lady in our community. She lives by herself and makes tonics. I don't think she's been to a gathering for a while. She keeps to herself pretty much."

"Sounds strange."

"*Nee*, she's a really nice lady. I've been with *Mamm* to visit her before."

"How far away does this lady live?"

"She lives a long distance away. *Dat* jokes it's in the middle of nowhere."

"As I said, I'd like to see you again very soon." Martha didn't say anything else.

When they got back to the Yoders' house, she looked over at him. "I'd better get inside." Why didn't she know what to say to him? Should she have said she wanted to see him soon as well, or would that have been too forward? She stepped down from the buggy.

He jumped out and ran around the other side to meet her. "I'll walk you in."

"*Nee*, there's no need." Martha glanced up at the house and saw Gabbie watching them from the window of her bedroom. It seemed her best friend had now become her rival in love. He followed her to the door, and when she turned, she found him closer than she'd expected. "I had a nice time, being with you today."

"Me too," Michael said. "And, don't forget I'm driving you and Gabbie around on Saturday."

"I won't forget. Do you want to come in?"

"*Nee*. It's late." Michael stared at her and she didn't

know what to do or say. Turning away from him, she put her hand on the door handle.

"Goodbye," she said before opening the door. Once she was inside, she heard his goodbye before she shut the door softly behind her.

She leaned against the closed door and wanted to cry. Every time she said something to Michael she was sure it was wrong.

When Martha went up to her bedroom, she knew she'd be faced with one hundred and one questions from Gabbie. When she opened her door, she saw Gabbie was in bed. Martha knew she wasn't asleep because it was still early and she'd seen Gabbie looking out the window. "Gabbie, come downstairs with me. We can have hot tea and cake."

Gabbie said, *"Nee,* I'm not hungry. I'll stay here and sleep."

"Do you want me to bring something up to you?"

"Nee."

Martha decided to go to sleep too. Changing into her nightgown, she wished she was more like Gabbie. Gabbie was never at a loss when it came to conversation. Even though Michael had asked her to the charity auction with him, he'd soon lose interest if she was boring to be around. She was always afraid of saying something stupid. That was her real fear and it kept her from saying much at all.

Gabbie knew that there was only one reason for Martha to want to speak with her, and that was to gloat. Martha had spent most of the day with Michael and she wanted to rub it in. Of course, she was upset, but she couldn't let Martha see that.

Maybe Michael likes her more, just like Joseph and Ilsa. Life is so unfair. When is a man going to want me?

Gabbie closed her eyes tightly, so she wouldn't cry. Michael asking Martha out had stirred up the sadness in her heart over Joseph's rejection.

Chapter Twenty-Three

On Saturday morning, both girls were excited Michael was going to drive them in his buggy.

"Do I look all right, Martha?" Gabbie asked.

Martha looked over at Gabbie who was pushing a few strands of hair back under her prayer *kapp*. She had borrowed Martha's brown dress, which enhanced her hazel eyes and her warm skin tone. *"Ach, jah,* you look lovely, Gabbie."

"Do you think Michael will think I look lovely?"

Martha looked over at Gabbie. "Of course he will."

"What are you going to wear?"

Martha looked down at the nightgown she was still wearing. She only had three dresses and since Gabbie was wearing her brown dress she had a choice of lemon or grape-colored. "I am going to wear my favorite grape-colored dress and my new over-apron. He won't be here for hours anyway."

"I know." Gabbie smoothed down her apron. "I'm excited to be looking around at all the things you've told me about. You don't think he'll cancel again, do you?"

"Nee, I don't think that he'd do that."

"I guess not," Gabbie said.

"I'm sorry I haven't taken the time to show you around."

"That's okay. Don't feel bad."

Martha pulled on her dress. "Come on, let's help with the breakfast."

"Okay, but don't you want me to braid your hair first?" Gabbie asked.

Martha laughed when she realized she hadn't brushed her hair or put on her prayer *kapp*. She always did that first thing when she woke up. "Would you? That would be great. We have to be quick because the girls will wake soon. Amy and I try to let *Mamm* have a good sleep-in."

"*Jah.* I noticed she spends most of her time in bed. I'll be quick. You're such a good person, Martha. You're always caring about other people. I wish I could be more like you."

Martha was pleased Gabbie thought that way of her. Sometimes she felt a little selfish. "You're caring too."

"Not really. I'm not."

Martha tried to think of an example of Gabbie being kind, but couldn't come up with anything. When they finished dressing, Martha and Gabbie raced down the stairs. It was usually the young girls who collected the eggs, but since there weren't any in the egg box, Gabbie collected the eggs while Martha set the table. Scrambled eggs and bacon were what they were having for breakfast. Bacon was a luxury reserved for Saturdays.

"I'm not going anywhere today, Martha." Amy held a letter in her hand.

"There's a surprise," Gabbie commented with sarcasm.

Amy ignored her and kept speaking to Martha. "Could you post this for me?"

"*Jah,* of course."

Gabbie reached forward and plucked the envelope from Martha's hands. "Who's it from?"

"From me." Amy giggled.

Gabbie frowned and looked at the letter. "I meant who's it to? Ah, it's to my *Onkel* Andrew. I knew you were still in love with him."

"Did he give you a message for her?" Martha took the chance to ask since they were talking about Andrew.

"Nee, he didn't, I'm sorry to say." Gabbie handed the letter to Martha. "I'll remind her to post it."

"Denke, Gabbie." Amy leaned over the kitchen table, grabbed a piece of toast and headed back to her room.

While in the middle of the morning chores, Martha realized it probably hadn't been a good idea to wear her best clothes. She should've put them on after all the work had been done. It was too late now, she knew, as she looked at her soiled apron. She did have a spare upstairs, which she'd change into before Michael arrived. Just as she climbed the stairs, she heard Michael's buggy.

The rest of the family, except for Amy, had left the house after breakfast, leaving Martha and Gabbie alone.

"He's here now," Gabbie called out.

"I'm coming. I'll be down in a minute. Don't leave without me," Martha joked.

Martha heard Gabbie laughing and then heard the front door click open.

While she put on her clean apron, she walked to the bedroom window and looked out to see Michael and Gabbie talking. Gabbie was extremely close to him, but Michael seemed more interested in tying up his horse.

Martha was pleased with what she saw and rushed

downstairs. Michael stood at the front door with Gab-bie behind him.

"Ready to go?" he asked.

"Jah, all ready, and Gabbie and I made a picnic lunch."

Michael threw his head back and laughed. "I was just telling Gabbie that my aunt packed food for the three of us too."

Gabbie stepped in front of Michael. "That's *wunder-baar;* we'll have a lot of food. Come on, Martha, aren't you ready yet?"

"Jah, I'll just get the picnic basket."

"I've already done that; it's in the buggy," Gabbie said.

Michael clapped his hands. "Okay, let's go."

Martha followed Gabbie and Michael out to the buggy, wishing that she was going alone with Michael. She immediately dismissed that thought; she didn't want to be mean and horrid; there was nothing wrong with Gabbie going with them. As usual, Gabbie made sure she sat right next to Michael. Martha wasn't upset, she had expected as much.

"Where to first, Martha?" Michael asked as he clicked the horse forward into a slow trot.

Martha breathed out heavily. She should've planned their drive; she had no idea where to go first. It was still a couple of hours before lunchtime, so she figured she'd show them all the farms and sights, and they could have lunch at one of the parks near the creek. "Turn right up here and keep going until I tell you when to turn."

Chapter Twenty-Four

While Martha showed Michael and Gabbie around, Amy had been collected by Olive and was now having coffee with three of her friends at the Coffee House.

Amy walked into the familiar place with Olive and saw her best friends, Jessie and Lucy. Claire wasn't there because she'd married Donovan Billings, an *Englischer,* and it wasn't right for them to associate with her too much since she'd left the community.

"Has anyone seen Claire?" Olive asked.

The girls all shook their heads.

"Does anyone have any news?" Amy asked, wondering why Olive had called this impromptu meeting.

"Tell them, Jessie," Olive urged her friend, and now, her sister-in-law.

Jessie giggled. "Okay."

The other two girls leaned forward. "Are you pregnant?" Lucy asked.

"I am."

The girls all squealed, and people turned around and looked at them.

Lucy put her hand on Jessie's tummy and Jessie hit

her hand away. "There's nothing there yet. Well, there is, but my stomach's still flat."

"Not for long," Amy said.

"I know. I can't wait." Jessie continued, "We told Elijah's family last night. That's how Olive found out first."

"I can't wait. This is the first *boppli* out of all of us," Lucy said.

Olive nodded. "I know. She beat me to it."

"You have Leo," Lucy pointed out.

"I know and he's such a blessing to our lives," Olive said, regarding her stepson.

All of Amy's friends were married and now one of them was pregnant. As much as Amy was happy for them, inside she felt empty and a touch inadequate.

"I'm going to be an aunt again," Olive said.

"So are we, kind of." Lucy giggled.

Jessie said, "You'll all be honorary aunts."

The only news Amy had didn't seem quite so important compared to Jessie's. "I'm so pleased for you and Elijah," Amy said.

Lucy asked, "What about you, Amy?"

Olive nudged Amy with her shoulder. "*Jah,* Amy, have you heard anything from a certain person?" All eyes were now on Amy.

"What do you mean?" She knew very well what Olive meant. Olive was always urging her to get back into contact with the man who occupied her thoughts every waking hour.

"Andrew," Jessie stated.

"Oh, Andrew. *Jah,* what's happening with him?" Lucy asked.

"I finally took your advice and I wrote to him."

Olive squealed, and patrons in the café once again

scowled in their direction. Olive turned away from the table, and told them, "I'm sorry. It won't happen again." Then she faced the girls and they all had a quiet laugh.

"When did you do that?" asked Lucy.

"Last night."

Jessie leaned close to her. "You posted it, right?"

"I gave it to Martha to post. She was going somewhere with Gabbie and Michael Glick. I didn't know I was going out today until Olive stopped by to collect me. Otherwise, I would've posted it myself."

"Good. It'll be on its way. It'll take about a week to get there and then when he writes back, that'll take another week. In two weeks, you should have an answer from him." Olive's face beamed with happiness.

"Well, I'm not holding my breath," Amy said. "He might've lost interest, but at least I tried."

"You'll find out soon. You've done the right thing," Lucy said. "At least you'll know one way or the other."

That's what Amy had been afraid of. She didn't want a letter back filled with news of what was happening in Andrew's community with no word about his feelings for her. Neither did she want to find out he'd met someone and was getting married. Maybe not knowing had been a blessing. It was possible that Gabbie had said no word about him because the news wasn't good.

After an hour of giving her tour, Martha said, "Michael, tie the buggy under that tree over there. There's a picnic spot a little walk from there."

"Not too far I hope." Gabbie turned to Martha. "Not too far; my leg is still sore. Michael might have to carry me."

Michael laughed. "I don't know about that, Gabbie.

If it's too far for you, you might have to have lunch in the buggy." Gabbie pouted.

Once Michael tied up the horse, he put the two picnic baskets one on top of the other. "You lead the way, Martha."

"Can you carry the both of them?" Gabbie asked.

"They aren't heavy. I just hope everybody's hungry."

"We won't need dinner tonight, that's for sure," Martha said.

Michael made his way down the grassy slope.

"It's so pretty here. The water looks crystal clear," Gabbie said pointing to the creek.

"There's a nice place for us to walk after we've eaten. The walkway winds all around the creek and through the trees," Martha said.

"How about here, Martha?" Michael asked.

"*Jah,* this looks like as good a spot as any."

Michael placed the baskets on the ground. Martha opened her picnic basket, pulled out a large blanket and spread it over the grass for them to sit on.

Michael opened the other basket. "Mrs. Glick went to a lot of trouble making all this food."

"That's so nice of her. Thank her for us, would you?" Gabbie poked around in the basket. "What do we have? Let's see; this looks like cold chicken, coleslaw, beetroot salad and fresh-baked bread. Is everyone hungry now? I know I am. Let's eat right now." Gabbie sat cross-legged on the blanket, covering her legs with her full dress, and Martha did the same.

"There's cider in here too." Michael pulled some cups and the glass bottle from the bottom of the basket.

"We forgot to bring something to drink, Martha," Gabbie said.

Martha screwed up her nose. "So we did. Just as well we've got Mrs. Glick looking after us."

As they helped themselves to the food, Gabbie said, "Do you know how long you'll be staying on here, Michael?"

Michael shook his head while he finished the mouthful he was chewing. "I'll have to wait and see, depends on my *onkel's* recovery."

"You don't seem to be doing an awful lot of work. I mean, we see you every two days or so," Gabbie said.

Michael drew his eyebrows together. "I do work very hard; I wake up before it's light and I put a lot of hours in. Why? How long would you expect me to work in a day?"

"Michael has had a lot of other things to do lately, Gabbie. Like, he took things to the charity auction for his *onkel.* And he does have to eat. We've seen him mainly for meals."

Michael smiled at Martha. *"Denke,* for defending me." Martha covered her mouth and giggled.

"We see you often, that's all." Gabbie carried on munching quite unaware she might have offended somebody. When she had finished eating, Gabbie kicked off her shoes and ran towards the creek. When she got there, she turned and yelled, "Are you two coming, or what?"

"We'll be there in a minute, Gabbie." Michael turned to Martha. "At last, time alone. You'll have to come on a buggy ride with me by yourself."

Martha looked into his beautiful face and smiled. She loved his soft brown eyes, the smoothness of his skin and most of all she loved the dimple in his cheek. She looked away when she realized she was staring at him a little too long.

"Well what do you say, Martha? Would you like to go on a buggy ride with me sometime; just you and me?"

Before Martha could answer, Gabbie was upon them. "Come on, you two, come down to the water."

Michael stood and put his hand out to help Martha to her feet. It was awkward for her to interact with Michael in front of Gabbie, but she couldn't help smiling at him as she placed her hand in his. He lifted her to her feet. It could have been a special moment but was ruined by Gabbie glaring at the two of them. Gabbie's arms were crossed as she turned back and walked to the water's edge.

They stood looking at the creek and Gabbie looked up at Michael. "It's a romantic place."

"It is indeed," Michael said.

"Let's walk off our lunch," Martha suggested. The three of them walked along the banks of the creek for half a mile and then back again. "I guess we should start heading back now; *Mamm* will want us to put the dinner on soon," Martha said to Gabbie.

"*Jah* and I've a few errands I need to run today," Michael said.

"Speaking of errands. We've got to post your *schweschder's* letter."

"*Ach,* I nearly forgot."

"We'll drive past a post box on the way home."

"*Denke,*" Martha said.

When they stopped at the post box, Gabbie offered to post Amy's letter. They couldn't park directly in front and it was a little way up the road. Martha hadn't insisted on popping it in the box herself and Gabbie knew she wanted the alone time with Michael. As Gabbie walked up the road with the envelope in her hand, she looked at it one more time.

When she got to the box, she glanced back to see Michael and Martha sharing a joke in the front seat. Anger seared through her like a hot knife through butter. Looking down at the letter, she wanted to rip it up. "Well, Amy, I'm sorry, but if I can't have Michael, you can't have *Onkel* Andrew. It's only fair." Next to the box was a trash can, so she promptly tore the letter in two and threw it in the trash before hurrying back to make sure Martha and Michael didn't get too close.

They arrived back at Martha's house and Michael carried the picnic basket into the kitchen for them. After he exchanged pleasantries with the family, he said goodbye to the girls. Martha and Gabbie watched him drive the buggy back up to the road.

"How was your day, girls?" Martha's mother asked when they walked back into the kitchen.

"We had a *wunderbaar* time." Gabbie clasped her hands to her heart not wanting anyone to see how annoyed she was. "Now, what do you want us to do for dinner, Mrs. Yoder?"

"You can shell the peas and grate the carrots. After you do that, you can set the table. First, you'll need to pick the carrots and the peas from the garden. I meant to do that earlier, but I forgot."

"You seem to forget a lot of things, Mrs. Yoder," Gabbie said.

Before Mrs. Yoder could respond, a breathless Amy, just home from the coffee shop, hurried into the kitchen. "Girls, did you remember to post my letter?"

"Jah, we did," Martha answered.

"Good, *denke.*"

The girls hurried off to do what they were asked. While they were there, the conversation led to Michael. "Do you think Michael's handsome, Martha?"

"Jah, he's nice. He's got a very good personality."

Gabbie laughed. "What? But do you think he's handsome?"

Martha turned her attention to the carrots she pulled out of the ground. It was hard to know what she should say to Gabbie because she often repeated things at the very worst times. *"Jah,* he is nice," she repeated the safest response.

"I had such a good time with him today. Do you think he likes me?"

"Do you mean as friends?" Martha asked hopefully.

Gabbie huffed. "I don't need any more friends. I mean likes me for his girlfriend."

"Are you going to collect the peas?" Martha asked.

"You're avoiding my questions, Martha."

"That's because I can't say how he feels. I don't know how he feels." Martha tried to hide the irritation welling inside.

"Well, I can't very well ask myself, can I?"

Martha laughed at the silliness of the situation. They both liked him; that was plain to see. Martha didn't know what to do. She had a feeling he might like her, but what if Gabbie had that feeling too? Romance and love were new to Martha, and she knew nothing of it. He kept asking her on a buggy ride alone, so he had to like her and not Gabbie. If he'd asked Gabbie on a buggy ride too, she would've heard about it by now. Today, she felt that Michael had gotten to know her better. She'd relaxed in his company and that had chased away her nervousness.

"The gathering is tomorrow, isn't it?" Gabbie asked.

"*Jah* it is. We'll see him again tomorrow if that's what you're thinking." She turned away from the carrots to look at Gabbie.

"*Jah,* I was just wondering when I'd see him again."

There was only one thing for it. Martha had to get the conversation away from Michael. One of them was going to get hurt; Michael could not court both girls. "That should be enough for the dinner now. Let's go inside," Martha said.

Chapter Twenty-Five

The rush on Sunday morning was hectic as usual. Martha's yellow dress was her only clean one. She pulled it on while thinking she would have to borrow one from her sister to wear the next day. She saw Gabbie was fast asleep. The awful situation of them both liking the same man had kept her awake all night. Martha decided to stay away from him the entire day. She needed proof that Michael liked her and her alone. If she saw any sign that he liked Gabbie too, Martha would know that he was not the man for her. Even though he'd asked her twice to go on a buggy ride, he'd never made a definite time or day. Martha knew Gabbie would enjoy the chance to talk to him alone.

From the start of the meeting, Martha carried out her plan of staying away from Michael. During the meal afterward, he made his way toward her, but she moved away to talk to some other people. Every time Martha glanced in Michael's direction, Gabbie was either with him or close by him.

As Martha poured herself a drink from the refreshments table, one of the younger boys pulled on her arm. "What is it?" Martha asked.

"That man over there," he turned and pointed to Michael, "asked me to give you this." He handed a folded piece of paper to Martha and left quickly.

Martha looked at Michael, and he gave her a quick smile. She looked down to the note pressed into her palm and slowly unfolded it. The note read, *Come on a buggy ride with me Tuesday night?* Martha smiled and crumpled the note in her hand. She looked back at Michael across the crowd, caught his eye and nodded.

Just before the singing was to begin, Gabbie raced to Martha. "Michael asked if he could drive us home." Her face glowed with excitement.

"Nee, Dat left us the buggy," Martha said.

"You go home in the buggy by yourself, and I'll go home with Michael."

"There's no need, Gabbie. I just said we could go home in *Dat's* buggy."

"Nee, I don't want to. I want Michael to take me home."

Martha shrugged her shoulders. "Do as you please."

"Okay." After Gabbie gave Martha a quick hug, she wasted no time in hurrying back to Michael.

Although Martha knew Gabbie deserved a fair chance and time alone with Michael, it didn't stop her being upset.

Now she wished she'd never agreed to the buggy ride.

Martha left the singing before it began; the mood had been ruined. As she drove the buggy in the dark, she had to wonder if Michael knew he'd have time alone with Gabbie or had he thought he'd drive both of them home? From what Gabbie had said, Michael offered to drive the two of them home. She couldn't blame Gabbie for seeing it as an opportunity to spend time with Michael.

Martha was caught in the middle, and more than ever, she missed the old Amy. The Amy before she'd gone to

Augusta. Now, Amy was a shell of her old self. Hopefully, Andrew would get that letter and ask her to come back and be his bride. That would be the best outcome for all concerned. Then Amy could be happy once more.

Martha couldn't confide in her mother, or her mother would most likely send Gabbie home, and she didn't want that. Her younger sisters closest in age, Rose and Mary, were too young to understand, and she didn't want to talk about something so personal with her friends. The horse's hooves continued their rhythmic clip-clop while she considered her awkward position.

She had agreed to go on a buggy ride with him on Tuesday evening. Things were confusing. How would she tell Gabbie about going on a buggy ride with him? Which one of them did Michael like? Didn't Michael know they both had a buggy there to go home in? When she got home, Martha unhitched the buggy and tended the horse, all the while fuming. Things would have been much easier if Gabbie had never come to stay.

Michael had driven Gabbie straight home after the singing. Martha was in bed when Gabbie walked into her darkened room singing. "Oh, are you awake, Martha?"

Martha sat up in bed. She hadn't been asleep. "I am now."

"He drove me straight home. What do you think it means? He didn't say much either."

This would've been a perfect opportunity for Martha to tell Gabbie that she was going on a buggy ride with him on Tuesday night. She couldn't bring herself to tell her in case she got upset and started crying.

Gabbie continued, "As soon as it was over, we left the

singing. And then drove here. He stared into the house. I think he was looking for you."

Maybe this was the best time to tell her. "Gabbie, tonight Michael asked me to go on a buggy ride on Tuesday night."

Gabbie's eyes grew wide. "I didn't even see you speaking to him tonight, Martha."

"Well I did, just briefly." There was no point in telling her about the young boy and the note.

"Strange he would take me on a buggy ride tonight, and you on one Tuesday night. It doesn't make sense."

"Is it late?" Martha asked.

"Nee, it's not. Are you coming downstairs?"

"I think I'll stay here and have an early night. You go downstairs if you wish," Martha said, lying back down on her bed.

"What about a cup of hot tea? I could bring one up to you."

"That would be nice, *denke,* Gabbie."

Martha pushed her head further into the pillow and closed her eyes. Sometimes Gabbie was annoying, but she was also her very best friend in the world. Why wasn't anything ever straightforward?

Gabbie stomped down the stairs. She knew that Martha was up to something. She had been watching Michael the whole night, and Michael hadn't talked to Martha. So, when did Michael ask her to go on this buggy ride? Would she have made it all up? She'd once thought Martha was a good friend, but she clearly wasn't. She was trying to take Michael from her. Maybe Martha had been the one to ask Michael. From now on, she'd watch Martha closely; she was clearly someone she couldn't trust.

Chapter Twenty-Six

The night of Martha's buggy ride rolled around. She was nervous and excited, and even Gabbie seemed happy for her. Gabbie helped her to dress and did her hair. As much as it was a happy time for Martha, it was mixed with feelings that her happiness came at the cost of Gabbie's. It was inconvenient they both liked the same man.

She knew she had to put Gabbie out of her mind so she'd have a good time with Michael. As soon as she heard the buggy, Martha closed the front door behind her, and went out to meet him. Her heart pounded more with each step closer to him. She breathed deeply to steady her nerves.

"It's a lovely night, Martha," Michael said, as she climbed into the buggy beside him.

Martha hadn't noticed the sky or the weather. It could've been snowing in the middle of summer and she wouldn't have cared. She glanced up at the dark night sky at the twinkling stars and the round luminous moon. "It is nice," she said. Martha knew she'd have to bury her nerves and talk so Michael could learn who she was deep down inside. Now was her chance to open up in a way she'd never opened up before. "Do you know where we're going?"

"Nee, I thought we'd drive around the streets." He laughed and looked over at her again. "I figured it doesn't matter where we go. I just want some time with you, and this is the only way I can get it, it seems."

Martha was glad he'd said how he felt. He drove the buggy a little way and they came to a T intersection.

"I think I'll go this way," he said, as he turned his horse to the left. "Tell me something about yourself. Tell me something I don't already know."

"There's not much to tell really," Martha said, frowning at her boring response.

"I know you do a great deal of charity work and that means you're kind and caring."

"That's nice of you to say. Well, you know about my family. My younger sisters and my baby brother, and Amy."

"I heard that your sister was sent to Augusta once to find a husband."

"She didn't want to go, but she didn't have any say in it. There weren't many men in the community for her, not any her age. That's what my *vadder* said, and I guess he was right to send her there."

"She's not much older than you, is she?"

"She's two years older than me. There are quite a few boys my age if that was your next question." Martha laughed, feeling more at ease.

"Are you telling me I've got competition?"

Martha giggled. *"Nee,* I didn't mean that."

"Then I have no competition? You will continue to go on buggy rides with me, and me alone?"

"Is that what you want?" Martha asked becoming bolder.

"Jah, Martha, I would like to see a great deal more of you."

Martha found it hard to get the smile off her face. The man she liked, liked her. Every time thoughts of Gabbie came into her mind, she pushed them aside. Tonight, it was her night to be alone with Michael.

"I've got a no-top buggy at home," Michael said. "It would've been lovely on a night like this."

Martha tried not to think of all the other girls he might've taken on buggy rides. She wondered if she should ask how many girls he'd taken in his buggy, then decided against it.

"Would you ever leave here?" Michael moved his buggy over to the side of the quiet road and then brought it to a halt.

"Nee, I don't think I'll ever leave my family. Not with *Mamm* being sick most of the time, and all."

"But what if things got serious between the two of us, would you move to Ohio with me?"

Martha swallowed hard. A cool breeze caressed her face, while she looked up the still, dark road. "It would depend if *Mamm* was better. If she was well and didn't need my help, I'd move to Ohio." Martha smiled and looked into his face.

"That's what I hoped you'd say." His eyes twinkled in the moonlight.

The way he looked at her made her breathless. "I have never been on a buggy ride before," she confessed.

"Haven't you? You're doing a fine job." He smiled at her and held out his hand.

She looked down and placed her hand in his. He

closed his fingers around her small hand. With a pounding heart, she looked back into his eyes. They held each other's gaze for more than a moment.

"We should go, before I kiss you," he said, which caused Martha to giggle again.

"I had better get home or *Dat* will come out looking for us."

He turned the buggy and headed back to her house.

Martha's heart beat wildly again once he stopped the buggy outside her house. How would they say their goodbyes? Would they hold hands again, or would he kiss her cheek? "I had a lovely time."

"Does that mean you'll come out with me again?" He moved a little closer.

"Jah." Martha knew she should get out of the buggy fast. At least one person would be watching them out of a window. "I had a lovely time," she repeated. *"Denke,* Michael."

"Me too, Martha, and I'm glad you came."

After she got out of the buggy, she turned to him. "Do you want to come in?"

He shook his head. "I'll go."

They smiled at each other for a moment before Martha turned and walked into the house. After she closed the door behind her, she saw her father on the couch. "You weren't waiting up for me, *Dat,* were you?"

"Jah, I was."

"Can I get you anything before I go to bed?"

He nodded his head toward a cup of tea. "I just got myself a cup of tea. I'm okay, *denke,* child."

"I'll go to bed now."

"Not so fast; sit down here with me."

Martha frowned, hoping she wasn't in trouble and sat down by her father.

"And what do you think of Michael Glick?" he asked, looking none too happy.

Martha hoped Gabbie wasn't listening in from upstairs. She spoke in a quiet voice. "I think he's very nice, *Dat,* very nice indeed."

"Was he a gentleman?"

Inwardly, she heaved a relieved sigh. It was just a general father/daughter talk. *"Ach jah,* very much a gentleman."

"I'm glad of that. You better get your sleep. You're taking your *mudder* to Nellie Byler's *haus* tomorrow."

That trip had been put off so many times. Martha hoped her mother would feel well enough to go. *"Jah* I know, *Dat.* I hope Nellie can help her."

"She will. She's helped before."

"Gut nacht, Dat."

"Gut nacht."

She left her father alone in the living room. He was always the last to go to bed, enjoying quiet moments alone with God as he read his Bible.

As soon as Martha stepped into the room, Gabbie sat bolt upright in bed. "Well, how did it go?"

Martha sat down and unwound her hair. "I had a good time."

"I'm happy for you." Gabbie threw herself down, pulled the covers around her neck, and did not ask another thing.

Martha tried hard not to concern herself about Gabbie and her feelings, but guilt bubbled within. She changed into her nightgown and slipped between the covers of her bed hoping sleep would come quickly. Martha was drifting off when she heard Gabbie sobbing. She knew that she was crying over Michael.

Martha rushed to her side. "Gabbie, what's wrong?"

Gabbie sat up and rubbed her eyes. "It's just that I'm missing Joseph."

"Are you sure that's all?"

Gabbie sniffed a couple of times and nodded. "And I can see that Michael likes you better than me." Her mouth turned down, and she cried uncontrollably.

"Sh, stop it, Gabbie." Martha felt sorry for her, but she also hoped that Gabbie's crying wouldn't wake the girls or Micah.

"I can't help it," she said sniffing again. "No one likes me, not even Joseph."

"Sh, it'll be all right."

"How will it be all right? I don't mean to cry. I feel silly. I'm just upset, that's all."

Martha rubbed Gabbie's back. "I know, Gabbie, I know."

After half an hour of Martha comforting Gabbie, both girls went back to sleep, but not before Martha had softly stroked Gabbie's arm to soothe her to sleep.

Chapter Twenty-Seven

The next morning, neither Gabbie nor Martha mentioned Gabbie's outburst from the night before. Martha dared not bring it up and was pleased they had the distraction of taking her mother to Nellie Byler's house.

On the way there, Gabbie asked, "Have you taken one of this woman's tonics before, Mrs. Yoder?"

"Jah, I have. I've been to her on and off over the years."

"What does she give you?" Gabbie asked.

Mrs. Yoder frowned. "I'm not sure exactly what's in the tonic, it's just a mixture of herbs."

"Last time when *Mamm* went to a doctor, he said she was low in iron. The medicine they gave her made her sick, but she got better after she had taken the tonic from Nellie," Martha said.

Mrs. Yoder drove the buggy over the bumpy roads. The roads near home were smooth but the closer they got to Nellie's house the worse the roads got. "I don't like doctors or hospitals. I prefer to stay well away from them," Mrs. Yoder said while doing her best to steer the buggy over the best sections of the road.

"We don't have anyone who gives tonics back home," Gabbie said.

Martha asked, "What do you do when you get sick?"

"We go to the doctor when we're really sick. We don't get sick often. My little *bruder* had a bad fever and had to be transferred to the hospital. They let him out two weeks later."

"Fevers can be dangerous, can't they?" Martha asked.

"Jah, they said his temperature went so high it was nearly the highest temperature they had ever recorded for someone his age."

"Did they ever find out what was wrong with him?" Martha asked.

"Measles," Gabbie said.

"Ach, that's not *gut.* Did it go through the whole *family?"* Mrs. Yoder asked.

"Nee, no one else caught it."

"I don't have anything like that; I'm just a little run down I'd say. Now that Amy's been preoccupied I've more work to do," Mrs. Yoder said.

Martha frowned. "I help you, *Mamm."*

"I know you do, and you're a blessing, but there's extra work now with Micah."

"Well, Micah can't be much of a burden because it seems to me that Amy looks after him mostly. He even sleeps in her room."

Martha was uncomfortable with the direction Gabbie was taking the conversation. "We're close now, aren't we?"

"She lives in that old house up there." Mrs. Yoder nodded her head to the left of them.

The girls looked across to the old house. As they drew

closer, they saw that the house's boards had no paint and were weathered gray.

"Look at the garden, all grown over. I've never seen such a thing," Gabbie said with disgust.

"I think they could be herbs or weeds she uses for the medicine," Martha said trying to recognize the plants as herbs or medicinal grasses and plants.

"I would never eat weeds," Gabbie said.

"Only some people call them weeds. *Gott* might've made them for our medicine, and people call them weeds when they grow unbidden in our flower beds," Mrs. Yoder said.

Gabbie raised her eyebrows. "I've never thought of it like that."

Mrs. Yoder chuckled as she brought the horse to a halt. *"Gott* has a purpose for everything, Gabbie."

Gabbie smiled and nodded at the older woman before both girls got out of the buggy. Mrs. Yoder tied the horse's reins, and they approached the front door.

"Nellie, are you home?" Mrs. Yoder stepped back as the door creaked open. She wandered through with the two girls close behind. "Yoohoo, Nellie, are you home?"

"Did she know we were coming?" Gabbie whispered.

"Nee, she's usually always at home." Martha looked around the room to see shelves on every wall, filled with bottles of dried herbs.

"She's not home then," Gabbie said.

Nellie stepped out of the kitchen causing everyone to jump. "It's the Yoders." She looked at Gabbie. "And…?"

Mrs. Yoder spoke, "This is Gabbie. She's staying with us and she comes from Augusta."

"Where's the little one?" Nellie asked.

"We left Micah with Amy," Mrs. Yoder said.

"Ah. What is it you've come to see me about?" Nellie stepped forward and peered into Mrs. Yoder's eyes and before she could speak, Nellie held up her hand. "Don't tell me. You haven't been yourself and you're tired constantly, and light-headed and often feel dizzy."

"Jah, that's right. How could you tell?" Mrs. Yoder asked.

"I can see it in your eyes, and in the color of your skin." The two girls looked at each other in amazement.

"How can you know that just by her eyes?" Gabbie asked.

"I've been doing this a long time. I read the signs just as you would read words on a page. Although, I think you might have more than one thing ailing you." Nellie picked up Mrs. Yoder's hand and pressed down on her skin.

"I was hoping you'd be able to mix me a tonic again," Mrs. Yoder said.

"Jah, I will. Now, what was it I gave you last time?"

"I don't remember. It was dark green and bitter. You had me take two tablespoons of it night and morning."

"Bitter, you say?"

Mrs. Yoder nodded.

"How long before you started to feel better?" Nellie asked.

"Just a couple days later, I was improved."

"I see, I see." The old woman walked down the bottle-lined wall.

"Are you a witch?" Gabbie asked.

Martha froze in shock and Mrs. Yoder said, "Gabbie!"

The old woman laughed and turned to face Gabbie. "I know nothing about witches, but it's not the first time I've been called one. People are frightened of the unknown." The old lady wagged a bony finger at both young girls. "Now, when I was a girl, we only had herbs as medicine. *Gott* gave them to us. We didn't go to doctors so much like they do today."

"I'm sorry, I said that without thinking," Gabbie said.

"As you do quite often, Gabbie," Mrs. Yoder snapped.

The old lady turned her attention back to her herbs. She hummed as she unscrewed various bottles to sniff the contents.

Martha was surprised to hear her mother speak so harshly to Gabbie. Martha turned her attention to Nellie and watched as she selected five bottles by smell. None of the bottles were labeled. She knew what they were by sight and by smell even though they looked exactly the same to Martha.

Nellie turned to see the three of them staring at her. "Sit, sit."

Mrs. Yoder and the two girls sat on the small couch that was really only big enough for two people.

"It'll take me half an hour to make this. Do you want to call back for it?" Nellie asked.

"Nee, I think we'll wait. By the time we get home, it'll be time to turn around. Can the girls take a walk?"

"Jah, there's a creek down by the trees. There's a bridge that runs across it and it's full of frogs." The old lady laughed.

"Come on, Martha." It seemed Gabbie couldn't get out of there fast enough as she grabbed Martha's arm and pulled her out the door. Once they were outside, Gabbie said, "That's the weirdest thing I've ever seen."

"Sh, she'll hear you."

"Nee, she won't. Let's walk down here." Gabbie pointed to the trees.

"She's okay. She seems a little strange, but she's harmless. There's nothing wrong with her at all."

"I shouldn't have asked her if she was a witch."

Martha laughed. *"Nee,* you probably shouldn't have. You must think before you speak."

"I guess." Gabbie looked over her shoulder at the old house. "I hope your *mudder* will be all right."

"She's just low in iron again, or something like that. That would explain why she's tired so often."

"My *mudder's* never been sick. I can't remember one day she's been sick in my whole life."

"Jah, my *dat's* like that; he's never been sick either," Martha said.

They found the wooden bridge and took off their shoes. Sitting on the low bridge, they dangled their feet in the cool water.

"You should come back with me when I leave, Martha."

"I don't know if I can leave *Mamm.* She needs my help."

"Ach, jah. I forgot." Gabbie gave a small giggle and looked back at the old house. "Does Nellie live there alone?"

"Jah, she's never married and she hasn't been to a gathering in a long time."

"My *vadder* always visits people who don't go to the meetings often."

"I guess that's the bishop's job." Martha stared into the water.

"If they don't go for a long time *Dat* tells them that they'll have to make a choice. I've heard him call them fence-sitters. It's not *gut* to stay away from the gatherings."

Martha scratched her face. "I guess not. I suppose she's had visits by the bishop and his *fraa*. I don't know." Martha kicked the cool water and looked to see if she could see any frogs, but the water was too murky.

"You girls aren't following me, are you?"

The girls jumped and turned their heads to see Michael.

Gabbie leaped to her feet. "Michael! What are you doing here?"

Chapter Twenty-Eight

Martha pulled herself to her feet by hanging onto the railing of the bridge.

"Nellie is my *grossdaddi's schweschder.* I've come for a quick visit," Michael said.

Martha smiled. He knew that she'd be there, and that's why he showed up today to visit Nellie.

"Why are you so surprised?" he asked both girls.

"We didn't expect to see you, that's all," Martha said. "Is Nellie related to Mr. or Mrs. Glick?"

"Neither, she's related through my *mudder's* side of the *familye* and the Glicks are through my *vadder's* side." Martha nodded.

"It's kind of in the middle of nowhere out here, and Nellie seems a strange lady. I thought she was a witch," Gabbie rambled, as she walked up the slight rise to meet him.

Martha held her breath. She'd only just advised Gabbie to think before she spoke. She hoped Michael wouldn't be offended. Martha gathered both sets of shoes and walked to catch up with Gabbie.

"I've just been inside to see that your *mudder* is waiting on a potion. They kicked me out and told me to come back in half an hour. Mrs. Yoder said you'd both be down here." He looked around. "I used to play here as a child. I stayed here one summer. I think I was about eight." Michael sat on the grass and Gabbie was quick to sit in front of him.

Martha walked forward and sat beside Gabbie, placing their shoes behind them. Gabbie was so interested in Michael that she was not aware she'd left her shoes. "What was it like staying with her?" Martha asked.

"I remember playing with frogs, and I don't remember much else. She cooked *gut* food, and she was kind to me. Is your *mudder* sicker now, Martha?"

"Run down is all. I try to help her as much as I can. She gets tired a lot."

Michael nodded and picked a long blade of grass.

"How are you enjoying your stay here?" Gabbie asked.

"I'm liking it. Although, I would like to get back to my old job. It's much better than farming."

"How did you play with the frogs?" Gabbie asked.

Michael's lips turned upward at the corners, and a dimple appeared in his cheek. "I'd take some frogs out of the creek and watch them as they hopped back into the water. I also gathered the tadpoles and watched them slowly turn into frogs."

"How far would you take them out of the water?"

"About five yards, that's all." He looked over at the creek. "I never caught any fish in there. I don't think there are any in there, probably too shallow."

"You could be a bad fisherman." Gabbie laughed.

He smiled and put the blade of grass in the corner of his mouth. "That might be why I never caught anything."

Martha tried to think of something to say but she

couldn't think fast enough. She felt calm and silent every time she was with him, but if she didn't say something then she might lose him to Gabbie. Gabbie got all the attention because of her constant chatter.

Gabbie suddenly lunged forward and clasped one of Michael's large hands. *"Ach,* Michael what happened to your hand?"

He pulled his hand away. "Just a little scrape. I did it this morning when I was hammering a nail back into the barn wall."

"It looks very bad," Gabbie said.

"It's not hurting or anything." He pulled his arm back even further. "Stop worrying. It's nothing."

"Maybe Nellie has something she can put on it," Gabbie said.

"I wouldn't bother her with something so small. I've had much worse injuries than this. I nailed my fingers together with a nail gun before I knew how to use it properly. See that?" He held out the fingers of his left hand to reveal two deep scars.

"Oh, that looks like it would've been painful," Gabbie said.

"It was, believe me." Michael laughed. "This little scratch is nothing."

Martha was disturbed to see the two of them looking into each other's eyes and talking about his hands. She had to leave. "I'll go back to the *haus* and see how *Mamm's* getting along. Nellie might be finished soon."

"We'll come too. It looks like it might rain." Michael jumped to his feet.

Gabbie reached out her arm for Michael to pull her to her feet. Michael grabbed her by her arm and pulled her to her feet.

Martha had already turned and walked away. Michael hurried to catch her.

"Wait for me," he said. Once he was level with Martha, they stopped and waited for Gabbie to collect her shoes, and then the three of them walked back to the house.

When Martha walked in, she saw Nellie pouring green liquid through a funnel into a bottle.

"You found them I see," Mrs. Yoder said to Michael.

"Jah. They were down by the bridge like you said."

Martha looked around the strange home once again. If they were at anyone else's home for that length of time, they would've been offered coffee, food or cool drinks. Nellie, although she was nice and kind, had offered them nothing. As Martha looked closer at the dried roots and leaves in the bottles, she considered that maybe it was a good thing she'd not offered them anything. Gabbie would surely have declined, she thought with a private smile.

Nellie looked up at Martha. "I'm nearly finished. I know how impatient you young people can be."

"How's your *onkel,* Michael?" Mrs. Yoder asked.

"He's *gut,* getting better."

After capping and shaking the bottle of green fluid, Nellie handed it to Mrs. Yoder. "Here you go."

Gabbie pulled a face. "I don't know how *that* could make anyone feel better."

Nellie ignored Gabbie's comment. "If that doesn't work, I want you to go to a doctor. You might need to have your thyroid tested. This will help if you have any dietary deficiencies, and that's all."

"Would that be serious if it's her thyroid?" Martha asked.

"I wouldn't let it go too long. Can make life awfully unpleasant."

Michael stayed on at Nellie's house after they left. Now, Martha was more worried about her mother. If the tonic didn't work in a few days, she'd take her to the doctor herself.

Sometime after cleaning up from dinner that night, Gabbie had disappeared. Martha was certain she'd gone to the bedroom, but she wasn't there. Not wanting to alarm her parents just yet, she quietly asked her sisters if they'd seen her.

"I saw her go outside after dinner," Rose whispered back.

Martha scratched her head. There was no reason for Gabbie to go outside in the dark. She'd never done that the whole time she'd been there. Guessing that Gabbie might be upset about something, Martha slipped out the back door to find her. The barn was the first place she headed. She saw the glow of a lantern coming from under the door of the barn. Breathing out heavily, she pushed the door open and saw Gabbie sitting on a bale of hay with a lantern by her feet.

Gabbie looked up at her. "I was coming in soon. I just wanted a little time to myself."

Her words were broken and Martha knew that she'd been crying. She stepped forward, kneeled beside her and looked up into her face. "I know you've been crying. Tell me what's upset you." Martha fought back tears as she saw her friend so upset.

"I miss home."

Martha kept looking at her and didn't say a word.

She knew it wasn't the truth. "You're upset about Michael, aren't you?"

Gabbie put her hands up to her face and sobbed. Martha sat next to her and put her arm around her. "Come on. There's nothing to be upset about."

"He doesn't like me. I've made a fool of myself. A complete fool. He likes you and not me."

"I think he likes both of us and can't decide." The words came out of her mouth before she could stop them.

Gabbie dropped her hands and looked up. "Do you think so?"

"Maybe." She didn't know what else she could say to make Gabbie feel better.

"Did he ask you on another buggy ride?"

Martha shook her head. It was the truth. He had said that he wanted to go on more buggy rides but wasn't specific about when. It was close enough to the truth for her to consider that she hadn't told a lie.

Gabbie sniffed.

"Come back inside before they notice that we're gone. We can go through the back door then up the stairs to the bedroom."

"Do I look as though I've been crying?"

Martha nodded. *"Jah,* and everyone will want to know why. That's the trouble with this *familye,* everyone wants to know what's going on."

Gabbie laughed a little and wiped her eyes.

Martha stood and picked up the lantern. "Follow me." They slipped back into the house and made their way to the bedroom with no one seeing them. Martha wrung out a washcloth for Gabbie to put over her red eyes. She could not let her friend be so upset. She'd speak to Michael as soon as she could and tell him that they couldn't see one another again. Not until Gabbie was happy about it, and Martha knew she might have to wait until Gabbie found someone of her own.

It was two nights later that Martha spoke to Michael. He stopped over after the Yoders had finished dinner, asking to speak to Martha. Martha stepped down from the porch to speak to him.

"What's wrong?" he asked. "I can tell by your face that something is."

"I can't see you anymore, Michael."

Michael looked down at the ground and then back up to her face. **"Why?"**

"You can't ask me that."

He frowned. "I have a right to know. I've become fond of you, and I thought you felt the same." When she was silent, he looked into her eyes. "Was I wrong?"

She couldn't lie to him and neither could she tell him the truth. If she continued to see him, she would hurt her best friend. She had to let him go. "I just can't, Michael."

He took a step back. "Would be nice to know why. Have I upset you, have I said something?"

She shook her head and looked to the ground.

"I'll respect your wishes." He turned and walked back to his buggy.

At that moment, she decided to tell him the truth. "Wait, Michael." She'd tell him she didn't want to see him until Gabbie had a boyfriend, or until Gabbie went home. He might think it silly, but she couldn't risk losing him forever.

He turned around. *"Jah."*

She licked her lips. "The thing is…"

"What?"

He was growing impatient with her, and she didn't

like the way that made her feel. "I'm trying to tell you the reasoning behind why I can't see you for a while."

"And, I'm waiting to hear it, but a man can't wait forever."

"It's about Gabbie."

"What about her?"

Martha swallowed hard. What she had to say would sound unreasonable, and maybe it was.

"What, Martha? Just say it."

"I'm thinking how to say it."

He shook his head. "Why don't we just end things? It shouldn't be this hard or this complicated. Goodbye, Martha."

She didn't wait for him to drive away. It would be too painful to watch the only man she'd ever liked drive away from her. She hurried back to the house and returned to her family, wondering if she'd just made a horrible mistake. Choosing between her friend and her potential boyfriend had been hard. By trying to keep everyone happy she'd made herself miserable, losing Michael.

"What did he want? Why didn't he come inside?" her mother asked.

"He wanted to speak to me, and we spoke." Martha walked up the stairs to her bedroom and closed the door. She needed to be alone and was glad Gabbie took her time in coming up to bed.

Chapter Twenty-Nine

Martha's father shook her awake before sunup. He whispered, "I've got to visit some people today and I'm making an early start. I'm worried about your *mudder* and I want you to take her to the hospital after the girls are at school."

Martha rubbed her eyes. "Okay." He continued, "Leave Micah with Amy." Martha nodded.

She had been so preoccupied with herself that she'd given no thought to her mother's health. The tonic hadn't helped and *Mamm*, rather than improving, was going downhill.

She woke her mother after the children had left for school. *"Dat* asked me to take you to the hospital."

"Nee, I'll be all right. Are the girls getting ready?"

"They've already left," Martha said. *"Dat* will be upset with me if he comes home and I haven't taken you to the hospital."

Her mother sat up. "Okay, I'll get ready. I can never talk your *vadder* out of anything once he gets his mind set on something."

Martha left her mother alone to get ready.

"I'll stay and help Amy look after Micah," Gabbie said.

"You don't mind?" Martha asked.

Gabbie laughed. "I love looking after Micah and playing with him."

"Okay, *denke.*"

Martha was glad Gabbie wasn't going to the hospital with them. Even though she was her best friend, she took a lot of energy out of her. Martha wanted to save all her strength to look after her *mudder* and concentrate on what the doctor had to say.

After waiting for hours in the hospital, they were shown to a room where they waited for another half hour before a doctor came to see them. Mrs. Yoder described her symptoms when she finally got to see the doctor.

"My best guess is postpartum thyroiditis. It's a condition in which the thyroid becomes dysfunctional after childbirth. With the hormonal levels varying during pregnancy and birth, it's a time where women become prone to developing thyroid dysfunction." The doctor ran through the symptoms and her mother had most of them.

They were sent to another waiting room to see another doctor and to have a blood test.

"I hope your *vadder* is happy about this. I hate needles and doctors."

"We need you better, *Mamm.*"

Just as the nurse called her mother's name, Michael walked into the waiting room. Mrs. Yoder looked shocked to see him, and then whispered to Martha, "You stay here, and I can go in by myself."

Michael nodded hello to Mrs. Yoder as she walked away.

"What are you doing here, Michael?"

"I called to see you and Gabbie told me where you were. I have to speak to you."

Martha raised her eyebrows, glad that he was still talking to her after their last conversation.

"I know why you said you don't want to see me. It's Gabbie, isn't it? I think she likes me, and you don't want to upset her."

Martha pressed her lips together.

"That's it, isn't it?" Michael asked.

Martha nodded. "I can't upset her. She's my very best friend. I do want to see you as much as I can too, but I just don't know what to do. Whatever I do and whatever choice I make, someone will be upset."

Michael smiled and leaned into the back of the gray vinyl chair. "Phew. I thought that might be it. I stayed awake all night thinking about why you didn't want to see me when we get along so well." He leaned toward Martha. "And you know what?"

"What?"

"It makes me like you even more that you are so considerate."

Martha smiled and said, "But I still can't see you. It would be awful for Gabbie."

Michael licked his lips. "Gabbie won't be here forever, Martha. I'll wait. We can wait until she leaves and then her feelings won't be hurt."

"Don't you have to go back home? I don't know how long Gabbie will stay."

She saw his dimple form in his cheek as he smiled. "I'm not going back to Ohio unless I'm taking you with me."

Martha couldn't stop the grin that formed on her face. "We'll have a secret."

"Jah, we will, but it won't be a bad one. When Gabbie goes home, we'll be together. I'll wait for you. How about it?"

Martha nodded. "I'd like that. I'll look forward to it."

"I'll go now. I have to get back to work, or Gabbie will spread rumors that I'm never at work." Michael gave a little laugh and bumped shoulders with her.

Martha smiled, then he jumped up and she watched him walk away. It was a perfect solution. She could enjoy the company of her very best friend and she'd have a wonderful boyfriend when her friend went home.

Her mother came back into the waiting room and sat down next to her. "What was Michael doing here?"

She couldn't tell her mother the truth about him. If *Mamm* found out about Gabbie and the couple of stunts she'd pulled, her mother would surely send her home. "He was visiting a friend, and he saw us, that's all."

Her mother arched an eyebrow. It had been a bad lie. The only people Michael would've known so far away from home would've been in the community and they would've heard if someone was in the hospital.

"Well, I'm all finished now," her mother said.

"What do they think's wrong with you?"

"You were there and heard that long term. It was just as Nellie thought; the blood test confirmed it. There's something wrong with my thyroid." Her mother stood up. "Let's go; I'll tell you more on the way." As they waited for a taxi outside the hospital, her mother continued, "Were you thinking about Michael, or were you listening to what the doctor said?"

"I heard what he said about your thyroid. Did he say what to do about it?"

Her mother smiled and shook her head. Martha felt

bad for thinking about a boy rather than listening to all that the doctor said, but when he had started using big words, Martha had zoned out.

"They're talking about putting me on hormone replacement therapy."

"Are you going to do that?"

"I guess I'll have to. It's only tablets; I don't have to have needle jabs except to recheck once in a while."

"Just as well *Dat* said to bring you here today." A taxi pulled up in front of them.

When they got home, Gabbie waited until she was alone with Martha before she asked, "Why was Michael so anxious to see you today? He came here asking for you and hurried away. Did he go to see you at the hospital?"

"Can I smell cookies?" Martha asked.

"I baked apple cookies and chocolate chip cookies. Let's have some now. I'll put a pot of coffee on." Martha followed Gabbie into the kitchen. "Well?" Gabbie asked when they were sitting down.

"Michael just wanted to talk to me about something to do with the charity event the other day, that's all."

"And he went all the way to the hospital to ask you about that?"

"Jah."

"You're a bad liar, Martha Yoder. I know he likes you and not me. It's okay, you don't have to hide anything. Anyway, I still like Joseph." Her lips formed a pout. "I wrote a letter to Sally asking her about Ilsa and Joseph. I'm hoping to get a letter back soon."

"You really think there's a chance they won't get married?"

"Jah, that's what I'm hoping." Gabbie stood and lifted

the fresh cookies off the baking tray and onto a plate. "Is your *mudder* coming down for coffee and cookies?"

"She's upstairs having a sleep before the girls get home from school. *Denke* for helping out when I took *Mamm* to the hospital."

"Anytime."

Chapter Thirty

Two weeks later, the mailman blew his whistle signaling the mail delivery. Gabbie ran downstairs and stopped in front of Amy, who was just inside the front door holding a handful of letters. "Anything there for me, Amy?" Gabbie made a grab at the letters.

Amy swerved out of her way, closed the door, and continued to ignore Gabbie's whining while sifting through the letters looking for one addressed to herself. *"Mamm,* mail's here."

"Ach, Amy, don't be cruel, you know how much I miss home." Gabbie tried to peek over Amy's shoulder at the names written on the envelopes, but Amy kept moving about. "Please?" This disruption to what Gabbie wanted annoyed her beyond reason, so she made another grab for the post.

"Where are your manners, Gabbie? Wait your turn, can't you? My *mudder* and *vadder* must have theirs first, then I'll look for yours."

"There's nothing there for you is there, Amy?"

Amy frowned at her. *"Nee,* there's not."

"Again!" Gabbie screwed up her face, too eager to

hear word from home to wait patiently like a mouse. Amy wasn't playing fair. With her third attempt, she managed to snatch the letters from her hands.

"Give those back at once, young lady," Mrs. Yoder said, as she stood behind her with Micah on one hip.

Gabbie ignored her, sifting through, throwing anything not hers to the floor, until she saw her name.

"What do you think you're doing, Gabbie? You cannot behave like this." Mrs. Yoder snatched the remaining letters out of Gabbie's hands. "Amy, pick up the letters on the floor.

"Gabbie, go to your room."

Gabbie was shocked at Mrs. Yoder. The woman was normally quiet and meek. The new pills she was on for her thyroid condition had evidently kicked in. "That's mine. You give it back." Gabbie's cheeks burned at the woman's nerve. That was her letter, and no one had a right to take it from her like that.

"Not nice is it, to have what is yours snatched from your grasp?" Mrs. Yoder said with a frown.

"Nee, so why did you do it, then?" Gabbie snarled.

"You will learn to wait for things, young lady. Patience is a virtue; you will need to learn that in life. Good manners are something I know your parents taught you."

Gabbie couldn't listen to more of her lecturing, she wanted the letter in Mrs. Yoder's hands, and she wanted it now. She didn't care about being virtuous or patient; she just wanted her letter. Gabbie snatched the letter from Mrs. Yoder and ran outside, shouting, "Sorry, I can't wait."

She ran to a spot under some trees at the end of the field closest to the house. After she ripped open the envelope she began to read:

Dearest Gabbie,

I hope you are well. I have some news and had to write immediately to inform you of something, which will no doubt make you rush back to us all if you are able to do so. Joseph is no longer engaged to Ilsa! You must be here to catch him before someone else gets to him first, or before he changes his mind and takes Ilsa back.

Come home, dear friend. Come home quickly.

All my love, your best friend,
Sally

Gabbie dropped the letter. Her heart beat so fast, and her throat clenched tight; she thought she might pass out from the intensity of her emotions. "I have to get home. I simply must get home." Moving into the light, allowing the sun to warm her cheeks, she sighed. "Oh, Joseph, I always said we were meant to be. And now, fate has given me an opening, a chance, and I will use it. I will."

A grin consumed her face; She part ran and part skipped back to Martha's house. Determined to write to her parents and beg them to allow her back home, she composed the perfect letter in her mind, ready for when she held paper and pen.

She'd been away from her home for long enough, and would convince them that she was worthy of forgiveness, had earned their respect, and had changed. She would do this by groveling, begging if she had to, because she must have Joseph at any cost.

But I'll need to convince Martha's family of it too, otherwise, they'll tell them what they think I'm like and I'll never see Joseph single again.

On her return, everyone was waiting for her on the porch. Gabbie started talking before they could. "Before you say anything…" She raised her hands. "Please let me apologize. My behavior over the mail was atrocious, especially taking off with my letter like that."

"Stop right there." Martha's mother frowned and her lips turned down. "There's no use misbehaving only to offer a quick apology. This is not the way to behave. This is why I keep telling you to stop and think before you act and speak." Irritation creased her face and reddened her watery eyes, but her husband patted her hand, offering silent comfort as always.

Where's my comfort? I won't get that until I return home and find Joseph. "Absolutely." Gabbie had to work harder, be more persuasive. "You're right. I shouldn't have allowed my utter sadness, and my silly homesickness to impede good behavior and good manners. I do so want to be better than this, and I feel as though this outburst has helped me to turn a corner." Gabbie lowered her head, but peered up at Martha and her parents, judging their expressions.

Mr. and Mrs. Yoder looked at each other and then Mrs. Yoder said, "If you're telling the truth, I'm both relieved and pleased to hear it."

"I'm so grateful for everything you've done for me, and for the advice you've offered. Truly, I am. I need to write home. I need to write to my *mudder* and *vadder*. I'm ready to go home."

Mr. Yoder had been silent up until now. "Write your letter while I discuss a fitting punishment for your bad behavior."

Gabbie nodded. "I will." She ran to Martha's bedroom and closed the door behind her. She took paper and pen from her suitcase and sat on a chair near the window to write:

Dear mother and father,

It's been a very trying time without my family, but I've faced up to harsh truths during my time away. My bad behavior is altered and I admit that I was a terrible girl back when you first sent me here.

At first, I resented you for it. It felt unfair. But now I realize you did what you had to do. After all, I left you with no choice.

I want you to know that I've benefitted immensely from your decision, and I thank you for making it. However, I now feel ready to face up to things, to become the young woman you need me to be.

If only I'd listened to you back then. The fact is, now I can appreciate this simple fact with hindsight to guide me, and I will bow to your greater wisdom from now on, without old resentments or hostilities.

For these reasons, and because I miss home so very much, I pray you make another wise decision by allowing me to return home as soon as you feel it is correct and good.
Gabbie.

When Gabbie finally went downstairs, she hoped her sorrowful apology resulted in a kinder, less severe punishment. She sought out Mr. and Mrs. Yoder who were in the kitchen.

"You'll not be allowed to a singing or any outings for a week," Mr. Yoder said.

Gabbie nodded. "Okay."

When she left the kitchen, Martha was waiting for her.

"Gabbie, I'll post the letter for you now."

Her eyes widened. "Would you?" Martha nodded.

"I'll go upstairs and get it. When you get back, I'll tell you what Sally said in the letter."

Now it was clear to Gabbie how important it was that letters got to people. She put herself in Amy's shoes and felt dreadful for throwing Amy's letter to *Onkel* Andrew away. As soon as Martha had gone, Gabbie sneaked out of the house and called her uncle at his timber mill. She confessed everything to him, not only had she thrown Amy's letter to him away in a fit of temper, also that she knew Amy had always loved him and was suffering being away from him.

There was silence from the other end of the phone and Gabbie hoped he still liked Amy. "Well, are you pleased?"

"I'm not pleased with what you've done, but I'm pleased you've confessed. You'll have to tell Amy what you've done."

"I will." *Yes, she would, but not just yet.* "But are you happy she loves you. Do you love her? I know you did once."

"My private life is my private life, Gabbie. I thank you for letting me know."

Gabbie heard the back door shut and didn't want anyone to know she was using the phone. "Gotta go." She promptly hung up the phone's receiver.

Chapter Thirty-One

Gabbie was more polite and refined three weeks later when another letter arrived for her. It was from her parents.

> Dear Gabbie,
>   We were very glad to hear you have grown from this experience and will return to us a young woman befitting this household and our good name.
>   It is with great pleasure we allow your return home at the Yoder family's earliest convenience. We have sent the required sum to purchase the train ticket and once we have secured the schedule for your journey, we will arrange to meet you here at this end. Hope to see you in a couple of weeks.
>   With love,
>   Your loving parents

Gabbie squealed, "Home, I'm going home." She ran down to see her hosts, smiling and waving the letter around.

"I know." Holding on to a bank note, Mrs. Yoder said, "Your parents wrote me too. Looks like we have a train ticket to purchase. Get your coat. We'll make the arrangements now."

The following week, while waiting for her departure day, Gabbie made the best of the time and spent it trying to learn about being ladylike from Martha, her sisters, and their mother. Mrs. Yoder had been livelier lately. Gabbie preferred the old Mrs. Yoder, the one who had little to say; she was more likable when she'd been tired and unwell.

On the last day, Gabbie was packed and ready to go hours before she'd needed to be. She reminded herself that to misbehave now would mean to lose Joseph, and her chance of going home. As annoying as it was, she would have to be meek, be grateful, and be patient.

Once at the station, she offered a hurried goodbye to Martha and Mr. Yoder. The rest of the family had stayed at home.

"We'll all miss you, Gabbie," Mr. Yoder said.

"Me especially," Martha said, hugging her tight.

Gabbie was a little surprised they seemed upset when she boarded the train. Perhaps they were telling the truth and they would miss her. All Gabbie cared about was getting on with the daylong journey.

She found her seat and looked out the window. Gabbie opened the window and called to the Yoders who were waving at her. *"Denke* for welcoming me into your home, Mr. Yoder." She looked at Martha. "You've been really great." *If a little boring.* "I'll miss you, Martha."

"Write to me, Gabbie."

"I will. For certain, I will."

"Be *gut* at home so you don't get sent back soon," Mr. Yoder said with a laugh. "I'm joking. You're always welcome, Gabbie. Come and visit us again soon."

Gabbie waved out of the window as the train left the station. Her long journey to her true love, Joseph, was just beginning.

After dinner that night, there was a knock on the door, and Martha held her breath and hoped it was Michael. She made sure she got to the door first and she flung it open to see her hope fulfilled; Michael, standing on the porch.

"Can you come outside and talk, Martha?"

Martha looked over her shoulder and her father gave her a nod. *"Jah,* for sure."

They both walked down the steps of the porch and headed away from the house.

"I've heard Gabbie went home today." He stopped still and turned to face her.

Martha smiled and looked up into his face. *"Jah,* we're not that long back from the station. She was excited to go home. I was going to come and tell you tomorrow."

"Do you remember what you said to me in the hospital, and our secret?"

She nodded. She had not forgotten one word of what they said that day.

"Do you still mean it?" Michael asked.

"I do."

"I told you I'd wait for you, and here I am. I want to see more of you, Martha."

"I'd like that."

"You are the nicest woman I've ever known. I've never known a woman to be so caring and kind."

Martha giggled. "What about your *mudder?*"

"Well…*jah*. Except for my *mudder.*" Michael chuckled.

"You're making out I'm something special, and I'm not. I love Gabbie and I didn't want to hurt her, that's all." Martha had done what she thought only fitting for a Christian woman to do and no more. If she had been selfish, things might not have worked out so well.

"You're so sweet, Martha. I don't want to leave here and go back to Ohio unless you come with me."

Martha swallowed hard. She had thought she might lose him and was glad that he waited for her. She knew he was a good man. He'd left his construction job he loved, and came from Ohio to help out on his sick uncle's farm.

Michael took hold of her hands and held them close to his heart. "I've thought about nothing else other than you these past few weeks. There are so many things I have to stop myself saying to you. I don't want to rush things; I want to take things slow."

They gazed into each other's eyes for a moment.

"I know you don't speak much, Martha, but you know how I feel about you. I never want to change you from being the quiet person you are. If you feel the same about me as I do about you, just tell me."

"I do, Michael, I do."

Michael laughed as if relieved and squeezed her hands tight.

They gazed into each other's eyes. Martha was thankful that everything had worked out for everybody. She was still good friends with Gabbie, and Gabbie was going back to see Joseph. Things couldn't have turned out any better. Martha said a silent prayer of thanks. She learned that when God is put first, all things find a way of falling into place.

Now, would *Gott* work a miracle for Amy? Amy was still desperately in love with Andrew. Where was he?

The trip from Lancaster County to Augusta had been a long one, and now, Gabbie Miller was nearly home. The letter bringing the good news that Joseph had broken off his engagement with Ilsa had not left her hand all day. As Sally had advised in her letter, she'd better get home fast before someone else snapped him up. Everyone had always said Joseph was handsome, and the best catch in the community.

When the bus pulled into the stop at Augusta, Wisconsin, Gabbie threw her suitcase to the ground. She followed it by jumping off and landing right next to it.

Her parents were there, waiting to collect her, and her mother tut-tutted at her. "Come now, what happened to the more ladylike behavior you told us you were committed to?" her mother asked, even before she said hello.

"Ach, sorry. I was so desperate to have my feet on solid ground that I clean forgot myself." Gabbie remembered that things went well for her when she told people what they wanted to hear. "Forgive me; I'm just an eager daughter happy to return to the bosom of her *familye."* The smiles on her parents' faces told her she hadn't lost her touch.

After playing the adoring daughter for half an hour during their buggy ride home, it was time; she had to find out about Joseph. "What's been happening? Any news from within the community?"

"Just the usual. Nothing noteworthy," her mother drawled. "You'll catch up on everything soon enough."

"Nothing startling happened then?" Joseph dumping his fiancée was enormous news for a small community such as theirs, so how could they not tell her? Her mother wasn't a gossip, but Gabbie knew a few who were. "Nothing new has rocked the community lately?"

"Nee. Whatever do you mean?" Her mother leaned back, folded her arms, and scrutinized her. "Everything is as it was before you left. Why on earth would you think otherwise?"

Her father rolled his eyes, uninterested in tales and idle gossip.

Gabbie soon grew irritated by her mother's lack of comprehension. "Sally wrote to tell me about Joseph breaking off his engagement to poor Ilsa." Gabbie attempted to show sympathy to a jilted woman, as it was proper to do so. "That's a big deal, isn't it? I thought the community would be troubled over that sort of thing." She smiled and blinked her large hazel eyes.

"That's not so at all." Gabbie's mother waved a disapproving finger at her. "Sally couldn't have been more wrong. They're still very much together."

Nausea cramped Gabbie's stomach and made her woozy.

"What?" she gulped. "What does 'very much together' mean?"

Her mother turned her eyes to the road ahead. *"Ach,* I shouldn't have to paint a picture for you, Gabbie dear."

Hoping against all hope, Gabbie suspected her mother misread Joseph's kindness for adoration. "You mean he talked with her, showed her compassion after the breakup? Because if that's what you were referring to, then everyone who talks and has compassion can easily be misread." Gabbie knew she was grasping at anything to make sense of the situation.

Her mother frowned and shook her head.

Gabbie continued, "They could have broken up as Sally told me but stayed friends. Joseph is very good like that; he's very kind."

"Is he really?" Gabbie's father asked, turning his head away from the road to look at her.

Gabbie screamed inside when her cheeks burned. "So I've heard, *Dat.*"

"Being the bishop, your *vadder* would be the first to know if something like that had happened. Either way, it's none of your concern, Gabbie."

"Your *mudder* is right, Gabbie. Keep your nose in your own business, and out of other people's business." Her father sighed and turned his attention to the road ahead, away from Gabbie and his wife.

"Well, *Dat?*" Gabbie asked.

He shook his head. "Stop it, Gabbie. They're still together. I didn't know you were so interested in other people."

"I am." Gabbie's voice softly trailed away as her imagination tortured her with images of Joseph and Ilsa being a couple. *Sick, I need to be sick.*

"And it'll be your turn to be engaged soon." Gabbie's mother nudged her arm. "Now that you've learned how to behave like a lady, we can look into getting you married off…er, I mean married too."

Gabbie gasped. What had she done? Her deceptions had gotten her home for what? To be "married off"?

"Are you well, Gabbie dear?" Her mother waved her handkerchief in her face. "You're awfully red."

"Fine, I'm fine." Gabbie grabbed her mother's hand, put it into her lap, and patted it. This did not satisfy her need to scream one bit, as she imagined herself throttling Sally for her lies. "I'll just be glad to get home, that's all. It's been a long day."

Her mother peered into her face. "Of course, you must be exhausted. We'll be home soon."

Gabbie's father said, "In around ten minutes I expect."

Gabbie stared into the darkness outside the buggy, her stomach so crippled with rage that it twisted like a hurricane.

Joseph is still not mine, my best friend is a liar, and they will try to make me marry someone else.

Chapter Thirty-Two

The following day, Gabbie couldn't eat breakfast. Her stomach was still churning, and all she could think about was seeing Sally. She had to get to the truth of the matter. She found her mother in the living room and said, *"Mamm,* I'm going to visit Sally." Gabbie wore her oldest dress and an over-apron that was once white but was now gray with age and wear. *What is the point in looking my best if Joseph is still engaged to Ilsa?*

"Are you, now?" Her mother looked her over, disapproval was written on her face. "Don't you mean to ask permission to leave this *haus?* Something like: '*Mamm,* may I visit Sally at some point today?'"

Gabbie stopped herself short before giving a cheeky response, knowing it would make her mother regret allowing her back home.

"Quite right, *Mamm."* She sat down on the couch, spine erect, hands folded in her lap. "I won't go then."

Her mother grinned. "Excellent. You can see her soon enough. Today we need to give your room a good cleaning. It hasn't been cleaned since you left." Mrs. Miller wrinkled her nose as she looked at her daughter's clothes. "What you're wearing can go in the rag basket. Go upstairs and change. You've got so many clothes, I don't know why you chose those."

Gabbie made to stand up, but her mother said, "Wait." She leaned over, and pulled Gabbie's prayer *kapp* back a little, and then shook her head. "You can also do your hair again; I can tell that you didn't even brush it before you pinned it."

"I was in a hurry that's why, and anyway, who sees my hair under the *kapp?* I promised Sally I would visit her as soon as I returned home, which was wrong of me considering I hadn't talked it over with you first." She could see her mother reconsidering the etiquette of such things, and poked some more. "It would be terribly rude not to go since that is what I told her." She peered at her mother. "Or have I got that wrong, *Mamm?"*

"Jah you have, Gabbie. You should know better than to speak words that you might have to go against. I've never liked saying *'I'll go here, or I'll go there'* when it should be *'if Gott wills it I'll go here, or go there.'"*

Gabbie nodded. "I know what you mean."

"All right you can go this time, but check with me or your *vadder* first next time to make sure it's okay with us. And never step a foot out of this *haus* looking like that, understand?"

"Jah, Mamm, I'll go change." Gabbie grinned and sprang to her feet. *"Denke, Mamm.* I'll clean my room when I get back, I promise. I mean, I will. If *Gott* wills it, I'll be back to clean my room." Gabbie frowned, hoping she was saying the right thing.

Mrs. Miller smiled up at her daughter, and said, "Be back early, in enough time to help me with the dinner. It'll be nice to have your help around here again."

"Will do." Gabbie changed into better clothes, and redid her hair. It was probably best she dress in a better manner just in case there was any truth in Sally's letter. She would want to look her best if she ran into Joseph and he was indeed single.

Once Gabbie was clear of the house, she ran through the forest and up the road to her friend Sally's house. She wanted to slap Sally for lying to her about Joseph and Ilsa and causing her disappointment. At the front door, she composed herself and knocked.

Sally opened her door, and as soon as she saw Gabbie, she threw her arms around her. "Gabbie! You're here. I'm so happy." She released Gabbie and pulled her inside by her sleeve. "Come in, come in." Sally dragged Gabbie up to her room and closed the door. "Sit, sit."

Without even a hello, or a bit of mindless small talk, Gabbie sniped, "Why? Why would you lie to me about something so important? I thought you were my friend."

Sally gaped at her for a while, before she said, *"Ach,* but I am. Please don't think I lied to you. I would never do such a thing. Please believe me."

"Then what happened to make you write me those lies? You said Joseph and Ilsa were not together anymore, but my *mudder* said that they are. Besides, my *vadder* would know if they weren't together anymore, and he agreed with *Mamm."*

"Well, the reason I thought they'd broken up was that I heard them fighting."

Gabbie pouted, wondering whether to believe her. "How did that come about?"

"I fell asleep in a barn, as I do sometimes. Something woke me up; voices, loud voices, you know? Anyway, I overheard a quarrel; well, I mean, it was all a little jumbled 'til I woke up a bit, so it took me a while to realize who was shouting." Sally wrung her hands and rounded her shoulders.

"I'm not great when I first wake up."

"What, Sally? Get on with it; what did you hear?"

"Ach, jah. Sorry." Sally rubbed her palms together. "Then I heard Ilsa yell at Joseph. She said, 'I'd be better off without you.'"

Gabbie raised her eyebrows. "She didn't?"

"She did, and he said, 'That's fine by me.'"

Gabbie swooned. "He's so masterful. He must be mine." She turned her attention to Sally. "And where did this take place?"

"At my *bruder's* barn after a gathering. Everyone had gone home, and I'd fallen asleep and their shouting woke me."

Gabbie tried to picture the whole scene as it would've unfolded. She pictured Sally's brother's house and his large barn. "Where was your *bruder?"*

"He was in the house with the rest of his *familye."*

"So, the pair was arguing in public?" It didn't sound like something Joseph would do. Gabbie had grown up with Joseph and knew him as calm and levelheaded.

Sally shook her head. *"Nee,* there was no one around except me, and they didn't know I was there."

"I can't even imagine that Joseph would shout."

"Not shout so much, but his voice was raised."

Gabbie tapped a finger on her lips. "And you thought they had broken up, but somewhere along the line they must have made up?"

"I guess so, but I didn't expect that would happen. It sounded as though they did not like each other anymore."

Gabbie nudged her. "What happened next?"

"Well, they both stormed off out of the barn, so I crept down from the loft to watch what happened outside."

"And?"

Sally frowned. "And nothing. They went off in separate directions."

"Ach?"

"Can you see now why I thought they were over?" Sally peered into Gabbie's face.

"I wish you'd made sure of your facts before writing to me. Couples fight though, don't they? Mind you, they don't shout at each other, but sometimes they have cross words. Don't your folks argue?"

"Not really, they don't talk enough to fight. And I thought you'd want me to write you the very next day to get the news right away."

"Jah, very good, *denke."* Gabbie could see that Sally was mighty upset by the whole thing. "When you found out you were massively wrong, why didn't you write again to set me straight?"

"I'm not so sure that what I said was wrong. I've been watching them, and I'm sure they're not in love. Anyway, it would've been too late to write to you."

Gabbie lifted an eyebrow. "You could've rung and left a message for me."

Sally shrugged her shoulders.

Sally was so pathetic sometimes that Gabbie despaired of her. "You did a bad thing. What if I'd seen Joseph before hearing they were still together? What if I had told him how I felt about him? Can you imagine the level of humiliation I'd have experienced? All because you assumed something and didn't correct that assumption when you found out that you were wrong. It was selfish of you."

Sally's cheeks flooded with tears, and Gabbie ignored her distress. "I can't look at you right now, Sally."

Sally wiped tears from her face. "Will you still be my friend? I didn't mean to cause you any trouble; I was just trying to help you."

"I shall think about it. Stop crying, Sally." Gabbie patted her friend on the back. "I'm sorry I've been so mean, but my parents are talking about marrying me off to someone now that I've come back."

"Nee." Sally covered her mouth. "Who will they marry you to?"

"Probably the first old fool they can find. I wish I'd stayed with the Yoders in Lancaster. There was a boy there I could've married, and now I'm sure that Martha Yoder has snatched him up. His name's Michael, and he was visiting from Ohio, and he's very nice. I didn't think it was a coincidence that we both arrived in Lancaster County at virtually the same time."

"I'm sorry, Gabbie."

"So am I, believe me. Martha saw that I liked Michael, so she liked him too. She as good as threw herself at him. It was embarrassing at times." Gabbie shuddered and threw her hands in the air. "Now, she's most likely going to marry him since I'm out of the way."

"Which man do you like best though, Gabbie?"

"I like Joseph best, of course. That's why I left as soon as I heard that Joseph was free. Mind you I would have stayed if I knew that he was still with Ilsa. I'm sure that Michael and I would've been happy together. It's most likely too late for that now. That goody-goody Martha will snatch him up as sure as trees are green."

After a silent moment, Sally said, "I'm sorry, Gabbie."

"It doesn't matter now. What's done is done. Now

I'm off to see what my cousin, Mary, has to say about the whole thing."

Sally twirled the strings of her prayer *kapp* around her fingers. "Aren't you going to stay longer? I haven't seen you for months and months."

"I'll come back soon and then we can do something together."

"Can I come with you to Mary's *haus?*" Sally frowned and leaned toward her.

Gabbie shook her head. "You stay here."

Gabbie ran to her cousin Mary's house. She was recently married, and Gabbie respected Mary more than anyone else even though she was only two years older.

Chapter Thirty-Three

Mary welcomed Gabbie as she always did, with a beaming smile and a big hug. "Come in. There's always tea and cake here."

Gabbie walked straight in and slumped into the couch. "Oh, Mary, it's so wonderful to see you. Everything's just so dreadful for me. *Gott* seems to have forgotten me."

"*Gott* doesn't forget anyone." Mary laughed. "He even knows when a tiny sparrow falls to the ground. Maybe He's trying to teach you—or show you—something, and you're not listening? He could be trying to get your attention."

Gabbie sniffed, wondering if she'd done the right thing in returning home.

"Are you still upset about Joseph getting married to Ilsa?"

Gabbie nodded. "I know I shouldn't be, but I am. I can't help it."

"It must be hard to love someone who can't love you back, but it's most likely for the best. But you can't meddle; you know that, don't you?"

"Mary, why would you say that?"

"You told me some time ago that you were thinking of trying to break them apart."

"Oh." Gabbie gave half a smile. *"Jah.* I wouldn't meddle; I wouldn't."

"Come outside into the sun; we can sit on the porch. Everything feels much better when sunlight warms the skin. You sit, and I'll put the kettle on the stove."

On the porch, Gabbie sat and waited for Mary to return. Talking to a good friend always made her feel better, and her cousin was even closer than a good friend. She hoped Mary had heard what was going on with Ilsa. Surely, if Mary had heard rumors that Ilsa and Joseph weren't getting along, she would have mentioned something already.

Mary placed a plate of cake on the table along with teacups.

"Do you want some help, Mary?"

"Nee, you stay there." Mary disappeared again and when she came back, she had a china teapot in her hands. She carefully poured the tea into two cups and sat down.

"Denke, Mary. This looks good."

"Taste the cake, and see if you like it. It's honey cake."

Gabbie broke off a piece of cake and popped it into her mouth. "It's good." She nodded.

"Right, then, tell me what the matter is," Mary said.

"Nothing, I'm just visiting."

"That's not what you said two minutes ago, Gabbie. A problem shared is a problem halved."

Gabbie took a sip of tea and then set the cup back on the saucer. "It's just that Sally's an idiot. She's humiliated me. Or she could have done if I'd acted on what she had told me. I'm livid, I tell you." Unable to be still, Gabbie got up and paced.

"What did she do?" Mary asked, watching Gabbie walk up and down the porch.

"She wrote me a letter, and in the letter, she said that Joseph and Ilsa had broken up. Of course, I wrote to my parents straightaway to reassure them that I was not only reformed but that I was also ready to be a good little lady. They believed me and allowed me to return. Now, I find out that they're thinking of finding a husband for me."

"Worse things could happen. I was sad and sorry for myself too until I married Sam. Now my life's complete."

"Things don't go well for me, Mary, they never have." Gabbie found it hard to breathe, her palms were sweaty, and her urge to throw a cup into the distance was threatening to overtake her. "What am I to do? My best friend is too stupid to be friends with, my folks will marry me off to some stranger, and the *mann* I love is going to marry a mouse. It's too, too much to bear."

Mary studied her quietly. "My goodness, Gabbie, sometimes you can be interesting and fun, but mostly you are intolerant of others. Ilsa is a very nice girl; you shouldn't call her a 'mouse.' Neither should you be rude about your good friend Sally."

As if her legs lost power, Gabbie fell into the porch chair, eyes wide, brows pinched. "Is that what you think of me? You think I'm rude?"

"Don't look so shocked. I'm not telling you anything you don't already know, deep down. You make it very hard for people to like you. Also, you don't think before you speak. You just blurt out the first thing that comes into your mind. More often than not, someone ends up embarrassed or with hurt feelings from your words."

"This is the worst day of my life. I have no friends, Sally is…"

"Stop dramatizing, will you? Honestly, can't you see Sally was trying to help you? She wouldn't have lied. What did she say exactly?"

Gabbie took a breath. "Well, she said she heard them break up, and I believed her."

"You asked her to keep you informed before you left for Lancaster?"

Gabbie nodded.

"That was your first mistake; you entered into an agreement to gossip, and you dragged Sally in with you."

Gabbie shook her head. "It wasn't gossip."

Mary put her hand to her throat and grimaced. "That's exactly what it was. It's normal for couples to argue. It sounds like Sally overheard them having nothing but a small tiff."

Gabbie looked down at her hands in her lap. "She shouldn't have got my hopes up. I was doing all right where I was, and I raced back here for nothing."

Mary said more, but Gabbie wasn't listening because she was thinking about Ilsa and Joseph. Was Sally wrong, or did the couple fall out, and then make up later on?

Mary's words finally registered in Gabbie's mind when Mary said, "Sally was only being a friend to you. Just forget Joseph for the time, and if it's meant to be, then something will happen."

"Sally should've…"

"What? Pitched up outside Joseph's window and spied on him? Questioned all of his friends until she got to the root of the matter?"

Gabbie nodded. *"Jah,* that would have been much better; that's what a true friend would have done."

"Don't be ridiculous, Gabbie. She passed on a message, and you acted on it as you always do. You gave no thought to the whys and wherefores. You charged at it like a dog to a dinner bowl, and you grew wild when the bowl was found to be empty. Your impatience makes you selfish, and consistently flawed, and you will soon be sent away again if you don't change your ways."

Gabbie jumped to her feet. "So, I cannot count you as my friend either, then?"

"Don't take what I say the wrong way, Gabbie. I am your friend, and that's why I'm talking to you like this, as a friend. If I didn't care about you, I wouldn't bother to say these things, but someone has to say it to you."

"Fine. I came here for support, not to be insulted." Gabbie ran from Mary's porch crying. She could hear Mary calling for her to come back, but she ignored her and ran into the forest.

Gabbie needed peace to make sense of her terrible day. Why was Mary being so horrid, and Sally so hopeless? Why should Joseph marry mousy Ilsa instead of her?

It wasn't fair. Life wasn't fair.

Looking out over the creek, Gabbie stopped thinking long enough for her rage to quiet down. She emptied her mind of troubling thoughts, and of all the people who irritated her. She welcomed the cool shade on her skin, smelled the damp wood, and breathed in the fresh air. Soon, Gabbie had calmed down, inside and out. The babbling sounds of the water, and being in nature, always soothed her whenever she was troubled.

Before long, her troubling thoughts crowded back in

on her. Mary had called her some horrible names. Gabbie recalled her own words and actions toward Sally and realized that Sally had only been trying to help. "Sally was just trying to be my friend, and I thanked her by leaving her in tears."

Gabbie licked her dry lips. "And now Mary thinks I'm awful and difficult to like. *Nee,* am I so bad? Am I all the things she said?" Gabbie lay back in the dirt, not caring about the twigs digging into her back, or the possibility of creeping insects crawling over her. "If I'm all those things, if this is how low I've fallen, then I deserve to be here in the dirt. Sally's not the fool, I am. Mary wasn't unfair, I was. I am."

Somehow, the discomfort of the cold ground made her feel better, as though nature itself was enforcing punishment. That way, she could atone in some way even if it were only by tolerating the sting of the twigs.

"I guess Mary's right; if things don't go my way, I want to scream and often do. I blame everyone but myself. When did this happen? Why am I so frustrated, so easy to disappoint, and so disappointing?" Gabbie's tears rolled back into her hair. "No wonder Ilsa gets a good man like Joseph. I'd reckon she's calm in a crisis, not running around falling out with her closest friends. I'd reckon she's perfectly behaved in all situations. I call her 'a mouse,' not because I know her, but because it suits me to believe she is imperfect, and that's mean of me."

Surrounded in unspoiled nature as she was, Gabbie felt close to God. *If You are trying to teach me something by making me miserable, please tell me, or show me, what it is.* She hoped that God heard her words even though she was sure He'd deserted her many years before.

* * *

Gabbie sat up and looked around once more at the only spot where she felt truly free to be herself. Here, there was no one to judge her, no one to seek approval from, and no one to impress. The dappling of light through the trees and the babbling of the creek soothed her. Her eyelids closed; she fell silent for a time listening to the water and the rustling of the breeze through the treetops.

Aware that time was slipping away, she stood and picked her way along the edge of the creek, carefully stepping from rock to rock as she went. The rocks were slick and mossy, but she'd been down this way many times, and little had changed while she had been gone. A cool breeze kissed her tear-stained cheeks, and she stopped to crouch on a large, flat section of stone.

Am I really that bad? Gabbie thought, as Mary's words rang in her head again. *I don't think I'm that rude or that selfish or anything like that.* Her nose wrinkled. *Mary must be wrong, but why would she say those things if she weren't being honest?*

Her thoughts stopped running in circles, and instead, turned inward, and dug deeper. There were times when she had been difficult, but she was a child then and didn't know better. Taking her brothers' toys, throwing tantrums when she didn't get her way, all of that was long past her. That was child's stuff, stuff she'd done years and years ago. Or was it? Her brow furrowed. Why had her family sent her away? Gabbie couldn't think of a reason off the top of her head, but as she gathered up flat stones and tried to skip them along the water, her thoughts grew clearer.

She didn't like to work hard as her brothers did. Even

though Gabbie didn't want to help out, she still did; she helped her mother all the time. Gabbie had to admit she never put more than the required effort into anything because nothing held her interest for long. Whenever she had to help her brothers with a chore, she never gave the full measure of effort. Often, they would have to redo whatever she'd just done. *How childish,* came immediately to her mind and her cheeks burned. Again, Gabbie saw the truth in Mary's words.

Running away when confronted with the truth? That was even more childish. Gabbie's cheeks reddened further with shame and embarrassment when she realized what she'd done. Her stomach sank, and fresh tears burned at the corners of her eyes.

"Ach nee. I wonder what Joseph thinks of me. He must think I'm an absolute terror," she muttered to herself. Gabbie was startled by the sound of her own voice, and immediately bit her tongue before she said more. It didn't matter that she was alone in the woods. She blew out a breath, allowing the remaining rocks to fall with a clatter onto the stones beneath her. She took a few more breaths to calm her nerves jarred by the realization of how she was viewed by others.

Nearby, something snapped; it was a twig or a small branch. She tried to take a step back, but her body was frozen to the spot. Her bottom lip trembled, as she said, "Hello? Who's there?"

Another twig cracked. Gabbie bit her lower lip, and stared toward the sounds. Was it a bear? There had been some sightings. She considered running, but realized that would do no good if it were something big and nasty. It didn't sound big and nasty, but she couldn't be sure. The sound of her heart beating in her ears made everything sound louder and bigger than it was.

"Hello?" A male voice sounded.

The sound of a human voice caused her to heave a sigh of relief. She squinted into the woods and saw the outline of a man. When he stepped closer, she saw that it was Joseph. "Joseph! That's you, isn't it? It's me, Gabbie."

"Ach, Gabbie." Leaves rustled and shifted for a few more moments until Joseph came into plain view.

He was every bit as handsome as she remembered him. Tall and dark-haired, with perfect blue eyes; the sight of him made Gabbie's heart throb all the more. She fought the urge to get closer, and instead, stood her ground while he approached.

"It's been a while, hasn't it? I heard you went off for a bit."

"I did," she said. "I've been staying with another *familye,* the Yoders, in Lancaster County. I'm back now." She couldn't fight the smile that claimed her lips, and she didn't try. "For good, I mean. I don't think I'll have to go back."

"I'm glad to hear it," he said with a soft laugh. "It was strange not seeing you around."

"Really?" Her eyes widened a little, and she forced herself to look away. "Did you miss me when I was gone?"

"Well, yeah." He ambled along the rocky edge of the creek just a few paces ahead of her. He stood there, his head tipped back with the weak afternoon sun scattered across his features. "This must be the best place in the world to think. I should've known I wasn't the only one to come here."

"I guess that's fair." Gabbie giggled. "I like coming here; it's always peaceful and quiet. It's easy to get lost in thought out here, but I really didn't know anyone else came here either."

Joseph nodded and murmured his agreement. He leaned down to collect a few stones, only to toss them one by one into the water. When he was done, he turned to Gabbie. "Anyway, I think it's something to do with the water. The sound of it, I mean. It's like it cuts out the rest of the noises up here." He tapped the side of his head with a knuckle and turned a lopsided grin her way. "Makes it easier to focus on what's important."

"That's probably it." Gabbie followed him, gathering her own handful of rocks. She stirred them around in her hand and picked through them to find the prettiest stones. "All I know is that I can lose myself in the sound of the water and let it wash all of my thoughts away with it."

He made a noise in his throat, and then tossed his last rock into the water. "The weather wasn't so good for visiting a while ago," he admitted. "But it's nicer now. A lot nicer."

"That's good." Gabbie dropped most of her rocks into the water and watched the surface of the water distort and ripple around the disturbance. The most colorful and smoothest rocks remained in her other hand. She studied them in turn, her lower lip caught in her teeth. One by one, even those were dropped into the steadily flowing waters.

Silence spun out between the two of them, against the backdrop of the bubbling creek. A single bird chirped in the distance, but the rest of the world was content to let the quiet moment stretch onward. Joseph finally stopped and stared into the gold-kissed waters, his features twisted with thought. He dug a toe into a small heap of pebbles and lifted a few with his toes to drop them into the water.

"Are you okay?" He didn't look at her when he asked; he didn't need to.

Gabbie pulled a face and turned away. She walked in the opposite direction, only to stop again when she realized what she was doing. *Running away? Now? Don't be a child, Gabbie.* She faced him, and said, "I guess I'm not okay." She bit her lower lip a little harder. "Mary and I were talking today, and she told me some things, and I just… I just ran away. It was stupid of me. I really should've stayed, but I just couldn't. It was terrible." She looked out across the water. "I'm terrible."

He said nothing right away. Instead, he studied her out of the corner of his eye. She squirmed just a little under his steady gaze before she looked sharply toward the water once more. She couldn't look at him any longer, imagining him judging her.

"It couldn't have been that bad," he finally said.

"I'm a horrible person, Joseph. I really, really am. I just didn't realize it until recently, that's all." She exhaled slowly and shut her eyes. Her shoulders bunched up tightly, and she folded her arms around her middle. It wasn't the same as the hug she desperately wanted from him, but he was there and that was enough.

"You aren't horrible, Gabbie. Truly, you aren't."

She could hear him getting closer. The rocks shifted under his feet, and a few fell into the water. She didn't dare look for fear he would disappear.

This can't be happening, she thought while funny

little tingles skittered down her spine. "I am," she said. "I…"

He cut her off with a firm, *"Nee.* Your *vadder* is the bishop. I can't imagine being raised with a *vadder* like yours. It's that kind of thing that would put a lot of pressure on a person, especially with you being the only girl—and the eldest. It's no surprise they'd push you hard to be perfect. I'm sure you suffer that burden every day."

He reached out and put a hand on her shoulder, and she tensed under his touch. His hand was warm, perfect, and just what she needed, but a thread of tension twisted through her all the same. "I know, I know. My *vadder's* a little disappointed that I wasn't a boy. My *bruders* just seem so much more useful."

"He practically has a herd of boys," Joseph pointed out. "He shouldn't hold you to the same standard that he holds them. You're a different person from the rest of them, and you're not horrible. You've got a spark that no one else has. People light up when you're around."

"You really think that?"

He smiled. "You're special, Gabbie." He gave her shoulder a squeeze, and she looked at him, only to look away again. His words had done nothing to quash the blossoming blush that claimed her cheeks, in fact, they'd fed it.

Embarrassment emerged again, and Gabbie pulled away from the comfort of his touch. As much as she desperately wanted to bask in that reassurance, and maybe, just maybe, get a hug—she couldn't. A terrible thought clawed its way out of the back of her mind and soured the moment with a single word—*Ilsa.* The very idea that Ilsa wouldn't approve was enough to throw cold water on the warm feelings that filled her. "I guess you're right. I just, I really shouldn't be telling you all of this."

"Why not?" Joseph's dark eyebrows drew together. "Is something wrong?" He reached for her, but Gabbie took a step away.

"I just don't think…" she began and then trailed off. She shook her head to clear it and then wore a smile she didn't feel, but thought it would look convincing. "You and Ilsa, you're about to be married soon. I don't think she'd like me talking to you about all of my problems. It also looks bad we're out here alone."

Joseph's features distorted, and it was his turn to look away. He said something just under his breath, but Gabbie didn't dare ask him to repeat it. Louder, he said, "It's fine, but I guess you're probably right."

She winced and bit her lower lip again. "I'm sorry, Joseph. I shouldn't have said anything to you about my problems." She didn't know what else to say. All she could do was wring her hands and look at him. Worry creased her brow, and she swallowed hard, ignoring the fact she could still feel the burn of her cheeks.

He glanced up at the overhead branches as though he were trying to spot the sky. Joseph's nose wrinkled after a long moment. "It's getting a little late. I should head back now."

"I should go too. Thanks for talking to me."

"Goodbye, Gabbie."

"Bye, Joseph."

He turned and walked back up the path he'd used. Soon enough, Gabbie was alone by the creek, filled with a mixture of emotions. She was pleased that they'd had a quiet moment alone, but she was no closer to him, and he was still going to marry Ilsa.

Chapter Thirty-Four

It was on the walk back home that Gabbie realized how much better she felt. Aside from putting Joseph in that awful position, it felt good to be heard for once and to have someone comfort her. Gabbie smiled as she hummed softly.

Joseph liked her; he had to. If he didn't, why would he even bother talking to her and why would he be so thoughtfully concerned for her? Her thoughts skipped around those ideas during the long walk home.

The sun was low in the sky, sending long shadows across her path. As she walked on, Gabbie marveled at the distorted shapes the late afternoon shadows made.

All of her thoughts waned once she approached the door to her house. She mounted the steps slowly, and grudgingly rested her hand on the doorknob. Opening that door would mean her peace was over. There would be chores, and she would have to talk to her parents. Her mother had asked her not to be late, and now she was, most likely too late to help with the dinner. She would have to face Mary at some stage too and apologize. Gabbie's stomach twisted with pain.

She sucked in a deep breath and then let out her breath slowly. Gabbie opened the door to be greeted by the sight of her father. He was seated in his usual chair, and he motioned to the empty chair opposite him. Wrinkling her nose, Gabbie stepped inside and shut the door behind her. Heavy steps carried her to the chair, and when she sat, silence lingered in the space between them.

Eventually, her father said, "Since you've come back, we've had to give a lot of thought to what we will do with you. Your *bruders* have a good hand on duties here at the *haus.*"

Gabbie shifted uncomfortably. "You won't send me back to the Yoders' *haus,* will you?" Her voice seemed tiny, distant and thin.

He shook his head and leaned forward in his chair. "*Nee,* but we are sending you to another *haus,* one that's closer and in much more need; Mrs. Kingsly's *haus.* Nancy Kingsly lost her husband not long ago in a terrible accident. She's left with four young *kinner* and a *boppli,* and all her *familye* are too far away to help. She's struggling to keep things together, and the community needs to give her more help."

Gabbie knew who Nancy was, although, being much younger than Nancy she had nothing in common with her. Gabbie could feel her face twist with displeasure. All she wanted to do was jump up and yell at him for suggesting it. She wanted to throw a terrible tantrum and get out of it; that's what she normally would've done when under so much pressure. And if not that, she would have schemed and plotted her way out of it.

Why should I help her? She wanted to cry. *Why can't I stay here and help Mamm?* She bit her tongue instead and waited.

Her father continued, "You'll be there every day to help. You'll do the cooking, cleaning, taking care of her *kinner,* everything and anything that needs to be done. She's a kind woman and I trust you'll do a good job while you're there. You know Nancy Kingsly, don't you?"

"Jah, of course, I do." Gabbie couldn't help but squirm restlessly in her seat. She forced herself to sit still, folded her hands and put them in her lap. In her sweetest voice, she asked, "How long am I going to be doing this?"

"Until she doesn't need the help anymore." Her father stood. "You'll not be paid for what you do, mind you. She hasn't a thing to spare. But, at the least, you'll have food in your belly, clothes on your back, and a bed to sleep in while you're there. It's a fine way to help someone who's unable to help themselves."

Inside, Gabbie could feel her anger bubbling. She bounded to her feet. "I'm to stay there—sleep there?"

Mr. Miller nodded. "It'll be easier that way."

"I understand," is what she said, but she didn't understand at all.

"I'm pleased that you're finally coming around to helping others in need." He stood up, smiled, and reached over to pat the top of her *kapp.* "Dinner's almost ready, Gabbie. Go see if your *mudder* needs help setting things up."

It was brought to Gabbie's mind again that she had said she'd be back in time to help her mother with the dinner, and she hadn't been.

Her father turned and left, leaving her alone in the room with her thoughts. Why did she have to do it? Why not someone else? Why did she have to do it without pay when she could've found an outside paying job? Why did they keep sending her away?

She didn't know how long she'd stood there, letting those thoughts twist and churn in her mind. It wasn't until her mother called her that she realized she was taking too long. Gabbie hastened to help with dinner, braced herself for chastisement over being late, and braced herself for what the next morning would bring at Nancy's house.

The next morning, she was sent off to the Kingsly house with a basket full of food and other odds and ends—soap, needles and thread, and assorted other things any woman would need to keep her household in good repair. Her father drove her there, and he promised to come and get her when she asked.

Gabbie had never been to the Kingslys' house before. When the buggy stopped in front of the house, she climbed out and saw that the house and garden were in good order. The recent tragedy was not reflected in the appearance of the property. She said goodbye to her father, shifted her grip on the basket, and approached the front door slowly, mindful of just how strange and quiet it was. Once she got closer, the illusion was shattered. A baby wailed, and she heard the other children making noise. *Children are like dogs, once one howls, they all do.* Her thought made her smile; she didn't know why.

Gabbie knocked on the door and was greeted by Nancy, a cheerful-looking young woman, maybe ten years older than herself. Strawberry blond hair poked through the front of Nancy's prayer *kapp,* and the bags under her eyes were masked by the brightness of her gray eyes. Nancy laughed, and that laughter was bell-bright, not burdened in the slightest by her arms being laden with children. A howling infant was tucked in the crook of one arm while an equally loud toddler was squirming down from where he had been held against her hip.

"Hello, Mrs. Kingsly."

"Hello, Gabbie. *Denke* for helping me. Please, just call me Nancy. Come in, now! Come in! Don't mind the little ones; they'll make room. They aren't normally this noisy."

Nancy stepped back, and Gabbie stepped inside looking around at the barely controlled chaos of the place. The children were all quite young and capable of making the most tremendous of messes.

"I'm so sorry," Nancy said. "I wanted to get some of this tidied before you came."

"Nee. It's okay. That's why I'm here," Gabbie said. Deep down, she gritted her teeth at the indignation of it all. Her parents were trying to test her; that was the only reason Gabbie could figure that she was there.

"The Wilsons sent along some bones for stock. It looks like we'll be eating soup for the next few days."

"Wait," Gabbie interjected; she couldn't help herself. "You're happy about having soup for days? Without any bread, or anything?"

"Oh," Nancy shrugged and finally released the toddler to play. "It's not so bad. Not at all. It just depends on how you look at things, you know? I like soup. They like soup. Why would having soup be bad?"

Gabbie handed her the basket of goodies and followed Nancy to the kitchen. "Well, it just seems like it would get kind of boring. Anyway, *Mamm's* sent some things along. There's plenty of bread and we could put some in the icebox for later."

"Denke," Nancy said, as she unpacked the basket and

sorted the contents. "I appreciate everything, Gabbie. I'm happy for the soup bones, too. You have to ask yourself if you'd rather eat and live, or starve. Living means things at least have a chance of getting better. Dead is just dead." Her voice had thickened a little.

Gabbie fell silent while she helped. Nancy's words weighed heavily in Gabbie's mind. Nancy had to be thinking of her recently departed husband.

The rest of the day was spent doing menial housework of the sort Gabbie always hated. And they were the scrubbing of the floors, washing curtains, doing laundry—all of those terrible chores that she always left to *Mamm*. Now, she had to contend with noisy children and the periodic cries of a baby.

Gabbie wasn't the only one working at Nancy's house. No matter what she was doing, Nancy seemed to be just as busy, and with a child at her hip or getting tangled into the mix. Even more surprising to Gabbie was the fact that Nancy was always happy, and endlessly patient with her children.

Gabbie finished her first day at the house exhausted and confused. She wished that she could go home and lie in her own bed. Nancy had organized that she had her own bedroom by squeezing some of the children into one room.

The baby slept in Nancy's room with her.

The next few weeks were more of the same. Gabbie would help out with whatever chores needed doing. Every day, she was increasingly more amazed at the fact that this woman with four rambunctious children and a baby and with little resources could still find joy in life. Having young children was sometimes a thankless chore. At first, Gabbie thought Nancy's happiness must have been some kind of show, but as she grew to know Nancy better, she understood that's just how she was.

Gabbie tried to improve herself by learning from Nancy's character and personality traits.

"All things work together for good," Nancy told her almost daily.

Gabbie decided to trust that whatever happened to her in the future was ultimately happening in her favor. The work did well to occupy Gabbie's hands, but her thoughts kept turning back to Joseph and their conversation by the creek.

She remembered the letter Sally had sent, and the rumors surrounding Joseph and Ilsa. She also regretted her argument with Mary.

Joseph had seemed to like her when they were at the creek. He had touched her shoulder and had uttered kind words to her. Would it be mean of her to hope that Joseph and Ilsa would have another tiff? She didn't dare give herself that hopeful thought just yet. Gabbie asked Nancy if she could have a spare afternoon to herself if she did a lot of work in the morning. Nancy agreed to let her have a free afternoon and Gabbie went to Ilsa's house thinking she'd go straight to the source to get her information.

Ilsa's mother, Hilde answered her knock, and her face split into a tremendous smile.

"Gabbie, how nice of you to come visiting. Come in. I haven't found out how you liked your stay with the Yoder *familye*. And you've been helping Nancy. How is she?" A barrage of questions came with a pull on Gabbie's arm.

"Things are good," Gabbie said. "I've been busy, and all, but that's good. Nancy's doing well too."

"Oh, I'm so glad. So, what brings you by today? Ilsa's not home; she's at the market 'till later today." Hilde set about getting a couple of glasses of water while Gabbie sat down.

"Oh. Well," Gabbie began. "You used to invite me over all the time before I left for Lancaster, and I never really had a chance to accept."

"Oh?" Hilde paused and looked over. "Well, we're planning a dinner this Friday if you'd like to join us. It will be absolutely delightful to have you with us. You can tell us all about where you've been, and all that you've been doing."

"That sounds wonderful, *denke*. I'll be by on Friday."

"There's so much I've wanted to talk to you about," Hilde said.

The conversation continued for some time along idle lines to do with the weather, farming, and uninteresting local gossip. Gabbie knew if she got into Hilde and Ilsa's good graces, she would find out the truth of what was going on with Ilsa's relationship with Joseph.

Friday was a busy day at Nancy's house. Gabbie spent most of it cleaning up after the children while Nancy prepared food and got things ready for a weekend without Gabbie's help. Gabbie would spend the weekend at her own home. She hurried to get there, so she could make a cake to take to dinner at Ilsa's house.

Gabbie's parents were happy that she was being sociable, but not happy when they learned she was off to Ilsa's house.

They warned her not to say or do anything she shouldn't.

When Gabbie arrived at the home of Hilde and Ilsa, she was pleased to learn that Joseph would not be coming to dinner. That way, she would avoid awkward moments as she tried to befriend Ilsa.

It was a perfectly lovely dinner, and Gabbie regretted not visiting Hilde and Ilsa more often. Hilde was an excellent cook, and Ilsa was shaping up to be just as good. The evening was full of lively conversation, and Gabbie was wrapped up in listening to all the stories the other guests had to tell. Gabbie shared her experiences at Lancaster County, and her more recent work with looking after Nancy's children.

"Ach, that poor soul," Hilde cried. "You're doing a *gut* thing helping Nancy. We're thinking of sending Ilsa over to help once in a while too, but there's just too much to do here."

"It's okay," Gabbie said. "I think we have things pretty well in hand now. It was difficult at first, but Nancy is nice and cheerful so that helps a lot."

"Oh, that's great. That's great." Hilde heaved a sigh of relief.

Gabbie thought about it for a minute and then turned to Ilsa. "I'm not helping Nancy over the weekend, Ilsa. Why don't we go for a picnic in the afternoon tomorrow?"

Ilsa's eyes lighted up. "That would be great fun," she said. "I can get a few things from here, and we can go out to the fields."

"The wildflowers are just coming into bloom out there, too," Gabbie said. "It looks so pretty in the fields already."

Ilsa smiled brilliantly and reached over to catch Gabbie in a warm, one-armed hug. "I'm so glad. It's been a long time since I've been on a picnic."

"Me too," Gabbie said.

Chapter Thirty-Five

Gabbie's morning had been chaotic. She was helping out at home and had finally gotten permission from her mother to go on the picnic with Ilsa. She dared not tell her mother that it had already been arranged. Her mother let her take one of the family buggies. Gabbie was pleased to hitch the buggy and take it out by herself, which was something she was rarely allowed to do.

As Gabbie pulled up outside Ilsa's house, she noticed Ilsa sitting on the porch with a large basket beside her. Ilsa waved, carried the basket over, and placed it in the buggy.

"Am I late?" Gabbie asked.

"*Nee,* I was ready early, so thought I'd wait for you."

"Phew. That's good. I had a little trouble getting away today. I think *Mamm's* missed me because I've spent so much time at Nancy's house."

"I'm excited to get out like this. I haven't been on a picnic in ages."

Gabbie resisted the urge to ask Ilsa if she had been on a picnic with Joseph. She'd find out soon enough about their relationship if all went according to plan on the picnic.

"I never thought you'd want to spend time with me," Ilsa said.

Gabbie leaned forward and blinked rapidly. "What do you mean?"

"I don't know. You always seemed like you didn't like me, that's all. We never really talked, and you wouldn't come over for dinner when my *mudder* invited you." She had spoken slowly, with a wary glance at Gabbie.

"What? *Nee*," Gabbie cried. *"Nee,* it's not like that at all. I mean, I used to be rude and mean, but I'm trying not to be. Not anymore. I'm sorry if I hurt your feelings before. I'm doing my best to change and become a new person."

Ilsa smiled. *"Nee,* it's okay. I understand. I'm just glad that you don't completely hate me, that's all."

"I never hated you!"

"It was hard to tell for a while, Gabbie." Ilsa's smile faltered. "But maybe I'm just worried."

"You don't need to be," Gabbie reassured her and reached over to touch her shoulder. "Besides, we're going to have the best picnic ever. Maybe we'll even find some wild blueberries out here."

"Maybe!"

Once they found a good spot to tie up the horse, they took the long and winding path to get to the old oak in the middle of the fields. The grass was tall and lush, and it whispered as they passed through.

"Who's that?" Ilsa asked, looking into the distance.

Gabbie squinted and shaded her eyes. "I think that might be Stephen Horst," she said. "It looks like him, doesn't it?"

Ilsa took her turn at squinting, and said, *"Jah,* it's the new boy, Stephen."

"He's not that new. His *familye* has been here for just over a year." Gabbie raised an arm and waved the young man over.

"Stephen!"

It was impossible not to see how cheerful Ilsa was. She was smiling so hard that she had dimples in her cheeks, and her eyes were brighter than Gabbie had ever seen. Gabbie looked from Ilsa to Stephen and back again. Ilsa had a blush of color on her cheeks.

"How are you?" Ilsa bounced on the balls of her feet. "We're just going on a little picnic out by the old oak tree."

"I'm fair enough," Stephen said, with a cheery face. "Just on my way to pick up some eggs for my *mudder* from the Joneses'. They said they have more than they know what to do with, and my *mudder* likes to have a *gut* supply of eggs."

Ilsa giggled. Gabbie laughed to be polite, but her thoughts were already clicking, figuring out how she could turn the unexpected meeting to her advantage.

"Stephen, did you want to sit with us for a while?" Gabbie asked with a sidelong look at Ilsa.

Ilsa's eyes widened, and she looked back at him, all but breathless awaiting his answer.

"I wish I could," he said. "But I really ought to go get those eggs and get them back home. Maybe, if you're still out here, I could join you later?"

From the way he looked at Ilsa, Gabbie was almost certain he would come back.

"Well, we'll hope to see you later then," Gabbie said, and continued walking toward the tree. Ilsa remained and talked to Stephen. Gabbie glanced over a shoulder at the two, and could tell that something was there. It was enough to bring a warm fuzzy feeling to Gabbie's heart. If Ilsa liked Stephen as much as she appeared to, then she might like him enough to call off her engagement to Joseph.

Gabbie got a few paces farther before she stopped, and turned to call, "If I get to the oak before you, I'm going to eat all of the sweet bread."

That got Ilsa moving, and she ended her conversation with Stephen. Gabbie noticed that the conversation ended with a laugh, and a mutual flashing of smiles. Stephen moved on, but Gabbie caught him looking back at Ilsa.

Good, Gabbie thought. *Very good.* And while Ilsa and Gabbie talked about life and everything else, the gears of Gabbie's mind hatched a plot. The scheming had only just begun.

The night of the picnic with Ilsa, Gabbie fell into bed with newfound satisfaction. Since she'd come back home from Lancaster, she had felt like she was unneeded and even unwanted at times. There was no doubt that most nights she fell asleep with sad thoughts on her mind.

The experience with Nancy had helped fight those feelings, but it wasn't until she'd hatched her new plan that she began to feel like her old self. She knew that nothing was a coincidence, and it hadn't been a coincidence when she and Ilsa ran into Stephen on their way to their picnic.

Gabbie knew that there was a spark between Ilsa and Stephen, and Gabbie understood why her friend felt that way. It was easy to recognize that she had the same reaction whenever she bumped into Joseph; her cheeks blushed and her hands always forced the movement to intertwine her fingers.

Gabbie's thoughts crowded in on her until she drifted off to sleep with the end result clear in her mind's eye. She would marry Joseph, and Ilsa would marry Stephen. Tomorrow, she would start phase one of her plan.

When morning came, Gabbie sprang out of bed, ready to take the sunshine in. Everything seemed more beautiful. The moist, green grass welcomed the sun, and the fresh morning air made everything seem as though anything was possible. Gabbie was too excited to stay lying on the bed. She took advantage of the hour to shower and brush her teeth. She arrived in the kitchen nice and early to help her mother with the morning task of bread baking.

Her mother looked up in shock. "Well, that's new," she said, and greeted her only daughter with a smile. The table was soon filled with fresh, oven-baked bread. Gabbie's father came through the back door with a bucket of fresh milk. The kitchen was soon filled with Gabbie's brothers, who were always ready to devour everything that was set before them. When the family was done eating, a rush of energy filled Gabbie's body. Now for her plan.

After the breakfast cleanup had been done, Gabbie called for her mother. *"Mamm,* I was thinking; Ilsa and I enjoyed a picnic yesterday, and I know there's a new *familye* in the community. Anyway, I got to thinking I should be friendly to the Horst family, and I wondered if you would mind if I invited the oldest boy for dinner one night, along with Ilsa? Would that be all right with you and *Dat?"*

"That's a *wunderbaar* idea, Gabbie. I'm sure your *vadder* would be agreeable to having some young people to dinner."

Her plan worked. *"Denke, Mamm."* Gabbie kissed her on the cheek.

"Oh, and I forgot to tell you that we just heard that Martha Yoder's getting married."

Pain stabbed at Gabbie's heart. "To Michael?"

"Jah, that was his name. I suppose you met him while you were there."

"I did."

"Your *vadder* and I discussed it and we'll send you back for the wedding."

Gabbie shook her head. "That's kind, *Mamm,* but I'd rather stay here. I'll write to Martha tonight and tell her how pleased I am for her."

"Very well."

As Gabbie wrote the letter, she remembered the worst thing she'd done in her life. Poor Amy! She had to put things right and confess to Andrew what she had done.

Chapter Thirty-Six

Martha Yoder and Michael Glick stood before the bishop and were pronounced married. Amy watched, pleased for her sister, but where was Andrew right now? What was he doing and who was he with? Had he heard the news her younger sister was getting married and did that make him remember what they once had?

During the meal, Amy had a chance to wander around talking to people she hadn't seen in a long time. That was, until her mother asked her to take Micah. Micah had begun to cry, and Amy knew walking soothed him. She patted him on the back while she walked to the edge of her parents' land. "Amy."

Amy knew that voice. Her heart nearly stopped beating as she swung around to see Andrew. Her mouth dropped open, and she wanted to run to him.

His eyes fell to young Micah in her arms.

Amy's breath caught in her throat—he might think the child was hers. Was Micah going to ruin her life once again? Him coming into the world was the reason she'd had to leave Augusta and stay at home once she arrived.

"I see you've been busy."

"*Nee,* he's not mine. I'm not married."

Andrew laughed. "I know. I've talked to your *vadder.*"

Immediately, she relaxed. "What are you doing here?"

"Since you won't come back to me, I thought I'd come to see you."

Amy sucked on her bottom lip. They'd hardly written to one another except at the start and then their letters dropped off. She had no idea what was on his mind. "You didn't write to me much," she said, trying to keep the hurt from her voice.

"You told me you'd return."

"*Mamm* wanted me to stay because she was feeling sick all the time with the new *boppli* coming. I had to look after the *familye,* that's why I couldn't come back."

"Why didn't you tell me that? I didn't know what to think."

"I thought you might've lost interest. You had said you were worried about me being so much younger." Micah started crying again.

"Can we go somewhere to talk?" Andrew said.

"Stay here. I'll give Micah to my *schweschder.* I'll be back in a minute."

Amy's heart beat hard and fast. Andrew was the man she wanted and no one else. She walked back toward him after she'd handed Micah to Rose. She blew out a deep breath in an effort to calm herself.

He smiled as she walked toward him, and when she reached him, he said, "It's so good to see you again."

"How did you know to come here?" Amy looked around them. "Did you get my letter?"

"I didn't. Didn't Gabbie talk to you about that?"

"*Nee.* What about it?"

"I'll leave Gabbie to tell you. She called me and told

me some things and when I heard your *schweschder* was getting married, I thought I should visit."

Amy screwed up her face. "What did Gabbie say?"

"She said you were very upset you weren't allowed to return. And good thing she did because that's something you never told me. When Gabbie got home, she said no one was courting you, and she suggested I come to the wedding."

Amy giggled. "I'm glad you're here."

"Let's walk."

Amy looked over her shoulder at the crowd. She'd fulfilled her duties as an attendant, and nothing required her to be any place in particular. "Okay."

When they were away from everyone, Andrew turned to her and held her hand. "I haven't been able to stop thinking about you, Amy. I know I should've written more, but I didn't want to find myself hurt or disappointed. My mind was filled with images of you married to someone else, someone your age, better suited." She remained silent, and he continued, "I figured it would be easier to forget about you considering the differences in age and the distance between your *familye* and where I live."

"I've missed you, Andrew."

"You have? You really have?"

Amy nodded, and he took hold of her and held her close. "I never want to let go." He released his hold on her to look into her eyes. "Will you come back with me?"

"I don't know if I can leave *Mamm* with everything. It'll be so much harder without Martha in the *haus.*"

"Amy, will you marry me? Your parents must solve that issue. I want you to come back and stay with my *bruder* again until we marry. I don't want another day to pass without you in it."

Amy wondered if she was dreaming. Things were working out for her just as she'd always dreamed.

She nodded. *"Jah,* I will marry you, Andrew."

He scooped her up into his arms and held her tight. "I'll talk to your *vadder* and have him see that you must return with me. This is what we both want."

"More than anything." With her head pressed against Andrew's chest, Amy closed her eyes and thanked *Gott* for answering her fervent nightly prayers. She stepped away from him. "I still can't believe you're here."

"You lighten my life, Amy. I don't want to be without you again." He held on to her hand and his eyes misted over. "We'll get married as soon as we can."

"I'd like that." Amy giggled. "I tried to forget you and I couldn't. I thought you'd decided I was too young for you."

He shook his head. "I was looking for reasons we mightn't be good for each other rather than reasons we would. As the months passed, I faced down my fears. I won't let my fear, your fears, or anything else, keep us apart."

Amy smiled as she looked into his kind blue eyes. "You've already met my *vadder?"*

"Jah, he's arranged somewhere for me to stay while I'm here."

"And you've met Micah, so come with me and meet the rest of them."

He took a deep breath and let go of her hand and then gave her a nod. Together they walked back into the crowd of wedding guests. As soon as he had met her family, she'd take him to meet her very best friends, Olive, Jessie, and Lucy. Claire hadn't been invited to the wedding since she was married to an outsider.

Chapter Thirty-Seven

Meanwhile, back in Augusta, Gabbie had plans for a special dinner.

The night of the dinner arrived, and Gabbie looked out the kitchen window to see that Stephen and Ilsa had arrived in their buggies at the same time. Gabbie rushed to the front door. As Gabbie waited for them in the doorway, she sensed chemistry between the pair, just as she had the day of the picnic.

As soon as the pair reached the door, Gabbie's mother quickly stood by her side, and said, "Here you are. Please sit in the living room. Gabbie, you can help me for a minute in the kitchen."

Gabbie greeted her friends and gladly obeyed her mother. It was as if her mother was in on her plan to force the pair together. If Ilsa liked Stephen, then she would break off her relationship with Joseph, and he would be free, free for her to swoop up.

"These apple pies smell lovely, *Mamm.*"

"You did most of the cooking, Gabbie." Her mother leaned in, and whispered, "What do you think of Stephen?"

Gabbie frowned. "He seems nice, but he's not for me."

Her mother raised her eyebrows. "We'll see."

Gabbie remained silent; there was no use in objecting further. "Shall I make tea and take it out, since dinner will be a little while?"

"Jah, do that, and we'll sit down and have a chat with Stephen and Ilsa."

Gabbie and her mother sat down with their guests and served tea.

After they had talked for a time, Gabbie's mother said to Stephen, "You could go and see if Mr. Miller is ready for dinner; he's with the horses. Sometimes he gets carried away and doesn't notice the time." She squinted her eyes and wrinkled her nose.

"Jah, I'll go and see if I can find him." Stephen took his last mouthful of tea and then rose to his feet.

"And the boys are all outside somewhere too," Gabbie said with a laugh.

The women waited until Stephen was out of the room until they started talking again.

"What a nice young man," Mrs. Miller said.

"He is," Ilsa agreed. *"Denke* for inviting me to dinner. It's nice getting to know new people in the community."

"I've invited Cousin Mary for dinner too," Mrs. Miller said.

"You didn't tell me, *Mamm."* Gabbie had hoped to have fixed any bad feeling she had with Mary before she would see her in a situation such as this.

Mrs. Miller frowned. "Didn't I tell you?"

"Nee, Mamm." Gabbie had run away from Mary when her cousin had given her opinion on her behavior. "I'll go and set one more place at the table." Gabbie left her mother and Ilsa sitting in the living room.

When Gabbie had set the table with an extra place,

she heard the clip-clop of hooves and knew that it was Mary's buggy. She'd have to go and apologize to Mary before they had dinner, and she would have to make certain that no one overheard their words. Gabbie raced past the living room and through the front door to meet Mary.

Her cousin had just stepped out of her buggy when Gabbie said, "Hello, Mary."

Mary looked up and smiled. "Oh, Gabbie, hello."

Gabbie was relieved to see the smile. "Can I have a quick word with you?"

"Of course, what is it?" Mary asked.

Gabbie spoke quietly. "I'm sorry about the way I acted the other day. You were right, what you said about me, and I'm sorry that I ran away. It was childish of me."

Mary smiled. "I'm glad you're not mad at me; I thought you might be. I was only trying to help you see that there are other ways to go about things. You're always trying to force things to go your way. I didn't mean to hurt your feelings."

Gabbie pursed her lips, and hoped that Mary wouldn't guess that she was trying to match Ilsa and Stephen. She would have to keep that information to herself, as she knew that no one would approve of her plan.

After Gabbie's younger brothers had washed up, everyone gathered around the dinner table. The Miller family and their guests sat, and closed their eyes for the silent prayer of thanks for the food.

Even though Gabbie had apologized, she still felt awkward with Mary's unexpected presence at dinner. Still, she gave Mary a crooked grin that could pass for a smile.

With some clever maneuvering, Gabbie had arranged that Ilsa sat next to Stephen. Baked chicken was on the menu, and Mrs. Miller had tried a new recipe of baked vegetables in a white sauce. As always, there was plenty of gravy, and fresh bread.

Stephen and Ilsa talked during the whole dinner, and laughed at each other's jokes. At one point, Ilsa even offered to clean the corner of Stephen's mouth where he had a dab of white sauce. Stephen flinched at Ilsa's touch, confirming Gabbie's hunch that the two of them would make a good pair. These two were in love; there was no doubt that they would carve their initials on a tree soon enough. After the white sauce incident, Mary tried to gain Stephen's attention by asking questions about his family, but after answering only two questions, his eyes were drawn back to Ilsa.

Apple pie was what everyone expected at Mrs. Miller's house, and tonight was no exception. During the mouth-watering apple pie, Gabbie felt bad about the prospect of breaking up a couple, and, of course, it was a wrong thing to do. Gabbie focused on the facts; Ilsa was the one acting like a single girl around Stephen. Stephen reciprocated her feelings, and acted the part of a potential boyfriend quite well. Stephen had even blushed at Ilsa's attention when they were in the woods before the picnic.

I haven't forced them to like one another, Gabbie thought when she caught her mother glaring at her. She looked away from her mother, and tried to engage Ilsa in conversation only to soften the words she knew her mother would have for her when their guests left.

Gabbie's brothers went to bed when the last of the guests left.

Gabbie was left alone with her parents. "Well, *gut nacht, Mamm* and *Dat.*" She took quick steps towards the stairs.

Her father's voice boomed, "Not so fast, Gabbie. Come and sit with us."

She spun around, and looked at the hard stares coming from both parents. Gabbie obeyed, and sat on the couch. "What is it? I've cleaned the kitchen, and every last dish has been wiped and put away."

"It's not about the dishes," Mr. Miller said.

"Nee, it's not." Mrs. Miller slumped down beside her husband. "It's about why you invited Stephen and Ilsa to dinner tonight."

Mr. Miller scratched his beard. "I know you have a fondness for Joseph and that's why we sent you to the Yoders' *haus* for a time. We wanted to stop you from doing something that you might later regret. You wrote and told us you had changed, and that's the only reason we allowed you back here."

Her mother leaned forward. "We didn't let you come back here so you could find a way to come between Ilsa and Joseph."

Gabbie scratched her chin and frowned. "Is that what you two think I've done?" Gabbie was upset that her plan was so transparent.

Mrs. Miller sighed. "That's exactly what we think that you've done."

Gabbie looked wide-eyed at both her parents. "I've become more friendly with Ilsa, and when we were on our picnic we ran into Stephen; that got me to thinking that I should get to know more people in the community. They both seem to get along well, but that's not something I could have foreseen. Especially not when Ilsa is betrothed to Joseph."

Her parents looked at each other, and then Mr. Miller said, "I hope you didn't do this in an effort to come between Joseph and Ilsa. No *gut* comes from interfering in other people's lives, Gabbie."

Gabbie nodded. "I have learned my lesson, I have. Now, can I go to bed?"

Mr. Miller exhaled deeply, and waved his hand. "Off you go."

Gabbie wasted no time getting up to her bedroom. She slipped under the covers glad that her plan had worked, to a point. Now, the friendship between Ilsa and Stephen had to grow. Gabbie fell asleep wondering how she could help the pair get closer—without getting herself into trouble.

Chapter Thirty-Eight

Gabbie woke to sunlight streaming into her room. She realized she must have overslept, so jumped out of bed. Today, she'd have to go back and help Nancy. She washed her face congratulating herself on her success of the night before. Gabbie allowed herself to dwell on her daydreams for a while before her mother broke the silence with a loud request that all her children come downstairs for breakfast.

Gabbie met one of her brothers at the top of the stairs. "I'll race you to the table."

"You're not getting the first pancake," he said, before he gave her a light push, and ran down the stairs in front of her.

Gabbie laughed at her brother and headed toward the kitchen.

"Hush children," Mrs. Miller called out.

When the boys and Gabbie were seated, their father came into the room. He was dressed like he had somewhere important to go.

"Where are you going, *Dat?*" one of the boys asked.

"Children," he began, hands on his hips in an odd

manner as though his body could not contain a secret excitement. "After you have finished the breakfast your *mudder* so kindly put together, go to your rooms and get ready. Today we're all going to a horse auction."

The boys squealed in excitement. Gabbie was pleased to see that her brothers were happy, but she had other things to do. Gabbie said, "I can't go, *Dat*. I'm to go back to Nancy's place today."

Her father lifted up his hand. *"Nee.* I've arranged for Mrs. Smith to take your place for today. You can go back there tomorrow."

"Denke, Dat." It meant a lot to her that her father would think to do that for her. Gabbie smiled while wondering whom she might see at the auction. If Ilsa were there, she could say nice things about Stephen, but maybe Joseph would be there, so she wanted to look her best.

Horse auctions were the family's favorite outings. Gabbie rarely saw excitement on her father's face, but today she saw joy.

At the auction, Gabbie's family took a whole row of seats between them. When Gabbie sat down, she looked around for someone she knew. She wasn't pleased that it had rained during the night because the grounds had become muddy, and mud had clung to her black leather boots. She picked up a stick and scraped as much mud as she could off her boots. When she'd finished that, she looked around the crowd once more to find someone she recognized.

Gabbie realized there must be someone she knew at the auction, so she left her family to take a walk around the sale yard. When she was halfway around the compound, she spotted Ilsa talking to someone. On a closer look, she saw that Ilsa was talking to Stephen. She couldn't have seen a better sight, and her fingertips flew to her mouth as she continued to watch the pair. Stephen whispered in Ilsa's ear while Ilsa looked at the skies and laughed.

Gabbie could scarcely believe what she had seen. Talking as they were was risky as many people from the community were there, and it certainly was not behavior that would be approved of. Neither Ilsa nor Stephen appeared to care that tongues might wag at their closeness.

Were things that bad between Ilsa and Joseph? How could Ilsa not care that she was speaking so closely with Stephen, as though they were a couple, above and beyond mere friends? Maybe Sally had been right to tell her about the conversation she had heard between Ilsa and Joseph. Being so friendly in plain view was outrageous. Gabbie could not wait to tell Sally about it.

Wondering what to do, Gabbie walked on until she came to the other end of the compound. She sat on a wooden bench, leaned over and picked up some small stones at her feet. She idly tossed them at a tree just four feet in front of her. Sensing someone behind her, she looked over her shoulder to see Joseph.

"We've got to stop bumping into each other like this. You must think I'm following you," Joseph said with a smile.

Gabbie smiled back but was lost for words. Did he know his fiancée was laughing and talking with another boy, and they weren't far away?

"What are you doing over here by yourself? The fun is over there." He nodded his head toward the auction.

She answered, "I am not much of an auction person. I've come over here where it's quiet. Last night's rain mixed with the horse manure is smelly. It seems this is the only dry place."

Joseph laughed. "I guess it is. Mind if I sit?"

"Of course you can sit."

Joseph sat close to her.

"Are you here to buy a horse?" Gabbie asked.

He shook his head. *"Nee,* not this time; maybe next time when I've saved a little more money. You here with your *familye?"*

Gabbie nodded. "They're over there." Gabbie wanted to move closer and put her head on his shoulder, but, of course, she couldn't. She closed her eyes for a moment and wondered how that would feel. "You here by yourself?"

"I'm with my *vadder.* He's around somewhere."

In all this crowd, he might not even know that Ilsa is here. What would he do if he saw Ilsa talking and laughing so closely with Stephen Horst? Gabbie thought. She wondered if she could bring herself to tell him. Was it her place to share that with Joseph? "How come I always see you alone, Joseph? I would have thought somebody getting married would be too busy to wander around forests and horse auctions."

"I don't know. It is not particularly easy. You know?" he answered, lowering his head.

"Why?" Gabbie asked, hoping he would say that he was no longer in love.

"Well," he replied, swallowing a bit. "There seems to be too much pressure on young people." He paused and ended the topic abruptly. "Like I said, it's not always easy." He looked into the distance.

Gabbie felt that her question had made him uncomfortable. Seeing him depressed like that made her think he deserved to know the truth. "You know Joseph," she began nervously, "I feel kind of weird saying this, but I believe it is the right thing to do."

"Go on." Joseph fixed his eyes on her.

Gabbie knew that there was no going back. She might lose him or she could win him.

"What is it, Gabbie?"

"I'm not sure if I should be the one to tell you."

Joseph rubbed the back of his neck. "You can tell me anything. Are you in some kind of trouble?"

He touched her shoulder gently, which gave Gabbie strength to speak. At first, Gabbie stuttered about seeing something, and after three stops and starts, she shook her head.

Joseph frowned. "What did you see? What is it, Gabbie? Just tell me."

She took a deep breath then blurted out, "I think there is something going on between Ilsa and Stephen."

Joseph's mouth fell open. "Stephen Horst?"

Gabbie nodded. "They came to our *haus* for dinner and didn't stop talking to each other. Now they're over there laughing and giggling for all the world to see."

Joseph sprang to his feet. "Why would you tell me such a thing?"

Gabbie opened her eyes wide; she understood she was in trouble.

Joseph continued, "What makes you think that whatever ideas run around in your head can be spoken?"

"I don't know." Gabbie looked down at the ground. She had hoped for a different response.

"You're way off, Gabbie." He scowled at her, and clamped his lips together. "Good day to you."

She knew she should have kept silent. If she had kept quiet, Joseph might have seen Ilsa and Stephen for himself, and then things would've been different. Gabbie watched Joseph until he disappeared into the crowd.

A pang went through Gabbie's heart. She'd turned away the one man she loved. She never imagined this would be the outcome. Seeing Joseph angry with her was too much.

Gabbie walked back to sit with her family and caught sight of Stephen who was now by himself. It was at that very moment Gabbie decided she would befriend Stephen. Maybe then he would confess his fondness for Ilsa. It was clear to Gabbie that Ilsa preferred Stephen.

Perhaps that's why Joseph was so angry with me. Joseph must know deep down in his heart that he and Ilsa are not destined to be together, Gabbie thought.

Chapter Thirty-Nine

Gabbie felt miserable for many days. She could not erase the image of Joseph's anger from her head, and it haunted her every time she sought a moment of peace at Nancy's or around the farm. Those moments of peace were few and far between especially at home when she could not get away from her younger brothers.

Every spare moment Gabbie had, she made an excuse to be with Stephen, and she surprised herself by their growing friendship. Their relationship was not romantic because Gabbie loved Joseph. She was still convinced that Stephen loved Ilsa, even though he hadn't admitted it.

Gabbie tried to make herself busy with Nancy, and with work around her own house. She was no longer sleeping nights at Nancy's *haus,* as the widow was managing much better now. As much as Gabbie tried to stop it, her mind continually drifted to Joseph. She kept busy on purpose to distract herself from worrying about Joseph, but she couldn't help but worry. Once Joseph got married to Ilsa, he'd be lost to her forever.

Maybe I should pay Joseph a visit. If I could explain

myself, he'd understand...but what could I possibly say to him?

When she'd finished helping out at Nancy's house, she came home and helped her mother with some of the dinner preparation.

Mrs. Miller put a hand on her daughter's shoulder. "Go clean up, and then come back and help some more after you've had a rest, Gabbie. You must be tired from helping Nancy."

"Denke, Mamm. I'm very tired. Every muscle in my body is screaming for a rest. I didn't know looking after small children could be so hard."

Her mother gave a little laugh and Gabbie left the kitchen to take a hot shower.

The water beating down upon her relaxed her tension for a while. Straight after her shower, it was time to help her mother in the kitchen again.

She was starving, and had hoped for mashed potatoes and veal. Instead, her mother had prepared rice with chicken and a special delicious tomato sauce with basil.

The family ate dinner, and then they all enjoyed Gabbie's favorite strawberry cake, their mother's surprise to them for dessert. With all the chatter from her younger brothers, Gabbie forgot all her worries over boys. She enjoyed her brothers' jokes and their laughter. Just as she was feeling better, her father cleared his throat, hushed the boys, and looked at her. Gabbie knew that he had something important to say, and she braced herself.

"Gabbie, I noticed you and Stephen have been spending too much time together."

Gabbie looked at the last bite of strawberry cake on her plate and set her fork beside it. Her last mouthful was ruined. "I don't know what you mean by that,

Dat. Surely, you mean just the normal amount, right, *Mamm?"* She looked at her mother hoping for support.

"Your *mudder* and I have talked about it already. We agree on the matter, Gabbie." Her father frowned at her. "I can't work you out."

Her mother put her hand gently on her husband's hand. "Maybe we should have this talk with Gabbie alone, after dinner?"

Mr. Miller nodded. "After dinner then."

Gabbie breathed out heavily. She knew their talk would be a serious one. After the boys were in bed, Gabbie and her parents sat in the living room.

Her father began by saying, "What I was going to say when your *mudder* stopped me, was that I can't work out what's going on with you."

"In what way, *Dat?"*

"When you had Ilsa here with Stephen, I thought it was good that you were more friendly. Now, I think that you were trying to match the pair together, which is a terrible thing to do since Ilsa is betrothed."

Gabbie screwed up her nose. "Why would I do such a thing?"

Her mother butted in, by saying, "It's no secret that you like Joseph."

"And now, you're spending far too much time with Stephen," Mr. Miller said.

"And we'd like to know why." Mrs. Miller glared at her daughter.

"It's just as friends. I'm allowed to have a boy as a friend, aren't I?"

"Only if you are careful about how you appear to others. We don't want others to think things are going on when they aren't. The Bible says that one should abstain from appearances of evil," Mr. Miller said, staring intently at Gabbie.

Gabbie heaved a sigh. "I'm not doing anything wrong." Mr. and Mrs. Miller exchanged glances.

"What are you up to, Gabbie?" Mrs. Miller asked. "You always have a plan for everything."

"I'm not up to anything. Can't you see that I've changed? I've been working hard helping Nancy. Is it so hard to believe that I haven't done wrong?"

Mrs. Miller looked at her husband. "She has been working hard helping Nancy, and then coming home and helping here."

Her father glared at her some more.

Gabbie squirmed in her seat. "I don't understand why being friends with Stephen is a problem. I'm friendly with a lot of boys, and girls too. I don't even like Stephen in that way. I don't like him as a boyfriend."

"As your *vadder* just said, it's how you appear to other people," Mrs. Miller said.

Mr. Miller nodded, and then said, *"Jah,* and as your *mudder* just said, we both wonder if you're up to something. You showed too much interest in Joseph, and that's why we sent you to stay with Mr. and Mrs. Yoder. Gabbie, we're not having this conversation again. It's not prudent to pursue a boy like you're a wolf stalking a sheep; it's not how you're meant to behave as a child of *Gott."*

Gabbie gasped. "I'm not acting like a wolf or anything of the kind."

"Don't forget that I'm the bishop, and my *familye* has to be an example to others, or I'll step down. If a *mann* can't keep his own *haus* in order, how can he keep *Gott's haus* in order? We can't trust you because you've lied to us in the past. Your *mudder* and I gave you the benefit of our doubt when you invited your two friends for dinner. During dinner, it became obvious what you were trying to do."

"Jah, you wanted to match the two of them, so that Joseph would be free." Mrs. Miller crossed her arms in front of her and leaned back in the couch.

Her father nodded.

"Nee, that's not right at all. Stephen Horst is new to the community, and I wanted to show him that we're friendly," Gabbie protested.

Mr. Miller frowned. "Why do you feel the need to lie to your *mudder* and me about it? Did you think we would not be able to see through your scheme?"

Gabbie looked at the floor; there was nowhere else to look. Her cheeks burned with embarrassment that the plan she had thought so clever was instead so obvious.

She was losing her touch. Her parents couldn't have heard any gossip about Stephen and Ilsa at the auction. Maybe she should tell them about the awful row Ilsa and Joseph had, which Sally had overheard.

Gabbie took a deep breath, calmed herself, and stopped herself from crying. In the back of her mind, she heard that her father was rambling on, giving her a series of warnings about her behavior. She brought her attention back to what her father was saying.

"If you continue this, you will end up marrying this boy. And that is not what your *mudder* or I wish for you. We believe you need an older man who is more mature minded."

Gabbie opened her mouth to ask whether he meant she'd have to marry Stephen or Joseph, but before she could ask, her mother spoke. "Your *vadder* and I have discussed whether you should go back to Lancaster County."

Gabbie held her breath, and looked at her two parents in turn. She could only stay still, quiet, and in secret pain, hoping they weren't seriously considering it.

Her father said, *"Jah,* we've discussed it, prayed about it, and we've decided to send you back to the Yoder *familye."*

Mrs. Miller looked at Mr. Miller, as if she were surprised, then covered it by saying, "I suppose that's best. They said that you're welcome back anytime; they loved having you. Martha will be pleased you're going back."

This news was worse than Gabbie's worst nightmare. She'd given up on the boy she'd liked in Lancaster County to come back to Joseph. Now, Martha had stolen Michael, the boy she had liked. How unfair could life and God be?

"This will be the best for you," her father added, leaning over to pat her on the arm.

Gabbie jumped up, and squealed, *"Nee.* You can't."

Her father and mother fairly trembled at her outburst.

"I mean, I cannot go there again right now. I've so much to do here; I have made a commitment to Nancy. She needs me like you wouldn't imagine, and I've grown to like helping other people. I've learned so much since I've helped Nancy." She wasn't lying, but she was stretching the truth in order to make the best argument.

Her father and mother looked at one another and smiled. Her father was the first one to speak. "That's what we hoped would happen. When we take the focus off ourselves, we can see what's important in life, and it's not petty worries that we might have."

Gabbie pouted. "Do I have to go back to the Yoders?"

"Well, we could negotiate an arrangement, of course," her father said, speaking slowly and deliberately.

"What your *vadder* is saying is that you're an adult, and you need to behave as an adult. You can't jump up and scream, as you did just now; that's what undisciplined children do."

"If you stay, then your responsibilities around the orchard will be more, and you will need to assist your *mudder* in the kitchen. She cannot be alone in taking care of the magnificent dinners."

Gabbie resisted the urge to tell her father that she did help a great deal with the dinners. *"Jah,* of course, *denke."* Gabbie sat down, glad that her outburst had, in a backwards way, saved the day.

"I'm not finished." Mr. Miller lifted his hands. "I want you to stop spending so much time with Stephen. I cannot have any of my *familye* be the subject of gossip. Understand?" Gabbie nodded.

Her father stuck out his chin and said, "This is not definite, Gabbie, we still might send you back to the Yoders. If you step out of line, you will be on the next train. You could benefit from acting according to the moral values you've been taught in this household."

"Jah, Dat," Gabbie answered, ashamed and saddened to hear what her father thought of her. Having secret schemes was one thing, but now that her parents had guessed them, she knew that they weren't too clever.

"Well, if we have all finished what we need to say, you can go upstairs, Gabbie. Or, you could stay here and read the Bible with us." Mr. Miller reached for his Bible on the table beside him.

"I'd rather read on my own, up in my room." Gabbie smiled at both parents before she walked up the stairs to her room. Her father's words were harsh, but she had stopped them sending her away. She would have to be on her very best behavior from now on.

Dat *didn't say anything about seeing Joseph,* she thought.

One thing Gabbie had not told her parents was that she had already made plans to see some people including Ilsa, Joseph and Stephen, the very next afternoon. She'd see them this one time, and then she would lay low and keep out of trouble. Her idea was that Joseph would see that Stephen and Ilsa had a special bond, and he would end his relationship with Ilsa.

Chapter Forty

On the way home from the afternoon with her friends, Gabbie was pleased that Joseph seemed to have forgotten his harsh words to her at the horse auction; it was as if nothing had happened.

Gabbie's parents had forbidden her from meddling, and also from speaking with Stephen. Gabbie tried to figure out what her parents thought she was doing spending time with Stephen when they knew that it was Joseph she liked. *I know they think I've been trying to match Stephen and Ilsa, but do they think that I like Stephen too, as well as Joseph?*

Gabbie wondered why her parents were so eager to send her away again. Her life might have been easier if she was just the usual bishop's daughter, all well behaved and meek. Possibly, her parents thought she was better off with other young girls, and the Yoder family had all girls, unlike her family where her siblings were all boys.

Maybe her parents needed all their energies to focus on her brothers to keep them under control and doing what they were told. Gabbie had always done whatever her heart, or her head, told her and not so much what her parents told her. Her mother had always labeled her as impulsive as if it were a bad thing to act quickly and suddenly.

Feeling guilty for having gone against her parents' orders of seeing Stephen, Gabbie jumped into chores and helped her mother with the dinner, as soon as she got home.

Moments before dinner was to be served, Gabbie's father stormed into the kitchen, leaving the front door to shut with a bang behind him. "Gabbie, I'm just back from visiting Stephen Horst's parents. Before I left their *haus,* I ran into Stephen, and he told me he'd just come back from seeing you, with Joseph and Ilsa. Would that be correct?"

"Jah, but only because it had already been arranged. That was honestly the last time I was going to see him, and Ilsa and Joseph too. Honestly, *Dat."* Gabbie knew from her father's swollen, red face that she'd overstepped her boundaries. She looked to her mother for help, only to see her mother shake her head, and look away. Her mother was equally as disappointed as her father.

"You will go back to the Yoder *familye,"* Mr. Miller said. "That's the only option."

Gabbie could not believe what she heard. She was to be sent away after all. "I've been so good. That's the only thing I did. I only was going to see them this one last time. Can't you believe me?"

"Your *vadder* asked you to stop, and you continued. You didn't tell us you had something arranged, and I'm not saying that would have even made a difference," Mrs. Miller said.

Mr. Miller held up both hands. "There will be no

more argument. I will telephone Mr. Yoder tonight and make arrangements for your return."

"But, *Dat,* why are you sending me back there again? I've practically just returned from there." Gabbie hoped she would think of something to say to change his mind.

"You had fair warning. It's better that you be away from us. You behave better when you're away from your *familye.* It's important that you grow up to have respect for authority." Her father's face was still red, but the rage causing his face to be puffy had lessened.

"Come on, *Dat,* you're being unfair to me, and you know it. Why can't I stay here? This is my home."

Mr. Miller shook his head. "Gabbie, don't answer me back. It's something that I have decided, and that's that."

Gabbie frowned and looked to her mother again, but her mother cast her gaze downward.

"Stop challenging my decisions. My mind's made up, and you will leave as soon as I can get you booked." Mr. Miller stomped out of the room.

Gabbie knew that any more effort trying to get her father to change his mind would be in vain. She was sure Joseph had feelings for her, and now her father was ruining everything.

That night, Gabbie couldn't sleep. She knew she should've left the situation with Ilsa and Joseph alone, but she thought she had to try at least something. She hated it when things were out of her control. And now, her father was making sure she had control of nothing—not only with Joseph.

Two days later, Gabbie was on the train back to the Yoders in Lancaster County. At the same time, Amy was on the train to Augusta to stay with the Miller family before her wedding to Andrew. A wedding and a love that Gabbie admitted she'd tried to hinder by tossing Amy's letter into the trash. Now she realized the gravity of what she'd done that day. She'd tried to rectify it by talking to Andrew, but what if it'd been too late? It made her feel horrid she'd done something so wicked. It was the most awful thing she'd done in her life.

She gazed out the window and thought about Martha, who was still in Lancaster County even though she'd married a man who said he was going to take her back to Ohio. She'd have to find out the real story behind that one. Being with the Yoders again would be a welcome change, she decided.

The soft rhythm of the moving train caused Gabbie to close her eyes. She remembered how Martha and she had both liked Michael Glick, and now, even if he hadn't married Martha, Gabbie wouldn't like him anymore at all. She'd left Martha to have him when she received that letter from Sally informing her that Joseph and Ilsa had parted company. Going home was all for nothing, just a big waste of time. *If only Sally hadn't jumped to conclusions and gotten my hopes up by writing that silly letter.*

When the train slowed, Gabbie opened her eyes to see a crowd waiting on the platform. Somewhere in the crowd of faces, she was sure she saw Martha and Mr. Yoder.

Gabbie grabbed her small bag, jumped off the train and hurried to her friends. She wrapped her arms around Martha's tiny waist and shook Mr. Yoder's hand. "I'm so pleased to be here again."

"How was the trip, Gabbie?" Mr. Yoder asked with a wide smile on his face.

"It was lovely, *denke*. The scenery is always nice to look at, and I filled in time with some needlework."

Mr. Yoder looked down at her small suitcase. "Is that all you've brought?"

"Jah, that's all. You didn't have to come to meet me. I could've gotten a taxi to your *haus. Dat* gave me enough money."

"We were looking forward to seeing you too much to let you get a taxi by yourself," Martha said, as she linked her arm through Gabbie's.

"Come on you two. You can talk all you like when we get home." Mr. Yoder took Gabbie's suitcase and headed toward the taxi rank.

When they arrived at the Yoders' house, and after Gabbie greeted the rest of the Yoder family, Martha walked up the stairs with Gabbie to help her unpack.

"Now, what's going on with you, Martha? You haven't written to say why you and Michael haven't gone back to Ohio."

"We'll be going soon. We're living in a trailer at his *onkel's haus.* I'm heading back there soon. When I heard you were coming, I wanted to see you again."

Gabbie studied Martha's face. She looked very happy, and at that moment, Gabbie was pleased she'd left Lancaster County when she had. "Is that so? Good for you, Martha. I hope you're happy and live a long and fulfilled life together with Michael."

"I thought you might be upset about us being married since you didn't come to the wedding," Martha said.

"Nee, not at all."

Martha breathed out heavily. *"Gut,* I'm glad you don't mind. And I was sad to hear that Joseph is still going to marry Ilsa. I know that was the only reason you went home."

"Denke, Martha, you're a true friend." Gabbie threw herself onto the bed. "Sometimes I've been selfish, I guess, but I'm trying to change."

Martha nodded, lying down on her stomach. "Well, I'm glad you're here, I've missed you a lot. We can have fun together."

"You seem very happy, Martha."

"I am very happy. I'm newly married, and we'll have our own home soon with *bopplis,* and everything."

Gabbie giggled. "You're a nice person, and that's why things are working out for you."

"Denke, Gabbie, that's a nice thing to say."

"It's true. You're nice, and I've been horrible, wicked at times."

Martha laughed and rolled onto her back.

"What's so funny?" Gabbie asked.

Martha sat up. "You're funny. You're not horrible, wicked, or any of those things. You're my good friend, and you're like another *schweschder.* I was hoping that you'd be back. I missed staying up late and talking."

It seemed to Gabbie that Martha was nice to everyone, and as a result, God gave her what she deserved, a nice family, and a husband who loved her. Gabbie was sure God gave her what she deserved, too, which was punishment for being selfish and deceptive. As she stared at Martha's sweet face, she wanted to change to be as nice as Martha. If she were sweet and wholesome, then maybe she would have good things in her life too.

Chapter Forty-One

Gabbie lay in bed. Her first night back in Lancaster County was over, and now it was early morning. She'd already decided to stop complaining and plotting. She'd let God guide her steps in life. God would reward her for the good things she did, she hoped, just as He had rewarded Amy and Martha.

Even though Gabbie hadn't been very nice to Martha's family the first time she'd visited, they were still pleased to see her when she arrived the second time. Mrs. Yoder had been cooking, and when Gabbie arrived in the taxi, she'd run out to meet her giving her a tight hug. As much as Mrs. Yoder's hug made Gabbie uncomfortable, it also made her feel wanted. It struck Gabbie just how much the Yoders had warmth and love to offer her, even though she'd been a difficult girl at times.

Gabbie wondered if she should do volunteer work to show God she was serious about changing her life. She remembered from her last stay that Mr. Yoder organized volunteer work.

After Gabbie had washed her face, she headed downstairs for breakfast. Mrs. Yoder sat drinking coffee at the kitchen table and looked up. "Scrambled eggs, or pancakes?"

"Pancakes for me, *denke,*" Gabbie said. "But, let me make breakfast for everyone."

Mrs. Yoder's eyes lighted up. "That would be a nice change. *Denke,* Gabbie."

"I'll help," Rose said when she came into the kitchen behind her.

While the girls made pancakes, Mr. Yoder came into the kitchen and sat at the table. "Morning, all."

"Morning, Mr. Yoder."

"Morning, *Dat.*"

Soon, the whole Yoder family was sitting at the breakfast table eating pancakes as fast as the girls could make them, with fresh butter and maple syrup.

"Mr. Yoder, I was wondering if you might have any volunteer work I could do?" Gabbie asked.

"Funny you should say that, Gabbie. I was going to mention it after breakfast. Mrs. Zook has had a bad case of stomach flu. Her niece has been looking after her, but she has to leave today."

Gabbie's face lighted up. "I'd like to look after her."

Mrs. Yoder frowned. "Are you sure, Gabbie? It's a big undertaking. Stomach flu isn't nice. There's a lot of cleaning up to do if you know what I mean."

Gabbie adjusted her prayer *kapp* thinking of what kind of messes she might have to clean up. *"Nee,* I can do it. I want to make use of myself."

"I'm pleased to hear it," Mr. Yoder said. "I can take you there this morning."

"Shall I stay there with her?"

"That might be best. Pack a few items of clothing,

and if she doesn't seem better, you might be best to stay there a couple of nights."

Gabbie nodded, pleased that her plan was put into action so fast.

When Gabbie and Mr. Yoder arrived at Mrs. Zook's house, Mrs. Zook's *Englischer* niece greeted them. She took Gabbie into Mrs. Zook's bedroom. Gabbie stared at the elderly lady asleep in her bed; she was small, frail-looking, and her long, silver-white hair was braided and draped over one shoulder. She hoped that the old lady wouldn't die while she was caring for her.

"She's asleep, but she'll most likely wake up soon," the niece whispered.

"What do I do? I've never really looked after anyone before. Well, except for my *bruders,* but they hardly ever get sick."

"Encourage her to eat the broth—I've got some on the stove—and help her drink water to prevent dehydration."

"Has a doctor been to see her?" Gabbie asked.

"She won't see a doctor. She refuses medical help of any kind."

"What else do I do?"

"Just basic cleaning; it doesn't need much." The woman ushered Gabbie out of the bedroom and showed her around the house.

"Okay if I leave you here now, Gabbie?" Mr. Yoder asked, interrupting the two women.

"*Jah,* Mr. Yoder, I'll be fine," Gabbie said.

Mr. Yoder smiled back, and added, "Mrs. Zook's got a phone in her barn, so call me when you're ready to come home, or if you run out of supplies."

Gabbie smiled. "I will."

Once Mr. Yoder had driven away, Mrs. Zook's niece told Gabbie there were plenty of supplies in the house. "And I'll give you my phone number." She opened her purse and handed Gabbie a white business card with silver writing.

Gabbie looked at her name, and the title under her name. "You're a caterer?"

"I've just started. I cater for small parties, and I've got two people working for me."

"Were you ever in the community?"

She laughed. "No, my aunt is the only one in the family. She married an Amish man and became Amish for him." Gabbie nodded.

"When she's better, I'm sure she'll tell you all about it. She's a talker when she's feeling well. Bye, and thanks, Gabbie."

Gabbie waved and watched Mrs. Zook's niece drive away in a small white car. This was the first time anyone had put so much trust in her. She was responsible for another person. Gabbie walked back into the bedroom to see that Mrs. Zook was awake.

Gabbie stepped fully into the room. "Hello, I'm Gabbie. Your niece has gone, and I'm looking after you." The old woman frowned.

"If that's all right?" Gabbie asked.

"You sure she's gone?" Mrs. Zook asked softly.

Maybe an elderly woman her age might be hard of hearing. Gabbie moved closer, and said, "Quite sure."

"Good." Mrs. Zook looked pleased with the news.

"Can I get you anything?"

"Nee." Mrs. Zook pushed herself up onto her pillows.

Gabbie stood next to her bed. "Your niece said to encourage you to eat broth." The old lady grunted.

"Is there anything you'd like?" Gabbie asked.

"No more broth."

Gabbie laughed.

She looked Gabbie up and down, and then said, "I'll sleep a little more."

"I'll leave you alone then."

The old woman lowered herself so that her head was flat onto the pillows before she closed her eyes. Gabbie backed out of the room. From what Mrs. Zook had said, she was pleased that her niece had gone. Gabbie walked into the kitchen intending to make a cup of coffee. On closer inspection of the state of the kitchen, she placed her hands on her hips and frowned. Gabbie decided to scrub the kitchen, and then she would make some fresh soup.

It was less than an hour later that she heard Mrs. Zook calling her.

Gabbie raced up the stairs. *"Jah?"*

"Got anything to eat besides that awful broth that tastes like horse pee?"

Gabbie put her hand over her mouth and giggled. "I'm making you some fresh soup, but it won't be ready for a while. I'll bring you something else."

Gabbie ran down the stairs to see what else she could find in the kitchen. She had fresh bread that Mrs. Yoder had sent with her, and thin slices of corned beef. In the cold box were lettuce, fresh tomatoes and a jar of pickles. She made Mrs. Zook a small sandwich and took it up to her with a cup of meadow tea. The soup would do nicely for dinner.

She placed the sandwich and tea on Mrs. Zook's nightstand.

"Gott has sent you to me, Gabbie. I prayed for that

awful woman to leave me, and for Him to send me some-one I'd like."

Gabbie smiled, pleased that someone was glad to see her. "Let me prop your pillows up a little."

The old lady pushed herself up into a sitting posi-tion while Gabbie supported her back with plumped up pillows.

Gabbie placed the plate with the sandwich onto her lap.

"Shall I call you Mrs. Zook or Betty?" Gabbie asked.

"Just call me Betty. You're not a child by the looks of you. I'd expect a child to call me Mrs. Zook, but I'd say you're close to twenty?"

"Fairly close to twenty years old."

"Now stay and tell me about yourself while I eat." The old lady took a mouthful of sandwich and looked back at Gabbie.

Gabbie sat on the end of her bed. "I guess there's not much to tell."

When the old lady continued to stare, Gabbie said, "I was sent here some time ago because my *familye* thought that I needed to grow up. I liked a boy, and my *vadder* thought I was going to make some kind of trouble."

Betty smiled and appeared to enjoy her story.

"I did like the boy, his name is Joseph, and I still like him, but he's engaged to someone else." Gabbie's shoul-ders drooped.

Betty raised her eyebrows. "Go on."

"Then I got a letter from my friend, Sally, saying that the boy I like had broken up with his girl, so I begged my family to take me back; I told them I'd changed. *Mamm* and *Dat* let me go back home, and then I found out that Sally had made a mistake."

"Oh dear." Betty looked saddened by her story. "Pass my tea?"

Gabbie helped Betty put the tea up to her and take a sip. Then Betty picked up a piece of her sandwich. Gabbie put the tea on the table and sat back down.

"What are you doing back here then?"

"My parents didn't believe I had changed. They thought that I was trying to match Joseph's girlfriend, Ilsa, with another man."

A giggle escaped Betty's lips. "Were you?"

Gabbie looked into Betty's brown eyes. *"Jah,* I was."

Betty gave a snigger. *"Ach,* my dear. *Gott* surely sent you here to cheer me up."

Gabbie laughed. "I'm glad someone is pleased to have me around. I'm not proud of what I've done. My life is awful now because of my wrong actions."

"I think I might be able to get out of bed and sit in some sunlight today."

"You're feeling better then?" Gabbie asked.

"I was very sick. I thought I would die, but now I think that I will live a little longer. *Gott* is not ready to take me home just yet, it seems."

"I'm glad. You're the only person who hasn't judged me or made me feel awful about myself."

Chapter Forty-Two

The next day, Betty and Gabbie sat in the sun drinking tea.

"You're rapidly improving," Gabbie said. "I expected to be cleaning up all sorts of messes that sick people have."

"I feel better. Now, what are your plans for this boy you like?"

"I've given up on planning anything. Nothing's worked out for me, and it got me sent here to Lancaster County far away from him."

Betty chuckled. "Things might be working out for you without you knowing it."

"Do you think so?"

Betty nodded. "When I met my Harold, he was betrothed to another woman."

Gabbie's eyes grew wide. "He was?"

"Jah. And I wasn't even Amish. My *vadder* was a blacksmith, and that's how I met Harold. Dad used to shoe a lot of the Amish buggy horses. We weren't Amish, but Harold was. He was engaged to an Amish woman named Daisy Morgan. A more boring woman

you couldn't even begin to imagine. I don't know how Harold could have ever thought about marrying a woman like her."

"How did he end up marrying you?"

Betty smiled, and her eyes lighted up. "We liked each other as soon as our eyes met. He told me he was engaged and said that he couldn't marry an *Englischer.*"

"How did things work out for you, since he was engaged to Daisy?"

"I planned that we would bump into each other everywhere. I think that Daisy got the idea that something was happening between us."

"You planned that?"

"Jah, I'm not proud of it, mind you, but I used to manipulate people into doing what I wanted."

Gabbie's eyebrows rose. "Just like me. I mean, I used to do that, but I'm trying to change and make myself better."

Betty leaned over and patted Gabbie's hand. "You've got a *gut* heart, Gabbie; *Gott* knows that."

Gabbie looked down. "I'm not proud of the things I've done." Gabbie looked into Betty's smiling face. "I'm glad things worked out for you doing things that way, but they aren't, or they didn't work out for me."

"All things work together for good for those who love *Gott.*"

Gabbie nodded. "Did you have a happy life with your husband?"

Betty blinked back tears and slowly nodded. "We had a blessed life. I wouldn't change one bit of it for anything. But things always turn out how they're supposed to. You might have had to learn your lessons so you could help other young people, or help them when you're older."

"Like you're helping me now?" Gabbie asked.

"I hope I'm helping you."

Gabbie nodded. "I think you're the only person I've met who understands me. You're the only person who knows what I've done and doesn't think that I'm bad."

"No one is ever bad, Gabbie. A person can do bad things, but that doesn't mean that they are a bad person. There's good and bad in us all. God has already forgiven our wrongdoing."

Gabbie's eyes opened wide.

Betty added, "It's our choices that define who we are."

"How do you mean?"

Betty took a moment to answer. "Whatever small choice you make sets your life on a different path. I try to make choices that will not hurt others. That's what my long years on this earth have taught me."

Gabbie had stayed a whole week at Mrs. Zook's house before she returned to the Yoders'. She was helping Martha in the garden when they both heard the mailman blow his whistle. Martha was at her parents' for the day while Michael was helping his uncle. For Gabbie it was just like the old days. As the two girls had always done when they heard the mailman, they ran to the front of the house hoping to reach the mail first. More often than not, Martha was the first one to reach the letters, and this day was no different.

Martha held the letters up high, to avoid Gabbie snatching them out of her hands. "I believe one is for you," Martha said.

"Really? From my folks?"

Martha passed Gabbie's letter over. Gabbie turned her letter over to see that it was from her friend, Sally.

"It's about time she wrote to me. I hope she's told me everything that's going on at home."

"The rest are for *Dat,*" Martha said with a sharp nod of her head.

Gabbie heard Martha say something and nodded, more interested in what her letter contained than what Martha had to say. She ripped the letter open and sat in one of the large porch chairs by the front door. In the letter, Sally told her that Joseph and Ilsa's relationship had fallen apart. She read the letter again carefully to make sure there was no way that she was reading it incorrectly.

After she reread the words, she dropped the letter into her lap. There was no mistake in what she read, but Sally had been wrong before, so she could be wrong again. Last time she'd heard this news, she had left the Yoders as quickly as she could, but this time she was a little older, a little wiser.

Martha plopped down in the chair next to her. "Well? What news does Sally send?"

Gabbie could not speak when she handed the letter over for Martha to read. Martha read the letter and then handed it back to Gabbie.

"Do you think it's true?" Martha asked, knowing that Sally had sent the same letter once before.

"I don't know. I really don't know if I can trust Sally again. You remember what happened last time."

"You're still in love with him, aren't you?"

"*Jah,* I am, but I can't take this letter seriously. I told you I'm trying to make myself a better person, and to run home is something the old Gabbie would do." Gabbie was silent for a moment before she added, "That's what the old Gabbie did do."

"Are you going to wait until you know whether it's true?" Martha wrinkled her nose.

Gabbie shrugged her shoulders. "I don't know what to do, except wait, and see what happens next."

"You really have changed, Gabbie. You were always a person to act first and think later."

Gabbie smiled at Martha. "I do want to be different." Gabbie wanted to speak to Betty. She trusted that Betty could give her some advice. Betty had lived a long life and had learned from making many mistakes. Even though Martha's father was a deacon, Gabbie did not feel comfortable talking to him about her life or about the boy she liked. "I think I'll go and visit Betty tomorrow and see how she's getting along."

"I'll drive you there. I've got to go into town to buy some supplies for me and Michael. I could take you there on the way and collect you on my way back."

Gabbie nodded. *"Denke,* Martha. I would appreciate that. Now, we'd better keep going with the gardening before we have to help with the dinner."

The rest of the afternoon in the garden, Gabbie had some quiet time to think things through. She was glad that she had gone home and hadn't stayed in Lancaster the first time she'd been there. She was also happy that Martha and Michael were married.

Betty was sitting on the porch when Martha's buggy pulled up in front of the house. Gabbie jumped out of the buggy, ran to her and threw her arms around her. "How have you been, Betty? Can I make you some tea?"

"Hello, Mrs. Zook," Martha called from the buggy.

"Hello, Martha." Mrs. Zook waved.

"Hey, Gabbie, you forgot the bread."

"Ach." Gabbie ran back to the buggy and grabbed the basket of food they had packed to bring Mrs. Zook. *"Denke,* Martha."

"I'll be back soon," Martha said before she clicked her horse forward.

"I'll put this in the kitchen, and then I'll make a cup of tea," Gabbie said.

"Denke, dear. What did you bring me?"

"We brought fresh bread, milk, butter, and eggs. Mrs. Yoder made you an orange cake. No broth or soup." Gabbie giggled, then made her way into the kitchen.

"Good." Betty laughed.

Gabbie brought two cups of tea out to the porch.

"I've something to ask you, Betty." Gabbie placed the tea on the low table next to Betty and then sank into a chair.

"You know you can ask me anything, Gabbie." She peered into Gabbie's face. "You look troubled."

Gabbie smiled. "Well, the thing is that I received a letter from my friend, Sally, telling me that Joseph has ended the relationship with Ilsa."

"Just like the letter she sent when you were staying here last time?"

Gabbie nodded.

"And you want to ask me what you should do?"

"Jah. In the past, I would've hurried back there before Joseph found another girl, but now I'm not so sure what I should do. I have to admit that the thought of Joseph being single made my heart rejoice, mostly because I knew I had nothing to do with their separation." Gabbie took a sip of tea. "I don't know if I should trust that this letter is truthful, or if it's just another false alarm. Maybe it's a test from *Gott* to see if I'm committed to changing

my ways. Should I ignore it entirely? But would I be a fool to ignore it, since Joseph is the only man I want?"

Betty picked up her teacup carefully, and took a good mouthful. "Ah, nice tea." She placed it down onto the saucer. "Gabbie, I can't tell you what to do. You must do what your heart tells you."

"Well, what would you do?"

"If it were me, I'd go back home if your parents were ready to have you back. You didn't manipulate this situation between Joseph and Ilsa, did you?"

"I couldn't have; I'm a day's journey away from them."

"This could be *Gott's* way of working things out for you. You've changed, and you've learned patience. The very fact that you're seeking advice shows that you have changed and have grown wiser."

Gabbie smiled at the elderly lady. "I don't feel as if I've learned patience."

"From what you've told me of your past behavior, you've always acted before you thought too much."

"Jah, that's true. I guess I can't go back home anyway unless *Mamm* and *Dat* want me back. You've been a real friend to me, Betty. When I was here looking after you, I didn't even care about myself. I only wanted you to get better. I've learned so much from you."

"And you've brought joy to me, Gabbie Miller. You must write to me when you go back home."

"I will write to you. I want to be just like you when I'm old."

Betty laughed.

"I mean when I'm older. Both my parents lost their parents early, so I never knew my grandparents. You're like my *grossmammi.*"

Betty placed her hand over Gabbie's.

Chapter Forty-Three

It was two weeks after her letter from Sally before Gabbie was on the train going home to Augusta. The decision to return home had not been a rushed one. Gabbie had received a letter from her parents allowing her to come back home. In the same letter, it was mentioned that Ilsa and Joseph were no longer together, so Gabbie knew for a fact it was true.

Gabbie was no longer a girl out for her own interests. Now, it pleased Gabbie to care for others and to be mindful of things that mattered to them. Looking after Betty and Nancy had enabled her to grow up.

Her favorite times in Lancaster County were when she had helped Betty. Betty had become a good friend even though Betty was old enough to be her *gross-mammi*. Betty knew who Gabbie was, and knew the terrible things she'd done, yet, there was no judgment within her. She would miss Betty, and Martha, as well as Martha's younger sisters. This was the second time she'd left Lancaster County, and this time she knew she had changed and become nearly a different person.

When she arrived back home, her father was waiting for her at the bus station. It had been a long ride on the train, not as long on the bus, but between the two, it was a tiresome journey.

When she stepped down from the bus, her father came forward and hugged her tight. He was not one to show affection openly; even with her mother he would sometimes appear cold and almost indifferent. Gabbie knew that her father had missed her, and it made her feel good.

"I've missed you and everyone, *Dat.*"

"We've all missed you, Gabbie."

"And I have changed. I'm no longer selfish and mean."

Mr. Miller laughed. "You were never that, Gabbie."

"Jah, I was, *Dat.*"

"Let's get you home." Mr. Miller took Gabbie's suitcase from her, and they headed to his waiting buggy.

Gabbie was pleased to see her brothers and mother, and also Amy, when she got home, but all she wanted to do was sleep. She went up to bed and changed into her nightgown. As soon as she put her head on the pillow, she fell soundly to sleep.

After breakfast the next morning, she tried to help her mother and Amy with the chores, but her mother shooed her away.

Amy said, "You have a rest today, Gabbie, after your long journey."

Gabbie agreed; she was tired. She'd missed home, and she'd missed her secret spot down by the creek. "I've something to tell you one day soon, Amy. Something about that letter you once wrote to Andrew."

"That's okay, Gabbie. Andrew already told me. We have no secrets."

Gabbie's mother spun around to face her. "What's this about?"

Amy said, "It's nothing really. Off you go and rest, Gabbie."

Gabbie wasted no time getting away before her mother found out the dreadful thing she'd done. She said a quick prayer of thanks that Amy wasn't holding anything against her, and then she decided to go back and visit the creek. It had always been a good place to clear her thoughts.

Her main problem was how she should approach Joseph without scaring him away. Or should she approach him at all? Should she wait until he made a move in her direction? Her head told her to wait, but her heart was worried that he might meet another girl, and be lost to her again. Pushing the dilemma out of her mind, she grabbed her coat from the laundry room and headed to the creek.

It looked as though it might rain. Even though it was morning, the sky was gray, and the wind was chilly. Gabbie didn't mind if it rained; she would shelter under the thick trees by the creek until the rain eased.

She arrived at her favorite spot and soaked in the beauty of the vibrant colors. Even in the gloomy weather there were purples and warm orange hues reflected in the cool waters. Being in nature made her feel close to the Creator, so she spoke to Him. "I'm sorry, *Gott*. I'm sorry for all the horrible things I've done, and the awful things that I've said about people." She closed her eyes while peace washed over her.

Not long after that, she heard a deep voice.

"You're back."

Gabbie gasped with fright, spun on her heel and looked directly into Joseph's face.

"Joseph. You scared me."

He chuckled. "Sorry; I didn't mean to. When did you get back?"

"I got back late yesterday."

"What are you doing here?"

Gabbie looked around. "Thinking. I always come here to think."

"I know, I've seen you here before, remember?" Gabbie nodded.

"Did you enjoy your vacation?" Joseph asked.

"It was good, but I'm pleased to be home. I guess I've missed lots of things since I haven't been around."

Joseph looked at the ground scratching his head. "Well not much has happened," he replied. "Things are mostly the same as they were when you left. Only small changes happened here and there. Nothing stays the same forever."

"Mm-hmm, I know what you mean. I've changed considerably since I've been away."

"You have?"

Gabbie nodded.

"How have you changed?"

"I've been a horrible person, Joseph."

Joseph chuckled softly. "I can't believe that."

"I used to tell lies and try to force things to benefit myself, without giving consideration to how it would affect other people. I had an experience in Lancaster, and it changed me, really changed me. I used to do some terrible things."

"Like the time you invited Ilsa and Stephen to dinner?

The time that you told me there was something going on between Stephen and Ilsa at the horse auction?"

Gabbie's mouth fell open. "Now I feel ashamed."

Joseph looked around, took off his coat and placed it on a fallen log. "Let's sit and you can tell me more." He sat and patted his coat, encouraging her to sit next to him.

She did so and then said, "I wasn't pleased with myself and I asked *Gott* to change me. I started helping Nancy out with her *kinner*. Things were so bad for Nancy, but she was always so cheerful, and she taught me to see things differently."

"What happened to make your parents send you back to Lancaster?"

"They weren't happy with my behavior over a couple of things. Anyway, I asked Mr. Yoder if I could do volunteer work, and I ended up meeting Betty Zook, a *wunderbaar* old lady. She changed my life. We had many *gut* talks, and I cared for her more than I cared for myself. For the first time in my life, I wasn't concerned with myself or any of my problems."

They were silent for a few moments, and then Gabbie said, "After the first days I spent taking care of Betty, her situation improved. She told me lots of stories, and we had a lot in common; she was very much like me. She could have been my own *grossmammi* we were so alike. Anyway, she helped me grow up and think differently about everything. When I got back to the Yoders' after staying with Betty, I could tell that I was a whole different person. Even Martha and her family noticed something different about me."

"It feels good helping people, doesn't it?" Joseph asked.

"It does, it certainly does."

"It sounds like Betty made quite an impact on your life."

Gabbie nodded. "It's like she's *familye* to me, closer than some of my real *familye*. I'm going to write to her every week." Gabbie looked into Joseph's eyes. "Or, have I changed? Here I am prattling on about myself, and you haven't told me what you've been up to. Are you okay? You look kind of troubled."

"You're right," he said. "Something did happen. I suppose you heard that Ilsa and I are no longer going to get married."

Gabbie nodded, blinking rapidly trying to hide her nervousness. "I heard."

"I suppose being the bishop's *dochder* you'd hear most things before anyone else."

"Nee, Dat would never tell us anything private. Mostly, I find out things from others."

"I didn't mean to say that he would repeat things. I guess that he wouldn't, or couldn't do that." Joseph rubbed his neck. "I guess things weren't meant to be between Ilsa and me."

Gabbie nodded. "I'm sorry, and I really mean that."

"Denke."

"Hurt passes in time, I've been told."

"You're probably too young to have been hurt, Gabbie."

"I suppose I am."

"You haven't asked what happened between Ilsa and me."

Gabbie's mouth fell open. *"Nee,* that's private. It's not for people to gossip about. Or for me to know any private details."

"Gabbie, when you went away again, I realized that… I missed you."

Gabbie looked into his blue eyes. "Like, really missed me?"

He nodded and swallowed hard. "It was then that I knew I couldn't go through with marrying Ilsa. We'd already had some arguments, which showed me we weren't suited. Still, I was reluctant to end things because I'd made a commitment."

"You don't need to tell me all this, Joseph."

"I do. The truth is that Ilsa and I had parted some time before we had made it known. We had agreed to keep the whole thing quiet, even from your *vadder,* the bishop."

"Why, Joseph?"

"I think we were embarrassed that we got engaged so quickly. We didn't want people to think that we were fickle."

Gabbie nodded, knowing how some people in the community liked to talk of others.

After a few moments of silence, Joseph looked at her with a softer face. With a quiet voice, he said, "You understand me, Gabbie, like no one else seems to. I hope you won't go away again. I don't want you to leave again."

Gabbie's mind blacked out for a second. His words were the ones she'd always wanted to hear from him. "Well, *jah,* I missed our conversations too. It's hard to find friends who can understand who you are sometimes." Gabbie tried to reply objectively even though her heart pounded.

"The truth is, I've liked you for some time, Gabbie. I was afraid to let you know because you're the bishop's *dochder.* I thought I wouldn't have a chance with you.

But now, I've decided not to settle. I will try to have what I want, and that is why I'd like to see you more often. I enjoy your company."

Gabbie swallowed hard. "You do?"

"Jah, I do, Gabbie. So, do you think that would be possible to see you again? Go on a buggy ride maybe, or just meet for a walk to start with?"

Gabbie could not stop the smile she knew was spreading across her face. "I'd like that, Joseph."

His blue eyes lighted up. "I like the way you say my name." She giggled.

"You're a woman who thinks deeply about things, and I like an intelligent woman." He tipped his hat back slightly. "I don't know why I asked Ilsa to marry me."

"We've all done things we regret. Well, I know that I have."

"What do you say, Gabbie?" He picked up Gabbie's right hand and covered it with the warmth of his.

Gabbie looked up into his eyes and nodded. A smile twigged at the edges of Joseph's lips, and his eyes crinkled at the corners.

Gabbie couldn't wait to write to Betty to tell her all that had happened. As Joseph squeezed her hand, she closed her eyes and said a quick "thank you" to God. She'd gone through some hard lessons, but with her eyes on God and off herself, she knew a wonderful journey had only just begun.

All of Amy's girlfriends from Lancaster had gathered for her wedding to Andrew at the Millers' house in Augusta. Even her friend Claire, who had married the *Englischer* was there, minus her husband who was too busy with work to attend.

Now, as Amy stood beside Andrew in front of Bishop John at their wedding ceremony, it no longer mattered to Amy that all her friends had gotten married before her. The past was behind her, and all that mattered was the present and the future.

As the bishop finished his talk and a man got ready to sing a hymn, Amy glanced behind her to see Gabbie wearing a grin from ear to ear and looking very much like she had a secret. In Amy's heart, she knew Joseph had proposed to Gabbie, and Gabbie didn't want to announce it just yet because this was Amy and Andrew's special day.

Then next to Gabbie was Amy's sister, Martha, who'd married Michael. Claire was sitting in between Olive and Jessie, who was cradling her new son, James. Olive's stepson, Leo, was on Olive's lap whispering something to his stepmother whom he now called *"Mamm"* since he and his father, Blake, had joined the community before Blake's marriage to Olive. Then on the other side of Jessie was Lucy, who was married to Joshua Hershberger and they were both dedicated to the movement to save the Amish farmlands.

Olive told Leo to be quiet and he frowned.

"Can I go over to *Dat?"* Leo asked.

"Nee, you said you wanted to sit with me. This is an important day for my friend. You have to be quiet."

"Why's it important?"

"I'll tell you soon. Now, hush."

"It better be a good reason." Leo turned around and looked to the front.

Olive shook her head. He was becoming a handful

and always wanted to know everything about everything.

As melodious baritone notes rang out from one of the community members, Olive's mind drifted to a couple of years ago when she'd had the idea that she and her four single and jobless friends should advertise their services as maids.

Who would've thought that one little decision would set them all on different paths and change their lives forever?

Call unto me, and I will answer thee, and show thee great and mighty things, which thou knowest not.

Jeremiah 33:3

* * * * *

WE HOPE YOU ENJOYED
THIS BOOK FROM

LOVE INSPIRED
INSPIRATIONAL ROMANCE

Uplifting stories of faith, forgiveness and hope.

Fall in love with stories where faith helps
guide you through life's challenges, and discover
the promise of a new beginning.

6 NEW BOOKS AVAILABLE EVERY MONTH!

LIHALO2020

SPECIAL EXCERPT FROM

LOVE INSPIRED
INSPIRATIONAL ROMANCE

*Intent on reopening a local bed-and-breakfast,
Addie Ricci sank all her savings into the project—and
now the single mother's in over her head. But her high
school sweetheart's back in town and happy to lend a
hand. Will Addie's long-kept secret stand in the way of
their second chance?*

Read on for a sneak preview of
Her Hidden Hope *by Jill Lynn,
part of her Colorado Grooms miniseries.*

Addie kept monopolizing Evan's time. First at the B and B—though she could hardly blame herself for that. He was the one who'd insisted on helping her out. And now again at church. Surely he had better places to be than with her.

"Do you need to go?" she asked Evan. "Sorry I kept you so long."

"I'm not in a rush. I might pop out to Wilder Ranch for lunch with Jace and Mackenzie. After that I have to…" Evan groaned.

"Run into a burning building? Perform brain surgery? Teach a sewing class?"

Humor momentarily flashed across his features. "Go to a meeting for Old Westbend Weekend."

What? So much for some Evan-free time to pull herself back together. "I'm going to that, but I didn't realize you were. The B and B is one of the sponsors for the weekend." Addie had used her entire limited advertising budget for the three-day event.

"I thought my brother might block for me today. Instead he totally kicked me under the bus as it roared by. He caught Bill's attention and volunteered me for the hero thing." The pure torment on Evan's face was almost comical. "I want to back out of it, but Bill played the 'it's for the kids' card, and now I think I'm trapped."

"Look, Mommy!" Sawyer ran over to them. A grubby, slimy—and very dead—worm rested in the palm of his hand.

"Ew."

At her disgust, Sawyer showed the prize to Evan. "Good find. He looks like he's dead, though, so you'd better give him a proper burial."

"Yeah!" Sawyer hurried over to the patch of dirt. He plopped the worm onto the sidewalk and told it to "stay" just like he would Belay. That made both of them laugh. Then he used one of the sticks as a shovel and began digging a hole.

"He's like a cat, always bringing me dead animals as gifts. I'm surprised he doesn't leave them for me on the doorstep."

Evan chuckled while waving toward the parking lot. She turned to see his brother and Mackenzie walking to their vehicle.

"Do you guys want to come out to Wilder Ranch for lunch? I'm sure they wouldn't mind two more. It's a happy sort of chaos there with all of the kids."

Addie's heart constricted at the offer. No doubt Sawyer would love it. She wanted exactly what Evan was offering, but all of that was off-limits for her. She couldn't allow herself any more access into Evan's world or vice versa.

"We can't, but thanks. I've got to get Sawyer down for a nap." Addie wasn't about to attempt attending a meeting with a tired Sawyer, and she didn't have anywhere else in town for him to go.

Evan's face morphed from relaxed to taut, but he didn't press further. "Right. Okay. I guess I'll see you later then." After saying goodbye to Sawyer, he caught up with Jace and Mackenzie in the parking lot.

A momentary flash of loss ached in Addie's chest. A few days in Evan's presence and he was already showing her how different things could have been. It was like there was a life out there that she'd missed by taking the wrong path. It was shiny and warm and so, so out of reach.

And the worst of it was, until Evan, she hadn't realized just how much she was missing.

Don't miss
Her Hidden Hope *by Jill Lynn,*
available May 2020 wherever
Love Inspired books and ebooks are sold.

LoveInspired.com

Copyright © 2020 by Jill Lynn

LIEXP0420

IF YOU ENJOYED THIS BOOK
WE THINK YOU WILL ALSO LOVE

LOVE INSPIRED SUSPENSE
INSPIRATIONAL ROMANCE

Courage. Danger. Faith.

Find strength and determination in stories
of faith and love in the face of danger.

6 NEW BOOKS AVAILABLE EVERY MONTH!

LISXSERIES2020

SPECIAL EXCERPT FROM

❧

LOVE INSPIRED SUSPENSE
INSPIRATIONAL ROMANCE

Someone is trying to force her off her land, and her only hope lies in the secret father of her child, who has come back home to sell his property.

Read on for a sneak preview of
Dangerous Amish Inheritance *by Debby Giusti,*
available April 2020 from Love Inspired Suspense.

Ruthie Eicher awoke with a start. She blinked in the darkness and touched the opposite side of the double bed, where her husband had slept. Two months since the tragic accident and she was not yet used to his absence.

Finding the far side of the bed empty and the sheets cold, she dropped her feet to the floor and hurried into the children's room. Even without lighting the oil lamp, she knew from the steady draw of their breaths that nine-year-old Simon and six-year-old Andrew were sound asleep.

Movement near the outbuildings caught her eye. She held her breath and stared for a long moment.

Narrowing her gaze, she leaned forward, and her heart raced as a flame licked the air.

She shook Simon. "The woodpile. On fire. I need help."

He rubbed his eyes.

"Hurry, Simon."

Leaving him to crawl from bed, she raced downstairs, almost tripping, her heart pounding as she knew all too well how quickly the fire could spread. She ran through the kitchen, grabbed the back doorknob and groaned as her fingers struggled with the lock.

"No!" she moaned, and coaxed her fumbling hands to work. The lock disengaged. She threw open the door and ran across the porch and down the steps.

A noise sounded behind her. She glanced over her shoulder, expecting Simon. Instead she saw a large, darkly dressed figure. Something struck the side of her head. She gasped with pain, dropped the bucket and stumbled toward the house.

He grabbed her shoulder and threw her to the ground. She cried out, struggled to her knees and started to crawl away. He kicked her side. She groaned and tried to stand. He tangled his fingers through her hair and pulled her to her feet.

The man's lips touched her ear. "Didn't you read my notes? You don't belong here." His rancid breath soured the air. "Leave before something happens to you and your children."

Don't miss
Dangerous Amish Inheritance *by Debby Giusti,
available April 2020 wherever*
Love Inspired Suspense *books and ebooks are sold.*

LoveInspired.com

Copyright © 2020 by Deborah W. Giusti

LISEXP0420